THE JADE
BUTTERFLY

THE JADE BUTTERFLY

A Dan Sharp Mystery

Jeffrey Round

DUNDURN
TORONTO

Editor: Shannon Whibbs
Cover Design: Carmen Giraudy
Cover Image: © Kompaniets Taras/Shutterstock.com
Printer: Webcom

Library and Archives Canada Cataloguing in Publication
Round, Jeffrey, author
The jade butterfly : a Dan Sharp mystery / Jeffrey Round.

Issued in print and electronic formats.
ISBN 978-1-4597-2185-2 (pbk.).--ISBN 978-1-4597-2186-9 (pdf).--
ISBN 978-1-4597-2187-6 (epub)

I. Title.

PS8635.O8625J33 2015   C813'.54   C2014-902956-X
C2014-902957-8

1   2   3   4   5   19   18   17   16   15

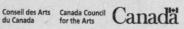

Conseil des Arts du Canada   Canada Council for the Arts   Canadä   ONTARIO ARTS COUNCIL
CONSEIL DES ARTS DE L'ONTARIO
an Ontario government agency
un organisme du gouvernement de l'Ontario

We acknowledge the support of the Canada Council for the Arts and the Ontario Arts Council for our publishing program. We also acknowledge the financial support of the Government of Canada through the Canada Book Fund and Livres Canada Books, and the Government of Ontario through the Ontario Book Publishing Tax Credit and the Ontario Media Development Corporation.

Care has been taken to trace the ownership of copyright material used in this book. The author and the publisher welcome any information enabling them to rectify any references or credits in subsequent editions.

J. Kirk Howard, President

The publisher is not responsible for websites or their content unless they are owned by the publisher.

Printed and bound in Canada.

VISIT US AT
Dundurn.com | @dundurnpress | Facebook.com/dundurnpress | Pinterest.com/dundurnpress

Dundurn
3 Church Street, Suite 500
Toronto, Ontario, Canada
M5E 1M2

For Arthur Rimbaud, Oscar Wilde, Marcel Proust, Jean Genet, Yukio Mishima, William Burroughs, David Wojnarowicz, and other assorted saints and sinners who got here long before me

"There are no homosexuals in China."
— Mao Zedong

Contents

Prologue

Beijing — June 4, 1989: Lost

It was already past midnight when they reached the Forbidden City and stopped outside the Gate of Heavenly Peace. The air blew hot and dry on the boy's skin. He'd been to the Red Dragon Restaurant with his sister and some friends to celebrate his eighteenth birthday. Amazing what a handful of *yuan* could buy these days for a gang of hungry students. The curried eel and scorpion kebabs had been especially fresh and tasty. And the ale flowing like wine! The four had indulged mightily. Then he surprised them by footing the bill: it was his gift to them.

He had plenty to celebrate. His real gift had come a few days earlier when he'd been accepted into the Beijing Institute of Foreign Trade. It was a ticket out of his impoverished past and into the world. A ticket to a new life. It also granted him exemption from military college, the prospects of which had loomed overhead for the past several years. Now he was free from that burden. This, of course, was only if he performed well in his studies. But if he did then he could leave this country one day. He could get beyond its ancient walls and dusty customs. Maybe he would even get beyond himself. He was still a boy in many ways. A boy who barely knew who he was or might become.

He glanced over at the others. Chunlan sat on a low stone wall, chewing gum, knobby knees exposed beneath the hem of her skirt. Ling had stopped to light a cigarette. Thin and ethereal, her face was pensive in the flare from the match. She took a drag then offered it to Wenwu, who pulled it suggestively through her fingers. The boy felt a flash of jealousy. When it came time to leave China, he would find a way to bring his sister with him. Only Ling knew who he really was. Only she understood him fully. Even more than he understood himself, he sometimes thought.

They continued on to Tiananmen, where the Monument to the People's Heroes was lit up with an eerie glow. A crowd stood around as though waiting expectantly for something to begin. It was hard to see over all the heads. They'd been gathering here for weeks, but it was a shock to see the numbers, well into the thousands, in the square alone. It was far more than any of the official reports said.

The boy had lied to his parents about where they were going. His father would be furious if he knew he and Ling were anywhere near the protests. Some of the student leaders had begun to talk about disbanding the movement, though the hardliners were advocating more drastic action, possibly even hunger strikes. *They should all just relax and go for a good meal at the Red Dragon*, the boy thought. *That would calm them down. Why all this fuss over a dead politician?* He signalled to the others to bypass the crowd, but Wenwu and Chunlan were already pushing forward. Ling followed them.

They seemed to burst into the square almost by accident. An unnatural calm hung in the air. Up ahead a tank rolled in, its treads steadily eating up the pavement. It stopped in front of the Mao Mausoleum. Before the night was over there would be many more, bringing death with them. The images would crackle around the world, spread by the international media. Estimates of the number of dead would be argued over for decades, ranging from official reports of hundreds to eye witness accounts of ten thousand or more, not to mention the unaccounted for casualties, the faceless ones who languished in prisons or were tortured and executed afterward.

The protests had been growing since the death of Hu Yaobang, former General Secretary, in April. Seen by party conservatives as "soft" and "Western," he'd been forced to resign two years earlier. A favourite with students, his demise sparked the first signs of resistance, not just in Beijing, but countrywide. The boy had seen posters eulogizing him all over the city. The calls for democracy and freedom struck a chord in him, as with so many others. It was because of Hu's influence that he was being allowed to attend a school for international trade. Such things had not existed in China before. Who knows? Maybe the West was not such a bad place after all. Perhaps Mao's China was finally coming undone.

The administration had reacted quickly, framing the protests as a direct attack on China's leaders and its political system. The *People's Daily* dismissed the disturbances as the work of a small group of opportunists plotting to overthrow the government. The next day, one hundred thousand students had marched into Tiananmen.

The movement grew. In Beijing, a million ordinary citizens joined the rally. *How could this be?* the boy wondered. He didn't know much about politics, but he'd been taught to believe the government was always right. Two days later, martial law was declared and the city went into lockdown. In spite of this, the protests continued night after night until the army withdrew.

As the students pushed their demands, several high-ranking government officials joined them in expressing pro-democracy beliefs, first privately, then publicly. A well-known general was removed from command for refusing to clear the square of protesters. Word spread as the army prepared to advance again, sending thousands of civilians into the streets to block the troops.

This was what the boy had walked into with his sister and friends upon leaving the restaurant. It was close to one o'clock as they made their way across the square with the crowds pulsing around them. People leaned from balconies all up and down the avenues, as though watching a command performance. It was almost impossible to move.

The boy had wanted to be home in bed by midnight. As things turned out, it would not happen that night or for nearly another two weeks. The sight of armoured vehicles in the square filled him with trepidation as well as admiration. *They are like powerful animals lying in wait*, he thought with a sense of foreboding. Suddenly, they all began to move as one. The crowd scattered.

Afterward, the boy would remember how quickly it happened. He watched in fascination as an arm stretched overhead and hurled a Molotov cocktail. The bottle smashed against a tank, rippling into blue-and-yellow flames. A soldier sprayed the air with machine-gun fire. Bodies crumpled and fell from the balconies.

The boy looked around in a panic. Wenwu and Chunlan had disappeared. Ling was up ahead, running from the tanks and glancing over her shoulder at him in horror. The gunfire continued in short bursts. As he turned to follow his sister, a fierce stinging seared his thigh. The crush of bodies held him upright a moment longer, then he sprawled on the ground, hitting his face on the pavement.

A forest of legs surged past, stumbling over his body. Instinctively, he pushed them away. The crowd receded and he was left lying there on his own. He clutched at the pain, then brought his hands before his face. Blood covered his fingers. Being crushed to death was no longer his chief worry: bleeding to death was.

From the corner of his eye, he saw someone heading toward him. An old man reached down and helped him to his feet before moving off.

The boy stood shakily against a wall. Bodies lay scattered around the square. Here and there, people were stooping to help the wounded, calling out in fear and horror. He looked around for his sister.

Ling was gone.

One

Toronto 2009:
The Complexity of Desire

Dan raised his head from the pillow. He'd been dreaming of crowds, angry and surging around him in a panic. The darkness receded. A vein pulsed behind his eye. He sat up and pushed the curtains aside, letting daylight stream over him. The dreams were getting worse, not better. It was to the point where he feared going to bed.

After a night like this, he woke feeling drained rather than refreshed. Sleep meant struggle and torment, not rest and a simple respite from the day. For most people, daytime was what they wanted to escape. Night was where they sought relief from their unfulfilled lives: bitter spouses, ungrateful children, and endless hours spent at meaningless jobs. It was the night Dan feared.

This was nothing so mundane as a wet dream coming to unsettle the prudish mind. These were dreamscapes filled with anxiety and dread. Sometimes they were of crowds, pulsing and restive. At other times they held a terror of the simplest things, fears that lay buried in his subconscious, overwhelming him as he lay in bed and burned, night after night, unable to wake.

Perhaps it came from too many years spent tracking people who vanished, often inexplicably and without a trace. People who left behind family, friends, and colleagues to wonder what had gone wrong in a country as advanced and enlightened as Canada, where such things were not supposed to happen. Lately, the dreams had taken on an even more personal tone, leaving Dan feeling vulnerable and exposed.

The worst was the dream of the empty bucket. It was hard to believe he was paralyzed by the sight of a child's pail sitting empty by the edge of the sea. Usually it was a variation on one he'd owned when he was four: galvanized steel, purple, with a plastic handle and a string of white seashells ringing the edges in soft undulations.

In his dream, the sun danced brightly on the water and the sand felt warm beneath his feet. But always, as he approached the bucket, a surge of despair overtook him like an unseen tide. He was consumed by an urge to grip the handle and lift it clear of the waves lapping at its sides. Then, to his horror, he watched as the water poured through the rusted-out bottom. Dan felt this presaged something dire about his life, as though it too could never contain anything for long. Somewhere in the distance, his mother was calling.

He turned instinctively from her voice, not wanting to see the breasts dangling beneath the open blouse. Not wanting to see her nakedness. If it was one of her bad days, she would be sloppy, her hair uncombed. Her breath would smell. On bad days, Dan was afraid of seeing her. He would try to hide from her in his dreams.

On nights like these he woke to sweat-soaked sheets, trying to clear his head and fight off a sense of numbing loss. *Amazing how the images can resonate in your mind for years*, he thought. He still remembered that trip to the beach, the wearing away of a hazy afternoon as his mother and a man who might have been his father got drunk. Then, later, stumbling on the pair in the bushes as she straddled the man lying prone beneath her. Dan recalled his fascination with her exposed breasts and something standing erect between the man's legs.

When they left the beach that day, he forgot to collect his pail. They were halfway home when he remembered. But the man would not go back for it, despite Dan's wailing. To quiet him, they stopped at the Dairy Queen and bought him a banana split. Dan still had a photograph of this outing, or one just like it, where he sat at the shore filling his pail with sand. It was the last summer of his mother's life. She would die at Christmas, locked out in the snow all night after a drunken argument with his father before succumbing to pneumonia soon after. It was one of a handful of memories he retained of her. By the time he was grown, she'd been reduced to an outline. Except lately, when she returned to haunt his dreams.

Mornings were never easy.

Dan lay in bed, hoping this false start wouldn't colour the whole day. The sooner he got up and tackled his duties, the sooner he'd feel normal. Whatever normal was.

He stumbled to the shower, first hot then mind-numbingly cold, till he felt revived. Next, he dried himself off and slung the towel over the shower rod. The glycerine-tinged eyes of some off-hours werewolf stared back from the mirror. A thin red line edged down the side of his face like a contour on an eleva-tion map, the reminder of a doorframe he'd encoun-tered when he was ten. Stubble had sprouted overnight, marking his face like a stain that could not be wiped away. His chest needed a clipping too, he noted, but that would wait for another day. He ran his fingers through his hair once, twice, then shook and pressed it into place. Wash and wear was good.

As he shaved, he listened for sounds of life from downstairs. None. His son had likely already gone to class. Lately he thought Ked had been avoiding him, getting up early and heading out before they could talk.

Not this morning, however. He came downstairs to find a handsome young man in pajamas sitting at the kitchen table, a ginger retriever near his feet. The dog looked up momentarily then turned away.

Dan glanced at the clock and frowned.

"Shouldn't you be getting ready for school?"

His son gave him a doleful look. "Earth to Dad — it's Saturday."

"Oh, right." Dan winked. "Just checking to see if you knew. You're lucky you have weekends, you know. I don't have the luxury."

Ked shrugged. "So take the day off. You're your own boss."

"Can't — too much to do."

Ralph grumped in the corner then turned on his side to catch the sun streaming through the French doors and across his tawny fur. Outside, the trees were filling in, buds popping into leaves, their branches growing heavy with green again.

"I can make pancakes," Ked offered after a moment.

"Sounds good," Dan said. "I'm hungry."

"You look grumpy."

"I'm not." He smiled as if to prove it. Probably not convincingly, after the tortured sleep he'd had.

His son stood and went to the cupboards. He brought down a box of mix and reached for the measuring cup.

"Buttermilk okay?"

"Works for me."

Dan watched as Ked prepared the batter. Darkness edged the boy's cheeks and chin, making him look older than usual.

"Saving on razor blades these days?"

"Ha-ha."

Ked glanced over, seriousness etched on his

features. His mouth twitched. He seemed about to say something, but the words weren't coming.

"What?" Dan said.

"Just — I don't know. How do you know when you like someone?"

"*Like?*"

Ked shrugged, turned back to the bowl of batter.

"You know."

Fifteen. It wasn't the easiest age. Teenage trauma, the turmoil at finding life's unanswered questions plotting your doom and staring you in the face each morning when you looked in the mirror or read it in the faces of others around you.

"Do you want the simple explanation or the complicated explanation?"

Ked shrugged again without looking over.

"Dunno."

"Okay, then let's start with simple. You go to school five days a week, more or less, and at some point you realize there's a face you see every day that stands out from the others. You start looking forward to seeing that particular face. It resonates with you. You feel excited when you see her in the crowd."

He watched his son. Ked focused on the bowl of mix, turned up the burner, dribbled oil in the pan.

"Good so far?"

"Yeah."

"Sometimes you want to talk to her, just her alone." Dan held up a finger. "But where you can talk to almost anyone else with no problem, this particular person seems like the hardest person in the world to get together with and just be yourself."

Ked's mouth grimaced.

"Sometimes you feel really stupid around her, no matter what you say."

His son sighed. "Yeah, that's for sure."

Dan tried to hide a smile, but Ked was too focused on the frying pan to notice.

"Why?"

"Why?" Dan thought this over. "It's hard to say. Nerves, hormones. It's chemistry. But now we're getting into the complicated answer. Let's say you're at a certain age where your body is starting to change and your personality is becoming more complex. You realize you want things you never wanted before. It's like you're going through training all over again. All the things that worked for you before are starting to have different results. You need to learn to drive all over again."

"I don't drive."

"Well, that's not the right metaphor for everybody. Let's just say things are looking very different from what you're used to. And because this person — this girl — is likely starting to notice you too, it matters more. Suddenly it's a big deal. You want to look cool. You want to sound smart when you talk to her, but you think you look like a jerk."

"Yeah — a real jerk."

"It happens to everyone, Ked. You don't need to feel bad about it."

The oil was crackling. Ked scooped a ladleful of batter and let it fall onto the pan where it sizzled on contact. Dan went to the fridge and removed the tin of maple syrup, then grabbed a peach and sliced it into a bowl. Setting everything on the table, he noticed the envelope with the Purolator label: MR. DAN SHARP, SPECIAL PRIVATE INVESTIGATION SERVICES. It sounded awfully formal.

"When did this come?"

"Not sure," Ked said with a shrug. "It was at the front door when I walked Ralph this morning."

Dan turned it in his hands. He could just make out the scrawl, but didn't recognize the sender's address. He slit the package open and a smaller envelope slid out. No markings, nothing to indicate what it was or who had sent it.

"So how do you know when she likes you?" Ked asked.

Dan picked up the smaller envelope, weighing it in his hands, then set it aside. He turned to his son. "You might see it in her face. The way she looks at you when you pass each other in the hall. Eventually, you'll know because it becomes the most natural thing in the world to spend time with her. Your heart stops racing and your tongue stops tripping over itself and you begin to like the way she looks at you when you look at her."

The pan was smoking. Ked seemed lost in thought.

"You might want to turn that down a bit."

"Oh, shit!"

Ked grabbed the spatula and turned the cakes, carefully, one after another. They were just right, Dan noted. Lacy edges crisping into brown, the centres lighter, off-yellow. A man and his son bonding over cooking. The twenty-first century was such a novelty.

"Why are some people confused about their sexuality?" Ked asked.

Dan flashed on the dream where he was equally revolted and fascinated by the sight of his mother's nakedness.

"Good question. The verdict's not entirely in on that one, but I think nature sets up a few taboos. You've heard of incest?"

"Of course."

"Well, genetics will tell you it's not a healthy thing, in the long run, if ever. So there's that. It's also partly because when it comes to sex most people are not properly educated. They're often told to fear the very things they desire."

"You're talking about gay people."

"I'm talking about sexual desire in general. If we're repeatedly told that sex is bad and that pleasure is bad then we don't get a chance to think things through for ourselves. That could be anybody, gay, straight, or other."

Ked slid the pancakes onto a plate and poured more batter into the pan.

"So, like religion, then."

"Religion, politics, morality. It doesn't matter. It's hard to decide what's right for you when the facts are distorted by other people's beliefs."

"That's messy. It can screw up your mind."

"That's for sure."

Ked fidgeted in silence for a bit, watching the new batch sizzle.

"What about you and Mom?" he asked quietly.

"What about us?"

He turned to his father. "Did you want to be with her? You know, when ..." He shrugged, embarrassed.

"When we conceived you?"

Ked looked down at the pan again. "Yeah."

Dan considered how to position this one. "That was not entirely desire on my part, but peer pressure. I felt I had to be manly, and at that age I thought being manly meant wanting to have sex with women. Because that's what I'd been taught to believe."

Ked flipped the pancakes while he thought that one over.

"But did you want to?"

"Well, I did want to be with her, but not entirely for the usual reasons."

Dan considered how far to take this conversation. He'd slept with Ked's mother just once. Kendra had made the first move. Dan followed through because he felt pressured, but also because he was infatuated with her brother, Arman, a fellow student in residence at university. He was saved from having to answer by Kedrick's further probing.

"What about now?"

"What do you mean?"

This conversation seemed unnecessarily abstruse,

Dan thought. Ked was usually more straightforward. He watched as his son placed a stack of pancakes on the table and sat across from him.

"I mean, do you want to be alone? Why don't you have anyone now? Don't you have those feelings anymore?"

Dan felt pinned to the wall like a butterfly. "No, I don't want to be alone. Some days it's just easier that way."

Ked stared at him. "But if you found the right person — the right guy — you would know?"

"I hope so."

Ked speared three pancakes with his fork, hearkening back to the days when they would try to see how many stacked slices they could fit into their mouths at once. He looked up after a moment.

"Dad, what's it like to be old?"

Dan smiled. "It's like, one day you look in the mirror and see that you've turned into the person you vowed never to become back when you were young."

He watched his son's face for signs of amusement. Ked seemed oblivious to irony, particularly when he was in such a serious frame of mind.

"Is that what happened to you?"

"Some days I think so."

Ked nodded. Silence invaded the kitchen. Ralph rolled over again.

Ked picked up the platter and offered it to his father. "Eat some more pancakes. It might make you feel better."

"Yes, son."

They finished breakfast in silence. Later, clearing the table, Dan saw he'd drizzled syrup over the envelope. He wiped his hands and opened it. It contained photocopies of newspaper clippings. Most of them were in Chinese, but one was in English. He didn't need a translator to know they were about the Tiananmen protests of 1989. Each carried a variation of the same photograph: a long line of tanks being held up by a single individual holding a jacket and travel bag in either hand. Tank Man. That was the name he'd gone by, though his true identity had never been confirmed.

Dan counted: there were five articles in total. He shook the envelope, but nothing further fell out. He was mystified. There was no clue as to why he'd been sent the clippings or who had sent them.

He checked his watch: it was getting late. Stashing the envelope in his laptop case, he headed for the door.

Two

Project Management

Donny sat perched on a high stool, chrome modern, overlooking the panorama from his living room window twenty-two stories up. Far below horns tooted, tail-lights winked, and pedestrians scurried over the pavement as though they were crossing a field covered by sniper fire. It was night-time in the ghetto as the Docent of Jarvis Street silently oversaw his domain, legs crossed, pants creased and crinkled at the knees. His top was light-coloured chiffon, short-sleeved, still early for the season, but massively in fashion with the younger crowd wanting to sport their biceps and tattoos. Ebony skin edged the cream a shade whiter by comparison. He was *Vogue* Superstar material in black. Tall and thin, a sepulchral shadow wandering the grounds of the necropolis when he moved. Tonight, however, he was busy doing what he usually did — dispensing advice with a cigarette sutured to his lips, while his icy stare evoked a final evening on board the *Titanic*. All hands on deck, but going down cool, his words calm, not frenzied. This was a serious discussion, after all.

"Your son was right to ask. He worries for you. But he is still a fifteen-year-old boy. He might be bright, but he's inexperienced. He sees the emptiness in your eyes and wonders. We all wonder, if you want to know. Ever since Trevor left." A quick glance over his shoulder to make sure he hadn't caused offence. "I don't know, though. A couple of head-on collisions in the *amour* department and you're ready to call it quits for eternity? Well, maybe you're right. I content myself these days with the boys at Slam."

"The strip club?"

"One and only. It's just that much easier. Both parties know what it's about before we engage in battle. And then it's over with. Real relationships are fraught with peril. They're inherently dangerous."

Assessment made, he took a long drag on his cigarette.

Dan laughed. "Dangerous? How so?" He'd never learned not to ask.

Donny eyed him dead on, fingers splayed and cigarette held at a distance.

"They take you places you don't always want to go. You can lose yourself there. Sometimes permanently."

"I think that's what Ked thinks. That I'm permanently lost."

Smoke exhaled into the night sky, a red spark set against eternity.

"I met the last one, didn't I? One night at Woody's? What was his name again?"

"Kelvin."

"Kelvin, that's right. Razor-sharp cheekbones. Nice eyes. Attractive, but a little stiff in the personality department. Somewhat lacking in humour, as I recall."

"That's him."

"Still, not important enough to get depressed over or give up on life for. So tell me about it."

Dan nodded, staring out across the same horizon as Donny, yet seeing something far different. More than the cityscape reflecting in his eyes.

"It was going really well …"

"They always do at first. Remind me again. This one did what?"

"Project manager at BMO."

"Sorry, you know me. I'm all about fashion here. What exactly does that mean?"

"Project manager? Kind of like heading up a task force."

"Like a platoon sergeant?"

"Sure, I guess. He oversaw the bank's website content. Customer protocols, et cetera. He described it as constantly looking for problems and pointing them out to the people under him."

"So, basically, Project Manager Kelvin criticizes the people under him, makes them sweat all day, and they no doubt resent him for it."

Dan smiled.

"That's pretty much how he described it. He didn't have much respect for his employees, by the sounds of it. And yes, of course they resented him."

"But you thought he would respect you, regardless?"

"I worked hard to earn his respect. And I think I deserved it."

Donny eyed him balefully. "So you wanted respect from a man who points out problems for a living. Did you think he wouldn't find any when he looked at you?"

Dan held up a hand. "Stop. I'm just giving you the back story."

Donny sniffed, took another drag. "Continue."

"You're not making this easy, you know."

Exhale. "Not trying to. Continue."

"Anyway, things went well for the first month. He seemed fun to be with. We had good conversations, enjoyed good food, both of us liked outdoor activities. The sex was great ..."

"Great? Not just good?"

"Great. The attraction was mutual."

Donny leaned forward, seemed to notice something disturbing in the distance.

"Must come from working in a bank. All that repression needs an outlet." He eyed Dan over his cigarette. "So we're not talking about straying, then. Not if you were both feeling fulfilled. Because that is the usual downfall of relationships in this cheerless little ghetto of ours."

"Not this time. But after a few weeks of dating, I started to get a creeping sense of disapproval from him. About little things, usually. I'd suggest doing something, but he wouldn't answer right away. After a minute, he'd hold my suggestion up for examination and revise it. The time we would meet or the movie I suggested. As though I couldn't be trusted to make the right decisions."

"Of course not. He's a project manager. He'd taken you on as a project. You had to be corrected and revised. That was his role. Not a bad idea in concept, but in reality you can't project-manage your boyfriends. They just don't co-operate."

"True."

"How about environment? What was his home like?"

"Big condo in the sky. Pricey. Lots of décor elements."

"Like mine?"

"No, yours is artistic."

"Ah!"

"His was fussy. Lots of art reproductions on the walls — nothing original. Oh, yeah — and artificial flowers in tall vases."

Donny shivered. "The kiss of death."

"He said they were expensive."

"No doubt he said it many times, since you probably didn't look impressed enough when he pointed them out the first time. That sort's always impressed with price tags."

Dan laughed. "True. He kept fishing for compliments every time I came over. He'd show me the latest cherry blossom branch or whatever it was. I'd tell him they were nice, but not my thing."

"Which of course pissed him off."

"If it did, he didn't show it. Well, maybe he did. He showed up at my place once with a big pink-and-white branch covered in blossoms. Silk, I think. He spent half an hour filling a vase with shiny balls and arranging the leaves till it dominated my living room from the fireplace mantel. I didn't know how to say I didn't like it."

"And now you don't have to."

Dan smiled. "When we broke up, he asked for it back."

Donny's face was pure outrage. "You're kidding! Did you give it to him?"

"I said if he wanted it he'd have to come over and get it. He accused me of acting like I was in high school."

"He asked you to return a gift and he called *you* high school? Sheesh! How did you last an entire month with this idiot?"

"I smiled a lot. Mostly during sex."

"What did he think of your profession? Did he like dating a missing-persons investigator? Because it sounds like there was a lot missing in his life."

"I told him what I did when we met. He was impressed that I was my own boss. He seemed to think that being a private investigator implied power.

Nothing like the reality, of course. Then I mentioned how hard I work for how little I make, and he pulled back. He said it was too bad I wasn't a success."

Donny slapped a hand against his thigh.

"He actually said that?"

Dan nodded. "He wasn't very subtle."

"I'm shocked." Donny checked himself. "But of course he would think that way. He works in a bank where success is measured in money. And you still went back for a second date?"

"I thought I could reform him. Besides, I was hot for him. We'd already agreed not to sleep together on the first night."

Donny rolled his eyes. "How quaint. But it just goes to show, that's how these relationships take root. If you'd slept with him on the first night, you'd remember how rude he was to you the next morning, then punch him in the nose and leave."

Dan laughed again. "Probably. Even though I was insulted by his comments, I was dazzled by the sex when we finally got around to it. I got completely hooked."

Donny frowned.

"Which proves you're a relationship junkie with sex addiction issues. If you'd just fuck them and toss them aside, you'd waste far less time and get hurt less often."

"Yeah, well …"

Donny shrugged. "Of course, perhaps I'm being too brutal."

"I really thought it would last. We had things in common. He had an abusive father, too."

"Not exactly the kind of thing you want to bond over."

"No, but it helps to understand the psychology."

The teacher sighed, impatient with the folly of his student.

"You already understand the psychology. I've pointed it out to you many times. You fall for emotionally damaged men who were psychologically wounded by their fathers when they were children. Case closed."

"But I need to get close to figure that out."

"And once you get close, do you like them more for it?"

Dan thought this over.

"No."

"You see? That's why I say relationships are dangerous. They lure you down into the deep end and leave you stranded."

"True."

"But that's only part of the picture." Donny looked over his shoulder at a wall clock. The skyline seemed to have lost its allure. "The other part is that you're positively cloistered. You live like a monk. You'll never meet anybody staying at home. When was the last time you went out and had a bit of fun?"

"I can't recall."

"Does Ked let you do this?"

"I don't think he notices. He's too busy dating.

Apparently he's becoming popular with the ladies. Besides, you know kids."

Donny did, indeed, know kids. Dan could vouch for that. Donny had taken on a temporary, support-a-kid project the previous year when Dan roped him into helping out with a stray he was trying to get off the streets. Lester, a lost boy from Oshawa, was a gay outcast on the run from his abusive parents. The rebellious teenager proved to be just what it took to turn Donny into a respectable parent. Donny and Dan were now on equal footing as fathers, although Donny's transition had been "without all the messy stuff," as he liked to put it.

The relationship had transformed Donny from a man at odds with himself to a man with a purpose. And while it curtailed some of his single-gay-man-on-the-prowl behaviour, it hadn't ended his activities entirely. He still felt Saturday nights were sacred to his routine. Lester was given movie money and sent out to enjoy himself with friends, while Donny checked out the scene.

"My advice? You need a big one to shake you up."

"You mean a big relationship?"

Donny took another cool drag and crushed the butt in a studied fashion.

"No, I mean a *big one*. I was referring to a more visceral experience." He jumped up. "Grab your jacket. We're going to Slam. You need therapy."

Three

Slam Bam, Thank You, Sam

The sign read *Gentlemen's Club*. None of the men making their way up the stairs looked particularly well groomed or well mannered. There wasn't a double-breasted three-piece or tux and cummerbund in sight. *Gentle* wasn't even in the picture. Most of them were heaving with age or with desire or just heaving to get to the top landing, all under the judicious eye of a brooding, muscular miscreant guarding the Gates to Paradise, or at least the down-low demi-paradise version to be found in Toronto's gay ghetto.

Donny discarded his cigarette at the foot of the stairs with a look of disdain for the injudicious by-laws afflicting the serious smoker. But then art had its price. Overhead, a marquee promised breathtaking performances from Messrs Orlando, Skye, Tyler, Little John, and Big Bad Captain Hook. One made sacrifices from time to time.

The conversation that had begun in Donny's condo continued. Donny was at his dismissive best as he wound himself up.

"What's the point?"

"Of love?"

"Of looking for it! Do you know? I gave up years ago." A fey hand on the heart promised all the world's truth and sincerity. "I never formally retired from love, of course. People can think what they like."

"I doubt they would believe you, even if you came out and declared it."

"Naturally, but I repeat: relationships are dangerous. Approach at your peril. Who wants to experience a train wreck or expire of utter boredom?"

Dan looked up at the marquee. "So this is your solution?"

"This is easier. It's soothing. It gets you through the night. It doesn't linger around and ask you to do the laundry or expect breakfast the next morning after disappointing you the night before."

"They can't all have been boring. Your boyfriends, I mean."

Donny stopped to consider.

"Maybe not. But I am now of an age — a *certain* age, as they say — where all the good ones are either taken or dead or desperate. Of the former category, one need not apply. Of the latter two categories there is nothing to be said."

They proceeded up the stairs and joined the line waiting to be frisked by a security guard who was, sensibly so for the management, a devastating looker. He embodied danger: pale skin, glossy hair and dressed entirely in black leather, right down to his fingerless gloves. Christian Bale crossed with the Hell's Angels. A gay man's death wish made flesh. Most of the clients seemed to anticipate his touch rather than fear it. Apparently they regarded it worth the heave-ho to climb the stairs just to be within his grasp.

Dan moved forward, arms raised for the patdown. "What about Philip?"

"Who?"

"Weren't you dating someone named Philip last year?"

Donny cast his mind back. "Describe."

The bouncer let Dan pass after what Dan regarded as a highly unprofessional frisk. The man seemed to have been checking out his personal apparatus rather than searching for weapons of the lethal sort. He turned to Donny, who was now undergoing a similar treatment.

"Delectable, lovely, charming. A beautiful, brown prince. Indian, maybe? You brought him around once or twice. He seemed very sensible. I thought you two got on well."

"Ah! You mean Not Philip."

"Not Philip?"

Donny smiled, looking his sphinx-like best.

"Yes, Not Philip. He was Sri Lankan."

The bouncer waved him through. Dan looked back over his shoulder.

"What was he checking for — cock rings and scrotum piercings? Since when did getting into a strip club become a porn audition?"

"It's all part of the fun."

"The joys of ghetto life?"

"Right. Anyway, he — meaning Not Philip — kept saying he had a secret. Not Philip made it sound like something terrible. An affliction of some sort. I kept expecting HIV or worse. I even checked out his medicine cabinet the first few times I stayed over. Nothing. Not even an eczema cream."

"So what was it?"

They were lining up again, this time to pay the inflated cover charge. Donny waved at a couple of faces in the line-up ahead and blew a kiss, all without breaking stride in the conversation.

"Two things, actually. First, his real name was Prabin, not Philip. He doesn't like to go by his birth name."

"It's a nice name."

"Exactly. He didn't live up to it."

"Not the most terrible thing, but it says a lot about him. And the second?"

Donny held up a warning finger: *Hearken — a note to the wise.*

"And second, he was forty-two years old and had never had a relationship last longer than two weeks."

"Ouch!"

"I think ours was the record at eighteen days."

"Congratulations?"

"No. Sympathy would be more in order. He was beautiful. Flawless, in fact. And he was heavenly in bed. All testosterone and sphincter muscles. His hair was superb, his skin irreproachable. Even his breath smelled fresh in the morning, no matter where his tongue had been the night before. But Not Philip was also not relationship material. At the first hint of my growing amorousness, he bolted."

"A fight?"

"No, more like a fright. And then no answer for days on end. From fast forward, let's-get-together-every-day to suddenly I'm-busy-all-the-time. I stopped calling after the first week. I became pathetic by the second. By the third, I wanted to go over and scratch at his door and beg him to let me in. I was totally gaga, head over heels. He wanted none of it."

Bills placed on the counter vanished in exchange for a stamp on the inner wrist. Dan looked down at a glowing smiley face. He assumed it was either a suggestion of the demeanour expected of each guest while on the premises or a highly optimistic prediction of how he would be feeling by evening's end.

He turned back to Donny. "Did you ever ask him what happened?"

A baleful glance. "I know what happened. I reached my Best Before date. I was stale meat. The next time I saw him was a month later. He was out at the Eagle surrounded by friends. I picked up my broken heart, dragged it across the floor by its chain, and went over to say hi. He actually acted glad to see me.

He slipped me the tongue and we practically made out in the middle of the bar for a full five minutes. The resurrection, la-ti-da. Then when I asked when I could see him, he just shrugged. 'We'll get together again,' he said. Five minutes later, I saw him snogging someone else. That was it. I never heard from him again."

"Somebody new on the scene?"

Donny shrugged. "I doubt it. He just doesn't get attached. For long, anyway. I mean, if you haven't had a real relationship by forty-two, what are the chances you're ever going to have one?"

"True."

They'd reached the club's inner sanctum, a rostrum where barely clothed young men wandered freely amongst the "gentlemen" to display their wares, such as they were. Dan looked around curiously. Many of the dancers were truly fetching. Skin tones galore and looks of every sort — from twinks to muscle gods and back again. It was a veritable catalogue of flesh, a modern-day slave auction. Only these boys were for the browsing and borrowing, not the buying.

"Anyway, to get back to you …"

"I thought you'd forgotten."

"… and your latest debacle."

They sidled up to the bar where Donny slapped a twenty on the counter. They watched a waiter turn, dip, and glide, pushing two pint glasses forward. Shirtless and wearing only tight shorts, he flashed a killer smile as he handed over the change, hinting that for a small price his affections might also be available. And maybe, for just a bit more, the rest of him, too. Donny pocketed the coins and left a five.

Dan glanced over. "Big tipper tonight."

"I'm a regular. It pays to treat the staff well."

"Big tippers get big tips?"

"Something like that. By the way, we're going to miss the show. Let's head upstairs."

They climbed the well-worn stairs, illuminated by a red light, and bordered by an intricately carved wood panel that might have come from the dungeon of the Marquis de Sade's last stand. Arcane, polished, and reflective, it bespoke of a century or more of hidden delights. A pseudo-mirror, with a patina shiny enough to fool the drunker patrons in a dim light.

Upstairs, they found a dancer's platform with boys lined up on either side. A glass backdrop overlooked a second stage one floor below. Double your viewing pleasure, double your fun. The MC stood, microphone in hand. His patter was quick, the music jaunty and upbeat as he offered the patrons a "Slam Bam Minute" featuring full frontal displays of the best wares the house had to offer.

Dan quaffed his beer and settled onto a couch beside Donny as the MC hustled his protégés for "a more intense encounter" behind the curtains at only twenty dollars per song. Considerably more than *Ten Cents a Dance*, Dan mused, but then this club had a reputation for being up-market. Who said romance was cheap?

On the dais, each dancer flashed his most prominent features. Many were attractive. All were charming. Heartbreak was the stock in trade here. Some were quite impressive — a young black man with the most differentiated set of abs Dan had ever seen, another with an elongated penis that, even slack, dangled nearly to his knee. Donny leaned over to confide that it had earned him the unofficial moniker, "Point of No Return."

"Colourful, that," Dan replied.

One at a time, the boys mounted the stage for the buying and selling of surreptitious looks; price no object when desire's on the block. Because what it comes down to, they seemed to say, is what have I got and how much can you afford? Once you're hooked, you'll keep coming back. No matter the prize, no matter your taste. Crack cocaine, cheap gin, rough sex, good times, a roll of the dice, the turn of a card. Everything's up for sale. Anything to blot out the despair of so long life, the pain of your miserable existence. A little magic to put the shine back in your eyes and the colour in your cheeks. Wind up the top and set it spinning on the floor once again. Your roll, friend. I'll undo my shirt just enough to make you squirm, show you the outline of a stiff prick in my trousers or push up a sleeve to flash the bulging vein just begging for a needle. Make me feel complete and I will love you forever. Or maybe just for a day or possibly even an hour. Well, long enough for a quick wank, at least. Because love's a sham, love's a lark. And we all know love is immortal. Or is it just immoral? No matter. While your need is strong my love is miles wide, a magic carpet to ride on straight to the land of your dreams. Who cares if it's only a few threads deep? But then five, ten, thirty years on and you're still trying to kick the habit. Where, oh where, is love? What is love, after all? Better to forget it ever existed. Better never to have known that dream at all. Time to drag yourself off home alone, once again. Ah, well, there's always tomorrow night.

The final dancer was one of the most dazzling Dan had ever seen. Sparkling blue eyes and chin-length black hair cut in a bob, he had a trailer-park body covered in tattoos, a piercing in every orifice, and a face with movie-star potential written all over it. He was anybody's amusement-park ride.

True to his word, the MC wrapped up the event in under a minute then leapt off-stage to allow the first dancer to give his all for art.

"You never said what ended the affair with Kelvin," Donny remarked, his attention revived now that the on-stage display was over and the music had returned to the normal tinselly state of a strip club-cum-brothel.

"His temper," Dan said.

Donny gave him a quizzical look. "Not yours? Shocking."

"Not mine. We'd made plans to get together on a Saturday and, as usual, he revised things at the last minute. He called half an hour before and said he was too busy to meet at four, as planned. He suggested a six o'clock rendezvous instead. I said I might be free then, but I would let him know if I was."

"And?"

"Turned out I wasn't. At five minutes past six, he called to ask where I was in a rather unpleasant tone. I said I was busy. He flew off the handle and called me irresponsible. I reminded him we'd agreed to meet at four and when he changed the time I said I would confirm if I was free. I wasn't. Ergo my no-show and no call. He seemed to think I'd kept him waiting on purpose."

"And did you?"

"No, but I purposely didn't rearrange my schedule for him because I was annoyed how he always had to have the last word. I wasn't going to give it to him. The next day I let him know I didn't like how he rescheduled all our get-togethers to suit him. He blew up. I told him to think about why he was really angry and hung up. I waited for an apology, but all I got was an email demanding that I return his shitty flowers."

Donny quaffed his beer and turned his attention to watch Point of No Return, who had just arrived onstage for a solo performance.

"He came in second in the Mr. Slam contest last month. Wait till you see his talent."

The boy's only attempt at dancing constituted something like jiggling back and forth from one foot to the other for a few seconds. After removing his last few pieces of clothing, he simply bent forward and tickled the head of his penis with his tongue.

"His real name is Sam," Donny offered, in case Dan wondered or cared.

"Good to know, I guess." Dan watched in fascination. "Is that possible?"

"Legally or physically?"

"Either. Both."

"It shouldn't be, but he's doing it, regardless."

"I'd be fascinated to know what talent the first place winner had."

"He rode in on a unicycle."

Dan looked over at the minuscule stage, trying to imagine it.

Donny turned to Dan. "Anyway, my summation of your latest affair is that Project Management Kelvin was trying to dominate you with all his revisions and criticisms. When he discovered he couldn't, it pissed him off. You're a nice guy. You're co-operative and generous. And you are never, ever irresponsible. That's obvious to anyone who knows you. He wanted your subservience. You didn't give it to him — and good for you — so it was over. He was rude and he owed you an apology. You didn't get one, you waited a reasonable time for it, and then made for the exit. I would have done the same, only sooner."

The music died and Point of No Return stood basking in the applause, lights glittering off all his piercings. Donny downed the dregs of his beer, looked over at the Ten Cents a Dance stage.

"And that is why both of us are alone today," he concluded with a nod at Dan's drink. "Another?"

Dan looked down at his glass, still half full.

"I'm good, thanks."

Donny patted him on the shoulder. "I know. That's your problem. You need to be bad again. Just now and then, for old times' sakes."

"Can't. You know the rules. I'm a reformed man."

Donny gave him a serious look.

"You know, they did this experiment with fruit flies. They put a bowl of alcohol in two different containers: one was filled with fruit flies that had just had sex and the other with fruit flies that hadn't had sex for a long time. Guess which ones drank the most."

Dan shrugged. "No idea."

"The sex-starved fruit flies. You should be lapping it up, if your current state of datelessness is to be believed."

"Are you saying I have the sex life of a fruit fly?"

"Something like that. If you don't want sex then at least have another drink. For old times' sake."

Just then Sam drifted by, smiling at Donny and four other men simultaneously.

"Speaking of old times' sake ... I'll be back."

Dan watched as Donny followed Sam to the private booths at the back of the bar. He knew they'd be gone for at least three songs' worth, which meant he was going to be a) very bored for the next fifteen minutes, and b) hit on by hungry street hustlers-gone-legit with their modicum of stagecraft, such as it was. Fortunately, he knew how to hold his own here.

He looked around the bar at the faces of the

perpetually frumpy clientele, saw the unsated hunger as they gazed at the dancers, at odds in a community where youth and beauty were crowns worn by princes and Cinderfellas. All others were ugly stepsisters at best.

Three songs unfurled in raunchy hypnotic beats. Dan managed to persuade two lap dancers that their affections were wasted on him. No joy in paying for something he could touch but not call his own or bring home for consolation later. He was thinking of leaving before Donny returned. *Too old for this sort of thing*, he'd say by way of apology the next time they spoke. He might have to endure a minor harangue for penance, but it would be worth it to escape this dismal palace of broken dreams.

Then he turned and felt a shiver go down his spine. Something about looking Fate in the eye without blinking. In this case, Fate stood alone in a dark corner, far from the light. Dan noticed him because of his stillness, his body rigid and upright, while everyone around him moved and gestured and shimmied with the beat. This man contained his own centre of gravity, holding himself apart from the rest of the room in a way that suggested superiority without making an issue of it.

Face like a statue. Sculpted cheekbones and deeply recessed eyes. An elegant brow, courtly nose, and slightly dissatisfied mouth. *Not white, but exotic in any language*, Dan thought. Here was exquisite beauty, the kind made for adoration, obsessive love, and suicidal urges contemplated in the aftermath of a touch. It was the legend carved in the foothills of desert towns and retold thousands of years hence. He'd seen a face like that once, a photograph of a young Serbian prince with just a hint of the gangster about him. The story went that both men and women had gone mad for him, throwing themselves off parapets and ramparts for his love.

Someone bumped his arm, spilling his beer. Dan turned as a short, pudgy boy reached a hand out in drunken apology, smiled sadly, then passed by on his search for some sort of oblivion. Dan's attention was distracted for only a split second. He looked back hurriedly, as though afraid the vision might vanish. The other was still there. Green laser sliced the air between them, hanging like phosphorous. Neither made a move as the dancers and bartenders and patrons slowly disappeared around them. All Dan saw was the face of the man staring back at him.

If Franz Mesmer himself had been in the audience, the attraction between the two men could not have been greater. Mesmer's postulation that an energy transfer occurred between animate and inanimate nature might have explained the rising and falling of so many priapic objects in the club's nether regions, where the magnetic property of money somehow magically transferred its powers to the various body parts moving in accordance with some mysterious principle. On the other hand, it would have had a harder time explaining the irresistible attraction between two men finding themselves alone in a crowded room, though it could have been defined as chemistry. In fact, it was a simple equation: two men who were hot for each other had just found their immutable object. Lust could be a beautiful thing.

Donny returned with a fresh mug of ale and an even fresher smile on his face. He saw Dan gazing off, looked over and caught the exotic features.

He set his glass down and shrugged. "Go for it, Romeo. You'll forget Project Management Kelvin in all of two seconds."

"Who?"

"My sentiments exactly."

They moved at the same time. Dan caught a gymnast's sleekness in the other's even stride.

"My name is Ren Hao," said the vision limned in white linen.

He held out a hand. There was no ring in the usual place, but there was a tan line suggesting it had been there recently. Dan suspected he was one of those beautiful Taiwanese businessmen on loan from their domestic lives, having a night out that the wife and kids would never have to know about, so far across the waves and on vacation from conventional morality.

"I'm Dan Sharp."

They shook hands, the desire for physical gratification only intensified by the contact.

Dan thought of his options: a long, boring conversation that might eventually lead nowhere or else taking charge of the situation, here and now. He recalled Donny's dismissive comment regarding the long road to consummation. Besides, he told himself, this one was definitely not a wait-until-later type. If you find a diamond on the road, you pick it up and put it in your pocket. Otherwise, it won't be there tomorrow when you return. Shiny things had a tendency to disappear quickly in the gay world.

Ren beat him to it. "My hotel is nearby," he said.

"Sounds good to me," Dan said, thinking it would turn out to be the Delta Chelsea or maybe the Towne Inn, both quietly functional accommodations that had hosted their share of late-night get-togethers of the vicarious sort.

Not so.

Four

Dangerous Liaisons

They left the strip club and caught a cab down to the financial district, dense and brooding, just a few blocks north of the harbour. A hub of traffic and commuter activity overlying fifteen tangled kilometres of underground shopping by day, it is eerily deserted at night. Walking alone here after dark has proved dangerous, but mostly to the unwary. Fog can crowd in unexpectedly. Footsteps echo on pavement in imitation of Jack the Ripper's London, silently admonishing: *Beware! Beware!* Those too drunk or naive to register the warning have ended up mugged or worse. Clubbers trip home in pairs and trios here. Your mother was right: there's safety in numbers.

Dan gazed out the window as the taxi slid along, sleek and predatory, a lone wolf cut loose from the pack. They paused at the intersection of Richmond and Peter Streets. Ren slipped the driver a few bills from a wad of cash as they exited.

There was no hotel in sight.

"It is nice to walk at night," he said, to Dan's questioning look as they stood together on the curb.

They came upon a cabal of kids at the next intersection. The smell of weed drifted toward them, the air rich with the fug-heavy sweetness. The group skeedaddled as the pair approached, two mature men looking very out of place in after-hours clubland.

Dan followed Ren's lead. Their talk was desultory. Ren's English was better than acceptable, Dan's Mandarin negligible. On the whole the silence between them felt comfortable, not awkward. Dan put it down to the fact they both had something other than conversation in mind. That was all right, as far as he was concerned. No need for pretence. It was far too long since he'd spent time with a man with nothing more than pleasure on the agenda. Ren fit the bill perfectly.

Dan was just beginning to think he'd misunderstood their destination when they rounded a darkened corner near the Air Canada Centre. He was momentarily surprised to see where they'd ended up. Long before lending his name to a highly successful hotel chain, Saint Germain was a penurious, sixth-century bishop known for his work with the poor. Canonized two centuries after his death, he was said to be as virtuous and austere as they came, a tireless reformer of peasants and royalty alike, setting all and sundry on the path of righteousness. So hardworking and generous was he that his monks once rebelled for fear he might give away everything he owned. The boutique hotels that bore his name, while equally fastidious, would never have welcomed the poor within their hallowed halls where a penthouse might cost upwards of a thousand dollars a throw. Dan had never spent the night here, but he knew this was fancy stuff. He was just starting to wonder what his pick-up did for a living, about to upgrade Ren from successful Taiwanese businessman to visiting Thai royalty, or even absconding drug lord, when they turned in at the demure, understated entrance.

A neatly dressed concierge glanced up discreetly. Dan caught the man's discerning gaze, registering them as Guest and Riffraff. Too late, he thought of his black jeans and chequered-shirt street wear. A second later, the man's face was a cipher. Whether he approved of early-morning trysts of the homosexual variety, or of any tryst at all, whether he was a proponent of the mixing of the races or an ardent admirer of Himmler's *Final Solution* was impossible to discern from his expression. No doubt, stashed somewhere deep in the vaults of the hotel was a mission statement dispensed to the staff in foreboding tones, outlining inappropriate fraternizing with the clientele and duly signed in blood. He'd probably been trained to memorize the face of each guest and admonished never to disturb them, no matter the hour, their states of dress or sobriety or, least of all, the company they kept. Anyone who could afford to stay at the Hôtel Le Saint-Germain could well afford the price of discretion.

Ren gave the man a curt nod then headed for the elevators, producing a pass card that made the doors whoosh open and shut again with minimal noise and maximal ease. The elevator gleamed like the inside of a diamond, mirrors positioned above and below, a self-referential little world designed with the professional voyeur or narcissist in mind. The ride was silent and smooth, as though nothing existed outside those walls. They could have been aboard a shuttle heading into deep space. It should have prepared Dan for the ostentation lying ahead. In fact, it was deceptive.

The doors opened onto a hallway that glowed quietly in a low light. Everything spoke of elegant understatement rather than flashy opulence. It was as if Germain's saintly austerity had rubbed off on the hotel's designers. Narrow rosewood shelves lined the walls at discreet intervals, with polished green apples set into slots in groupings of sixes and sevens. Real-life design motifs, each perfect and unblemished. Waxy tropical flowers, newly opened, thronged on side tables, spotlit in slender shafts of radiance like captive moonlight. All was hushed, solemn, and serene.

Dan followed Ren to room 1101. A binary code. In mathematicians' lingo, that was akin to a religious experience. Another swipe of the passkey and they entered what seemed a church's velvety interior. A more impressionable man might have knelt and genuflected. A wall of windows overlooking the lake resembled a giant mural where a freighter moved slowly, inexorably in the distance, passing out of the harbour and on to its destiny.

A final slicing of the passkey activated a relay of overhead pin-spots. The room was immaculate, a monk's cell designed for maximum comfort and efficiency. A wide bed had been tucked into a corner, like a ship at berth. An imposing black-and-white photo, oversized and mounted above, showed an athlete straining to achieve, biceps pumping and legs piston-like as he strove for glory or perfection.

The glass cubicle rising like a decompression air-lock at the room's centre was its most surprising feature. Transparent on three of four sides, the shower's blackout blinds could be operated from within for decency or raised to allow the voyeur pleasure from without. Your partner could lie in bed observing, waiting for the pivotal moment to strip down and join in, both of you watching the city go about its to-ings and fro-ings as you washed away your cares, your sins, or just the dirt of everyday living. All of this designed to bring you one step closer to the immaculate state of a sixth-century monk who wanted nothing more than to give away everything he owned, divesting himself of the constraints of the material world. *Not too shabby*, Dan thought.

He turned. Ren stood behind him, watching Dan watching the harbour. They moved slowly, like ships attempting a coupling for ease of boarding, Ren's body tight and compact, Dan's hard and expansive. Thighs grazed, arms held. Lips met with sudden force. Not in comradeship, but hunger. Dan sensed a man starved for sex. The kiss ended and they pulled apart, regrouping for a counterattack. Dan felt as though he might become absorbed by this man's need if he weren't careful.

Ren put a hand to Dan's face. Fingers closed over his eyelids, traced the outline of the scar that angled down his temple like caught lightning, given to him by his father when he was late coming home from school at the age of ten. The hand retreated and Dan opened his eyes again. Ren cocked his head, a grin transforming his features.

"You are a tough man, I think."

"Yeah," Dan said. "I am a tough man." *Right now I am anything you want me to be*, he thought.

He reached out to touch Ren's chest. A reptilian reflex twisted the hand up and aside. Dan felt the pain, his wrist pinned against the wall behind him. He didn't resist, curious to see what else this game presaged.

Ren's lips twitched, perfectly formed half moons joined by a silver thread. His breath was fragrant, a surprising rose garden at midnight.

"What you like to do to your lovers?"

Dan shook his head, denying the burning pain in his wrist. "Not to. *With*."

Ren tightened his grip. The half moons crumpled, turned cruel. "No, tough man. What you like to do *to* them."

Dan leaned forward.

"I like —" their lips met and parted again "— to kiss … to intoxicate them."

A tingling in Dan's groin said this was going to be

one of those rare sexual encounters that would make all his synapses come alive. An energy transfer, pure animal magnetism. This was the beginning of real sex, not just a simulacrum of pleasure. Deep and devastating. A dance through fire. A shedding of defences, shattering and annihilating. He'd experienced it a handful of times before. It was like giving yourself up to the soft caress of Death and seeing where it led. All the while knowing you were doomed, no matter where it took you.

His hands slid down Ren's abdomen, strayed along a waistband, slipped inside. A quickening of desire as his fingers crept into the warm cleft behind. Ren's hand stole up to Dan's throat. They stood, combatants armed to the death, each waiting for the other to strike the fatal blow.

Dan felt his breathing constricted, surprised to find himself lifted off the ground, his back pressed into the smooth wood behind him. Sparkles outlined his vision as he encountered that brief separation of reality and unreality that presaged the beginnings of a blackout. Entering a new realm of experience. He wasn't sure he wanted to know what lay on the other side. If Ren didn't release his grip soon ... Dan raised his leg and kneed him in the groin, sending him reeling across the room.

Ren fell to the floor and lay there, looking pleased.

"Tough man," he said, his eyes glittering with satisfaction. "I like you."

Dan pulled him up and pressed him against the wall, yanking his shirttails free from his trousers. He knelt, pressed his mouth against Ren's tensed belly, licking his way up to the pectorals, hard and smooth, the nipples like dark opals on a field of amber.

An erection strained Ren's briefs, hard and fat. Well-dressed men were always dirtiest out of their clothes, Dan knew. There was something about an expensively tailored businessman that melted before his rough-and-tumble appearance. A sweaty T-shirt peeled over taut muscle charged the eagerness of a manor lord sneaking off to the stables for a brief romp with the stable boy under cover of darkness, slipping away at break of dawn with bits of straw clinging to his back and in his hair.

In the light, a gash gleamed across Ren's thigh, the wound healed long ago. It was startling, like a worm revealed at the heart of a perfect rose. Before he could examine it further, Ren's hands pushed him aside, forcing Dan's face into his crotch.

Dan struggled to his feet. Together, they stumbled to the bed. Silk sheets, an Aladdin's boudoir. *No surprise there*, Dan told himself as they tumbled down and over the ersatz stage. Inhibitions quickly gave way to feelings of euphoria that might otherwise have taken a great deal of alcohol to achieve. They slipped aside those restraints, pressed flesh against flesh, as daring lapsed into daring.

Dan was pleased by his lovemate's body, a superb machine, its movements smooth and piston-like. Caught in the wall mirror, Ren's dreamy eyes suggested a lineage of cultivated excess, a descent from opium eaters. This was a man born for pleasure, but one who knew how to trigger it in return, gauging the smallest seismic tremors to leave his partner trembling.

The condoms lay nestled inside a bedside drawer, a small stack encased in an ebony box. Dan expected no less from such a man. He ripped the package open with his teeth and spat out the wrapper.

Ren lay on his back looking up, his torso taut with the raggedness of his breathing. Dan shook his head.

"Not here," he said, yanking him up and splaying him before the window.

Nerves jangling, Dan gripped Ren from behind and eased himself in. Ren tightened, twisting to experience all that Dan offered, as though his sensory antennae had been set to maximum.

When they finished, Dan peeled off the condom and let it fall to the floor with a soft *plop*. As far as he was concerned, rich men taking a brief detour from their family life should be able to afford discreet valets and chambermaids as well as discretionary concierges. If they couldn't, then they shouldn't be out playing around after dark.

A clock built into the headboard read 3:33 a.m. He'd have to dispense with the stagey shower. Maybe save it for another time.

"That's what I like to do to my lovers," he said, pulling on his pants and grabbing for his shirt.

"I like you, tough man," Ren said.

"I'll leave you my number." Dan reached into his wallet and extracted a card.

Ren took the card and placed it on the bedside table without looking at it. There was a glazed look in his eyes. He was unlikely to call, Dan knew. Having served his purpose, he would quickly be forgotten — discarded like the used condom. Ren would soon be flying back to wherever he came from, returning to the wife and children and quiet suburban home waiting for him in whatever country he'd left.

Ren walked him to the door, standing in the soft light. His muscles gleamed with sweat, quivering softly like a racehorse after a particularly well-run race. There was no goodbye kiss, as Dan knew there wouldn't be. Kissing was for arousal, not comradely communing or a parting thanks, no matter how well done the job.

A brief nod, the barest acknowledgement of what had transpired between them, and the door clicked shut. In the hallway, Dan grasped an apple, hefted it from the slot and bit into the tart sweetness, the juice running down his chin. A clanking alerted him. At the far end of the hall, a man with a cart was replacing the green apples with white pears. Of course, wealth had its rewards. It was only then that he realized he still had no idea what Ren did for a living.

Downstairs the desk clerk looked up, barely noting his passage through the lobby. Dan exited the shushing doors and wandered home through the misty streets, marvelling at the city's stillness, as pleased with his recent conquest as any teenager on a first date. Little wondering where it all might be heading.

Five

A Good Girl Gone Bad

Getting up after four hours of sleep is one thing when you're a nineteen-year-old university freshman recovering from the sundry joys of a pub crawl with your dorm mates the night before. Pretending you can do the same thing and keep a productive schedule while approaching forty is simply folly or, at best, self-delusion. Dan got up because he had to. There was a rising, but little shining to go with it.

Once again, his son sat at the kitchen table. Ked glanced up, noted his father's restive features, the glazed eyes. His expression turned to a look of concern.

"Dad, you're not drinking again, are you?"

Dan shook his head then decided on full disclosure. "One beer only, I promise. Though I stayed out far later than I should have."

Since his "troubles" in recent years, his son had been demanding of Dan's sobriety, and rightly so. Dan had been on a path to self-destruction when Ked intervened. Following a period of self-imposed abstention, they now had an agreement — occasional social drinking was fine, but not to excess. So far, Dan had kept the faith.

"I was out with your Uncle Donny, if you want an alibi. At least for the first part of the evening."

"What happened after that?"

Dan grabbed his keys and wallet and checked his watch.

"No time for the third degree right now," he said. "But I swear I didn't overdo it. No secrets between us, remember?"

Being a good father was one thing, but trying to lead the life of a single gay man and keeping the two paths separate was nearly impossible with an inquisitive teenager in the house.

"I believe you," Ked said cautiously. "I'm just curious."

"I know. And thank you for your concern. I'll see you tonight."

Dan closed the door behind him before his son asked any more awkward questions.

Dan preferred to walk to work when he had the time and inclination. Today he decided to take the time. Spring was late, but the sun was at least making an effort to break through. If it could then so could he. The walk revived him somewhat.

His office was in a warehouse at the foot of

Broadview Avenue, a red brick fortification surviving from the period just after Confederation. It had been modified and made chic enough to attract an IT operation, several independent design companies, and an import-export business. The area was in an enclave just far enough away from the rising towers of downtown to afford open vistas and an unimpeded view of the city's skyline. To the west, a lone church stood out against the meagre, miserly flow of the Don River.

The plaque on the outside door bore his name. Below, it read simply PRIVATE INVESTIGATIONS. The lettering was small and discreet enough, and the neighbourhood fashionable-unfashionable enough, that Dan wasn't regaled with requests from people trying to get the goods on their unfaithful spouses. He invariably turned those down. There was low and then there was too low. Messy karma stuff. That wasn't how he wanted to make his living.

Inside, all was quiet. The premises were modest, but they suited his needs and income. In fact, he was lucky to be renting from a former client, an international shipping agent for whom he'd once done a favour. He gratefully accepted the unused space directly over a warehouse where a treasure trove of tagged and numbered cartons rested briefly on their way to and from the airport. On any given day they housed premium artwork, fine furniture, family heirlooms, fresh flowers, exotic foods, pricey liquor, and even Cuban cigars prior to being transferred from their original cartons to more innocuous-looking boxes — transformed from contraband to sanctioned goods, from crooked to straight, with a simple change of dress that meant they could easily be transported across the U.S. border and resold in their new guise.

That he hadn't been given front and centre in the building's operations suited Dan's needs perfectly. Despite being shuffled off to the far end, he did not feel himself a pariah in the bustling world of importing and exporting. To make him feel more at home, he'd been given access to Sylvia, the matronly secretary who lorded over her domain like a deposed queen just trying to make the best of things under diminished circumstances. Among her chores, both official and unofficial, Sylvia added to the ambience with a talent for baking.

Dan's office was a soothing grey-blue, a statement of earnest sobriety. Two modest murals chosen by Donny added a personal accent. While Donny's taste in art tended toward the modern, the pieces were refined enough not to bewilder the average viewer yet without being reduced to mere decorations. There was ample room for a filing cabinet, a desk, and two client chairs. The overall impression was just one step away from Philip Marlowe, but Dan was glad to quit his study in leafy Leslieville and head out to this place each morning. It felt like a giant step up, no matter the cost or size.

He grabbed a coffee in the lobby then checked in with Sylvia for messages and a cinnamon bun. She gave him a smile that stopped just short of flirtation.

Both of them spent far too many weekends there than was good for them, though Dan knew nothing of her personal life. He knew she liked to mother him, but maybe a glimmer of sexuality spiced up her day. There was nothing pressing, she said. Anything important would be waiting for him on his office phone. He headed down a long, echoing hallway — the trademark of a true industrial building — and unlocked his door, depositing himself at his desk before a discreet grouping of files that contained the bare facts of the lives he'd been hired to restore to something like a state of normalcy, inasmuch as that was possible.

He flipped through the top three to see what he could reasonably update. All those sad stories with no happy endings in sight. Some people left behind families, careers, and cars abandoned in empty lots. Others left full suitcases and empty bank accounts. The variations were endless, as were the reasons for vanishing. It all spelled heartbreak and despair. No matter the circumstance, there was always someone who wanted to know the why of it, even if they were saddened to learn that the incurable addict had preferred to wind up dead in some alley with a needle in her arm rather than spend a life in and out of rehab.

The stories seldom ended well, even when Dan found his quarry alive. Some expressed a desire to return to their former lives, but few were able to do it. Going back home was a tough act to pull off. Moses knew a thing or two about that. So did Noah and Thomas Wolfe. Whatever their reasons for leaving, people who reinvented themselves did not remain the same afterward, even when the vanishing was by choice.

He found it difficult to keep focused on work. Before long it was clear the morning would not go well. Concentration was not in the cards. Thoughts of the previous night's tryst stayed with him like memories of a drunken debauch. Intoxication was one word for it. His senses were on fire, his heart pounded each time he drifted off into reveries of what he'd experienced. The images shimmered on the edge of his mind, distant and unreal. Or maybe what he'd felt the previous night was real, while the rest of life's modest little expectations were just an anteroom in which he waited for reality to catch up.

The phone jarred his nerves. He caught the name of a police contact on the display: Sergeant Ian Cunningham. He couldn't recall having made an inquiry of this particular officer, at least not recently. His hand hesitated over the receiver: answer or don't answer. *Better to answer*, he told himself. Police intel didn't come easy. It was best to take it when he could.

In fact, the officer wasn't responding to an inquiry, but hoping for a favour. After an awkward greeting, he explained that he was looking for information on a young woman who had disappeared not far from Dan's neighbourhood. After a few prudent queries, it turned out she was the officer's daughter and had vanished following an argument about boyfriends and drugs and a salacious Facebook posting. The tale quickly unfolded: piercings, tattoos, and constant back-talk to a formerly much-respected father currently at his wit's end. This, followed by a few angry, over-heated words now much-regretted.

"Teenagers, eh?" the rueful father said.

"I've been there," Dan replied.

"A good girl gone bad," the officer lamented.

Aren't we all? Dan thought, though he kept it to himself.

A simple request: *Would he keep an ear open for word on the street?*

Dan said he would do what he could, asked for the girl's photograph to be forwarded, and put the phone down. Before he could return to the pile of waiting cases, it rang again. It was Donny.

"One waits, trembling with anticipation."

"Ask all you like. I may not admit everything, though."

"Was it as wonderful as it looked from an envious distance?"

"It was good, but a bit disconcerting."

"Do tell."

"You know me, I prefer discretion. Let's just say he likes it rough, but I won't go into the details."

A pause ensued. "Rough or violent?"

"It's a thin line, but I managed to walk it. So far just rough."

"Name? Occupation?"

"His name's Ren. My guess is he's a Taiwanese businessman."

"Your guess? You obviously didn't go in for more than the basics, if you don't even know that."

"We had other things to discuss."

A demure pause. "No doubt. Will you see him again?"

"Probably not. I left my number. He didn't offer his."

"Too bad. He was unbelievably yummy-looking."

Dan paused, wondering whether to divulge more. Mischievousness won out, knowing Donny's predilection for the frills and fripperies of life.

"He's staying at the Saint-Germain."

There was a pause.

"An extremely wealthy Taiwanese businessman, then."

"I didn't snoop in his wallet …"

"And you call yourself a detective."

"… but that's my guess, too."

"Anyway, it sounds like you struck it rich. I wish you luck."

"I know you better than that."

"Okay, you're right. I wish you a brief but memorable fling before you come crawling back to the fold of the Lonely Hearts Club. I can't be stranded here all by myself forever."

A buzzing interrupted the line.

"Gotta go. I've got another call coming in."

"Keep in touch. Don't leave town suddenly."

"I'll try not to." He hit the reset button. "Dan Sharp."

"Hello, tough man."

Dan felt the smile creep over his face.

He settled in the chair and lifted his feet onto the desk, visions of himself splayed across silk sheets dancing before his eyes.

"Hello yourself, Ren. It's nice to hear from you."

"Thank you. You left your card. I thought it perhaps not inappropriate to call."

"Not at all."

"I wished to tell you I am very glad I went out last night instead of staying in my hotel. I think this is what is called serendipity, is it not?"

"Something like that," Dan said. "It doesn't matter what you call it, but it was a good encounter."

"I should like to see you again."

"I'd like that, too."

"Perhaps not just for the personal, but also for business reasons."

Dan felt himself shift from casual to cautious. "I see."

"You are a private investigator."

Dan swung his feet off the desk and onto the floor. "That's correct."

"Then we must talk," Ren said. "Perhaps with the more personal to come afterwards."

Dan was silent. He wasn't sure what he thought of mixing business with pleasure. It spelled complication.

"Unless this is not the usual protocol?" came Ren's voice.

"You read my mind. We'll have to leave it at that until you tell me more."

"Very good. Shall I come to your office? I am free this afternoon."

Dan glanced around the small, cramped space and thought again of the sumptuous Hôtel Le Saint-Germain.

"Let's meet somewhere else."

"When?"

He opened his appointment book: blank.

"How about an hour from now?"

"Very good."

Dan looked over at his notice board and rattled off an address from a lunch flyer. "I'll see you there," he said, feeling a pleasant lightness at the prospect of meeting Ren again so soon.

Six

Doing the Dannie

Toronto's Danforth Avenue is to Greeks what Santa's Village is to elves, with the scent of grilled calamari, the tangy kiss of *tzatziki*, and the crackling burst of *saganaki* flames to astonish the uninitiated before the ritual dousing in lemon juice. Then too there are the waiters, centaur-like with their crisp linens and protuberant buttocks, who smile and crinkle winsomely, but always leave you wanting more. Not everyone needs a stage to break a heart.

Ren was seated near the back, dressed in a suit and tie. Armani, and not the cheap kind. At Dan's arrival, he stood and gave a vigorous nod, his smile broadening. The greeting seemed oddly reverential. No matter, Dan liked eagerness in his dates, whether business or pleasure. He studied Ren's face in the daylight: the flat cheekbones, silky skin, and pouting mouth. *Late thirties*, he decided, though he could pass for younger. Maybe because of the desire he saw etched there.

They shook hands with a show of formality. Had it been two North Americans who'd slept together the night before they would have embraced, brothers at arms, revelling in the instant familiarity gays accord one another, no matter how disparate their backgrounds. Once you slept with a man, you were connected with him in some ineffable way that non-sexual comrades never could be.

"It is a distinct pleasure to see you again so soon," Ren said.

"Thanks. Good to see you, too," Dan replied.

He would allow Ren his awkward formality for now. If he steered toward the weather and last night's baseball scores as topics of conversation, Dan might rethink his strategy, but a bit of stiffness was fine for the moment. How straight men tolerated the nonsense they bonded over was beyond him, though maybe it was just a shallow connection they were seeking and not true intimacy. But one look at that angelic face atop a satyr's body promised to be worth any amount of small talk he might endure.

"I had a good time last night," Dan ventured, trying to push things in a more palpable direction. "I hope you did, too."

Ren actually blushed. Dan was charmed.

"Yes, I enjoyed myself very much," he said, his voice lowered and eyes darting, as though worried they might be overheard.

It's Toronto in the twenty-first century, Dan wanted to say. *We don't need to hide it here.* But he wouldn't risk Ren's discomfort. He had no idea of his social conditioning, the boundaries he needed to observe to keep on an even keel, especially if he was a married man stepping out on the sly.

A waiter approached. Ren looked at Dan.

"Please, will you order for both?" He caught Dan's surprised look. "I am open to many things."

Dan resisted a smile, nodded, and turned to the menu. He rattled off a few dishes, hoping they would offer a range of appeal. The waiter gathered up the menus and left.

"Thank you," Ren said. "Your hospitality is most appreciated."

"So was yours last night. I'm just returning the favour."

This time there was no blushing.

"That was also my pleasure," Ren told him.

"We didn't get much chance to talk," Dan said. "I don't even know where you're from."

"I am from mainland China," Ren replied. "But I am abroad a great deal."

Visions of the Taiwanese businessman slipped away and were replaced by countless questions on Dan's part.

"I am here as a representative for my country," Ren explained, as if anticipating his thoughts. "I am a cultural ambassador. I meet with members of your government and business community for trade and tourism purposes."

"That sounds impressive."

He smiled his disarming smile. "It is not really very interesting, I am afraid."

"I'm also impressed by your English. Did you learn it in school?"

Ren shook his head. "Not as a child. Later, I went to a school for international trade relations. There I had an English teacher from Canada. She was extremely effective. This is one of the reasons I am allowed to come here. My government considers me to be a much-valued asset." Almost as an afterthought, he added, "Of course, many people wish to leave China and come to the West."

"Do you?"

A smile flickered and died. Ren held Dan's gaze. "There are many things I would like."

"Such as?"

"I would like to change certain things. For instance, there is almost no homosexual life in China. What is there is purposely hidden. For many years, I did not even know such things existed. No one spoke about it. Chinese say it is a Western disease."

Dan nodded. "I believe Mao claimed that homosexuality was the result of a corrupt capitalist society."

China's great leader, Dan knew, was just one in a long line of politicians who had used scare tactics to intimidate people, equating the inferred slur of homosexuality with corrupt political practices. Ironically, both sides in the communist-capitalist debate fostered the same kind of fear, with gays caught in the middle, as usual. The infamous red-baiter, Senator Joseph McCarthy, went so far as to defend his beliefs by saying that anyone who stood against them was "either a communist or a cocksucker," neither of which most Americans wanted to be called at the time. On the other hand, a committed communist named Harry Hay, founder of one of the first gay liberation groups in the U.S., was subsequently kicked out of the Communist party for being a homosexual. In an almost-farcical turnaround, he was expelled from his own Mattachine Society for being a communist. For queers, there was just no middle ground.

Dan smiled. "You can blame anything on money, I guess."

Ren nodded shyly. "This may be true, but I did not grow up rich. My family came from Chengdu in Sichuan province. Although my father was in the military, we were still very poor."

"Well, there you go," Dan said. "You were gay and poor. So neither assertion is correct."

"Yes."

Ren's face grew solemn.

"Thank you for coming today," he said, as though addressing a will reading. "I would like to discuss a matter with you for professional reasons."

He pulled an envelope from his pocket. A single black-and-white image slid onto the table. Dan picked up the photograph. A massive sculpture of a lion filled the background, while two teenagers stood in the foreground. Ren's nascent beauty was already palpable; the girl beside him seemed ghostly, pensive.

"This is me with my sister, Ling. She died in Tiananmen."

"My condolences."

"Thank you. I would like to hire you to find her."

Dan shook his head. "I'm sorry, I don't understand. You want me to find a dead woman?"

Ren shook his head vigorously. "Excuse me, please. Perhaps she is not dead now. I have found her on the Internet. I believe she lives here, possibly under a false name."

Dan's expression must have been comical, because Ren suddenly began to laugh.

"Yes, it is a mystery!"

Dan flashed on the envelope that had showed up at breakfast two days earlier, the one filled with clippings on the Tiananmen massacre.

"You sent me photocopies of articles on Tiananmen."

Ren smiled shyly. "Yes, I did this. It is true."

"Why?"

Ren's face was all seriousness now. "I did not know if you would be acquainted with the history of my country and the student revolts."

"Tiananmen was famous. Everybody remembers it. Everybody who was alive then."

Ren shook his head. "In my country, it is already being forgotten. It is buried along with the past."

Dan's mind was backtracking as he studied Ren's face. "Then you already knew who I was when we met."

"You will please forgive me. I tracked you down, as they say in the West."

"Is that why you slept with me?"

Ren looked chagrined. "No. Please do not believe this was to take advantage. I was pleasantly ... surprised to find myself attracted to you. Only because of this did I sleep with you, I promise."

"Sorry, that was rude of me." Dan glanced down at the photograph. "You had better explain what this all has to do with your sister."

"When I learned my government was sending me to Canada, I investigated the Internet to learn about Toronto. To my surprise, I found a Chinatown with many Chinese people."

"More than one," Dan said, thinking of the second Chinatown in Riverdale close to his own neighbourhood, as well as several established Asian neighbourhoods in the city at large.

"I believe I have found a picture of my sister at the Kowloon Bakery."

The name sounded familiar. Dan thought he recalled such an establishment from his student days. "I think I know it," he said.

"In the picture, my sister is sitting at a table eating with other customers."

"Are you sure it's her?"

Ren nodded. "I am very sure it is her."

"When did you last see her?"

"At Tiananmen Square on the night the fighting started."

"Tell me what happened."

"It was my eighteenth birthday. We were at a

restaurant called Red Dragon. Ling, myself, and two friends from school. On the way home, we heard the noise of many people gathered in the square near the Mausoleum of Mao Zedong. We already knew there was unrest and anti-government protests, but not the fighting. I said to my friends, 'Let us go and see what is happening.' We all went. Then the tanks arrived. When the fighting started, we tried to escape. I was shot."

"You were shot?"

Ren gripped his thigh. "Here."

Dan remembered the scar he'd seen on Ren's leg, the worm at the heart of the perfect rose.

"I fell down. Others were screaming and yelling. My friends ran away. When I got up, Ling was gone. I never saw her again."

His expression was subdued.

"I loved my sister very much," he said softly.

"What happened after that?"

"I hid until the fighting was over. Some people took me in. I could not go home for two weeks. There was no telephone. My mother was very scared, but my father was angry. He beat me when I came back without Ling."

"And your leg?"

"It healed eventually. It still hurts sometimes."

"I'm not surprised," Dan said.

The waiter returned with drinks. Dan waited till he left again before continuing.

"Tell me about your sister. What was she like?"

"Ling was a well-behaved girl and always obedient to our parents. She obtained very high marks in school. My sister was very smart and exquisitely beautiful."

"Older or younger than you?"

"One year older. Ling was extremely intelligent and liked to read. In fact, we were both good readers. When we were children, our father brought us books from the military library. We would read each one together. When we had finished all the books in the library, he went on his bicycle to another town to get more books. Especially English authors."

Dan looked at him in surprise. "I thought they would have been banned by your government."

"Not all. Only propaganda. If something criticized the Western world and the exploitation of workers, such books were allowed. Charles Dickens, for instance."

Dan smiled to think that Pip and Oliver Twist were Chinese heroes.

"How did you find the picture of your sister at the Kowloon Bakery?"

"When we were children, there was a calendar in our home. It was from the Kowloon Café in Hong Kong. Ling and I said that one day we would go there together. When I saw the advertisement for the Kowloon Bakery in Toronto, I clicked on it from simple curiosity."

"It sounds like your sister decided to go there without you. Did you print a copy of the picture?"

Ren shook his head. "No, this was not possible.

Authority figures would be curious why I should want such a thing. But I was so surprised to see her, I cried out loud."

Dan studied Ren's face. "What makes you sure the woman is your sister?"

"It has to be. If I think how she might change in twenty years, then this is precisely what she would look like today."

Dan's experience told him that was not always the case, but he was willing to hear the full story before making a judgment.

"Would you be able to find the site again?"

Ren nodded slowly. "Yes. I am sure I can find it."

The waiter returned. Dan and Ren sat in silence while he placed a basket of bread before them, plates piled with salad on either side. The boy stepped away from the table with a brisk nod. Dan almost expected him to click his heels and pivot.

He nodded to Ren to begin then picked up his fork and dug in. Fresh oregano, olive oil, and vinegar clanged against his taste buds.

"Supposing I find her? What then? What if she doesn't want to see you?"

Ren looked surprised.

"You have to be prepared," Dan cautioned. "These are the difficulties I always advise my clients to be ready to face. Tiananmen was what — twenty years ago? If your sister has lived in Toronto all this time without trying to contact you, there may be a reason for that."

A tremor passed over Ren's face. Hurt, possibly.

Or disbelief. Perhaps it hadn't occurred to him that his sister was fleeing something, or else she simply had no desire to see her family again. The logic was sometimes beyond comprehension. There was often a valid reason, if only in the mind of the person who had gone missing. Unspoken resentments, unexpressed fears. Intolerable secrets. It was impossible to say. There didn't even have to be a reason, just a lack of desire to be in touch with the family again. You couldn't make anyone go home again, not if they didn't want to. Sometimes it just took one thing — an accident, a revolt — and you realized the moment had come to make a choice: go through that brief window in time or wait for a second chance that might never come.

"She will wish to see me," Ren insisted.

"I hope she does, but I can't make her," Dan told him. "You have to understand that would be between the two of you. Assuming I can find her after twenty years. I just want you to be prepared, no matter what."

"I am a rich man. I can pay."

"I gathered."

A Chinese national with money to burn was a rare thing, Dan knew. Once an impoverished nation that could barely feed its population, the economic reforms China implemented over the past three decades had given it the second-largest economy in the world. While the average citizen remained below parity, an energetic private sector had created a small pool of millionaires whose status ranked alongside political officials. Ren's lodgings alone said he was special in that regard. If he was well set up with his government, there was no telling what he had at his disposal.

Dan pushed his salad plate away. A late lunch crowd arrived, filling the tables around them. The noise grew.

"I have to admit, I'm intrigued."

"And what of the other?" Ren asked softly. "Will you still want that from me?"

Dan smiled. *You don't find a diamond every day*, he reminded himself. For Ren, he was prepared to break a few professional rules, maybe even a few personal ones. While he didn't believe in love at first sight, he had no doubt about the powerful attraction between them, remembering how fully alive he'd felt the night before. That didn't happen every day, either.

"Maybe we need to check out what kind of fruit is in your hotel this evening."

Ren gave him a curious look. "Please?"

Their food had just arrived, mountains of it.

"I'll explain later. Let's eat."

Seven

CPTSD

Dan was back in his office by two o'clock. At four, he wrapped up the files he'd been mulling over and shut down his computer. Then he got in his car and headed downtown.

Women's College Hospital loomed at the north end of Hospital Row. He drove by it twice, like a soldier on reconnaissance deciding where and how to make his approach.

In the lobby, a small boy clutched a large bouquet of purple tulips to his chest. The flowers screamed a silent protest at their young abuser, who seemed undaunted by their sorry state. Mute as they were, the best they could offer was a creased, abused look of protest over the maltreatment.

Dan wasn't afraid of death, but he disliked hospitals. He had visited numerous graveyards and spent countless hours in morgues identifying bodies for people too delicate or timid to do such things themselves. In his professional life, he maintained a scientific demeanour, an objectivity he thought unshakable. Yet he could not come near a hospital without suffering trepidation at the thought of spending time there. Rushing through to drop off gifts and dispense good cheer while on the run would have suited him far better than having to sit and relax. Whenever he had to pay a visit, self-consciousness held him immobile in his seat, anticipating the moment when he could stand and walk down the hallway, retracing his steps out the front door and down the street where he could breathe, breathe, breathe once again.

Until then, he was stuck.

This time, however, he was the patient. Like it or not, he would endure the place till it was done with him. He crossed the lobby, bypassed the boy smothering his purple offerings for some mother/sister/aunt/grandmother, and headed to an elevator that stood empty but for one elderly woman with a fresh hairdo and an anxious face. She wore a standard-issue black dress and shiny necklace. Clearly a visitor and not a patient, then. At least, not yet. But Death had sent his calling card in advance. One arm leaned on a cane. The other trembled as it rose to select the floor button.

"Let me help you," Dan said.

"Six, please."

She smiled and retreated into her solitude. The incidental companionship of others, helpful as it might at times be for pushing buttons, was often too much to bear otherwise. Dan understood that. He pressed six and eight then settled in to await the slow journey to whatever lay above them. At the last second, a hand thrust itself between the doors. They juddered to a halt then slowly reopened, mindful of the weakened physical state of many patients or perhaps of the untoward cost of lawsuits these days. Dan glanced at the out-of-shape man in a suit and tie who apparently couldn't be bothered to wait for another car. An overdressed business exec, by the looks of it. Impatient, self-absorbed.

"Sorry," the man said, without addressing either of them in particular.

The old woman winced at the sound of his voice, frowning to herself as though this disruption might jeopardize whatever awaited her on the sixth floor.

"No problem," Dan told him.

The man scowled at his fingernails as though they were in need of a manicure. Dan studied his profile. A long, slender nose rescued what was an otherwise unremarkable face from obscurity. The newcomer eyed the numbered panel then looked away, seemingly satisfied with one of the buttons lit in an orange glow.

They stood in silence as the elevator hummed and pinged its way to the sixth floor, settling at last. The doors opened. The business exec hesitated, looking to Dan as though awaiting a cue. Behind him, the old woman suddenly shuffled to life, making her way out onto the floor. The doors closed again and they resumed their upward journey.

The man threw another glance at Dan then back down at the panel, staring in mute concentration.

"Forget which floor you're on?" Dan asked.

"Sorry," he said, as if he was one of life's permanent bunglers. "I can never seem to remember."

Overhead, the numbers slid from seven to eight.

"You can always ask at the desk," Dan said.

Brown eyes flashed warily at him. "What?"

"If you can't remember which floor you're visiting, you can ask at any desk. They're friendly here."

"Right, of course. You come here a lot?"

Dan shook his head. "Just a check-up."

"Oh?" He seemed to find the news surprising.

The door pinged again as the elevator opened onto one of the inner rings of purgatory. Worn faces looked blankly to see if anyone had come to say hello or perhaps to rescue them from their eternal wanderings. Several patients used canes to get around, while others clung to walkers. Still others, the brave few, moved about with IV stands trailing saline lines, shuffling alongside these sepulchral companions to remind them of the eventual destination of all.

Dan made his way down the hall to reception. At the desk, he smiled his bravest smile. A young woman glanced up like a guard dog on the alert, as though a man in a women's hospital might betoken something ominous.

"I'm here to see Doctor Chronos," he said, proffering a crumpled form.

The nurse frowned as she scrutinized it.

"It's *Chranos*," she said, shaking her head and striking a line through the offending *o* that separated Father Time from his mortal cousin. She referred to an appointment book. "You can take a seat. She's a little behind today."

Dan steeled himself as he sat and looked around at his fellow detainees. Here, the faces were grimmest of all. One or two smiled to acknowledge his presence before turning back to magazines or the television screen glaring overhead. Dan wasn't sure if he should bother to spend energy trying to appear optimistic. A young mother not much older than Ked jiggled a fat baby on her knee at the far end of a bench. Beside her sat a worried-looking matronly woman, perhaps the young mother's mother. Her job seemed to be to watch the baby jiggling up and down and sigh with concern. Only the baby appeared unconcerned, bouncing like a ball of suet while the older women exuded a convincing mix of joylessness and disapproval.

The baby let out a sudden shriek. The older woman's face contracted in an expression of wounded dignity. She raised a finger to her lips, shushing the child loudly. The baby glanced up, startled, then settled down again to its giddy movements, as though the world were no more than a series of broken revolutions centred around the piston of its mother's knee.

Dan turned to the window. Outside, the day was still bright. The sky seemed to beckon him onward, tempting him with the possibility of escape at the last moment rather than spending the afternoon in this theatre of sickness and death.

Time ticked. Dan picked up a magazine, browsed through it then put it down again. He heard his name spoken softly and glanced over at the desk. The clerk was pointing to a door at the far end of the hall.

"She's ready for you."

He nodded and headed for the door. A silvery voice welcomed him in. He found himself facing an attractive Asian woman his own age or possibly a little younger. She smiled.

"Have a seat please, Daniel."

He sat without speaking. She looked straight at him, not at the open file on her desk or at a spot elsewhere in the room.

"I'm Doctor Chranos. I understand you've been referred by Doctor Harding. How are you feeling today?"

"I'm fine. Nothing critical at the moment."

She nodded, as though this agreed with her own assessment of the man she was observing.

"Everything okay at home?"

"More or less."

"Good." She smiled again. "I just like to be sure before we start to talk. I've reviewed your file. As Doctor Harding may have told you, he and I are personal friends and I am seeing you as a favour to him. Women's College Hospital has a long waiting list for people in your situation."

"I understand. Thank you for seeing me —"

She cut him off, "So we can talk today and then discuss your options, depending on what assessment I make. Are you fine with that?"

"I guess so."

She waited.

"Yes. I'm fine with that."

"Good. Doctor Harding referred you to us because of the emotional turmoil you've been experiencing and how it relates to your ability to function. The file says you have a history of angry outbursts, but not a history of violence, per se. Is that correct?"

"More or less. I've been inclined to kick a filing cabinet or two, but I don't hit people. At least not without provocation."

Again, she waited. Her cues were silent, but Dan could feel the prompt as plain as a tap on the shoulder.

"I'm a private investigator. Sometimes I'm forced to defend myself against physical violence, but I don't have a history of unprovoked attacks on others."

"Okay." She nodded vigorously, maintaining eye contact with him. "What causes the outbursts? In your own words."

"Frustration, anger, unfairness ..."

"Unfairness," she repeated. "Does that mean toward yourself or toward others?"

"Either. I dislike it when I see people abusing other people."

"Does that happen often?"

"All the time."

She smiled. "Okay. Anything else that comes to mind?"

"Not especially. I think of myself as a peaceful person, for the most part. I can be impatient, however, and often I realize it's not justified. I snap at my son from time to time. I dislike myself for it and I always apologize afterwards."

She smiled again. "He's a teenager, I understand. I think a lot of parents would say something similar."

Dan relaxed a little. "Yes, I've heard that before."

She took a breath.

"I understand you had a difficult childhood. We don't need to go into it. I've read the file. Your father was an abusive man, an alcoholic. Your mother died when you were four." She paused. "I also read that you have frequent dreams about her."

Dan nodded. "Dreams, nightmares ... whatever you call them. And yes, they're frequent."

"Are you an insomniac?"

"That's for sure."

"Your doctor was concerned because you asked for some very heavy sedatives to help you sleep. Do they work?"

Dan shook his head. "Not really. I take them and find myself sitting bolt upright from some nightmare or other about four hours later. I can't always get back to sleep after that. But I'm too groggy from the pills to concentrate, so I can't do anything productive at that hour. Until it wears off of my system, it sits there like a chemical burn on my brain."

"Are you still taking the medication?"

"Not consistently. Only if I'm feeling totally wired and need to knock myself out to get into bed."

She looked at him.

"You might try a drink."

He smiled.

"Not a good idea. I used to drink too much. I don't think drinking myself to sleep is really an option."

"What was that like? The drinking."

"It felt like a necessity then. I couldn't get through the day without it. I stopped drinking heavily more than a year ago. I promised my son I wouldn't go back there." He shook his head. "I don't want to go back there."

"Good." Her voice held a tone of practised sympathy, all honey and mellifluousness. "It sounds like you were drinking to escape. Trying to get away from your feelings and your memories."

"I ..." He stopped. He wasn't going to argue. "Maybe."

"How many years did that go on?"

Dan looked away. "I don't really know. It's not like there was a starting date. Sometime in my late twenties, I guess. I was alone. I had a son to raise, largely by myself. His mother didn't neglect him, but I did ... I *do* ... most of the work."

"So you drank heavily for what ... roughly ten years?"

"Yes."

"What were your relationships like during that time?"

A bell rang clearly inside Dan's head. "Not good. Except for my son."

"Why except for your son?"

"Because that's pure. It's not tainted."

He waited, hoping for reassurance. She gave him none.

"What about other relationships?"

"Not good. I sometimes wonder if I really know how to love other people, apart from my son."

"Why is that?"

"Maybe I don't know what it means. To love. If my son … if my son died, I think my life would be over. That's love. It has to be. It's so total. But with other people, I'm not sure. Even with Ked's mother, Kendra. I would miss her if she died. She's a good person, a sensible person. But I don't know if I love her."

She was watching him with her relentless scrutiny. "Do you need to love her?"

"She's the mother of my child. Shouldn't I?"

"I can't answer that. Do you want to love her?"

"Yes. I want to love people. Some people. I have a best friend, perhaps the person I'm closest to in the entire world apart from my son, but I still don't know if that's love. I enjoy being with him and I would miss him terribly if he died. I would feel like I'd lost a piece of myself, but I don't know if that's love or just a selfish need for company."

She watched him with something like a smile on the corners of her mouth. Dan felt like a specimen studied behind glass. It didn't feel insulting or degrading, merely strange.

After a pause, she said, "Is there no one you feel you might love apart from your son?"

Dan thought of Ren. "I recently met a man. I'm very attracted to him. I'd certainly like to spend more time with him. Maybe I could love him, though it's too soon to say."

"Don't confuse love with infatuation."

Dan looked up. "Is that what I'm doing?"

"Perhaps. It's not for me to say."

She looked over at her clock.

"What are the nightmares like?"

"They're aggressive. Relentless. They won't leave me alone. Even when I manage to go back to sleep afterward they're still there, waiting to get me."

"What is waiting to get you?"

"The people. My mother, more often than not. Her name was Christine. She's usually with a man by a seashore where I'm playing. I pull my bucket out of the water and the bottom is rusted out. It leaves me with a feeling that my life is empty and meaningless. That I'm incapable of love."

"How do you feel when you wake up?"

"I can't get out of bed. I don't want to go on. I don't feel good about anything. It leaves me feeling shattered, like it's useless to keep trying. There's a hopelessness attached to it. It makes it hard to get through the day when you wake up with a hornets' nest inside your head."

She looked at him for a moment.

"That is possibly the best description I've ever heard of it."

Dan stared at her.

"Of what?"

"PTSD. Post-traumatic stress disorder."

Dan stared at her, grasping for comprehension.

"Excuse me? Are you telling me I have post-traumatic stress disorder? I thought PTSD was something only soldiers suffered from."

"A popular misconception, but far from the truth." She nodded. "I think you are suffering from CPTSD. Chronic or complex post-traumatic stress disorder. It's longer-term, and sometimes more difficult to diagnose."

Dan frowned. "But how could I have it? I've never been to war."

"You don't have to go to war to live in a warlike state of mind. I've reviewed your file. You've got the classic triggers of PTSD. An abusive father, a tragic end to your mother's life. You came of age during the AIDS crisis and no doubt lost friends —"

"True."

"And then there's you."

"Me?"

"Your life has been directly threatened on several occasions in the course of your profession. Am I telling you anything you don't already know?"

Dan shook his head. "No. I just never thought —"

"As I said, it's hard to diagnose. It's also intermittent.

The symptoms can come and go, depending on the stress factors in your life."

"So, if you're correct, what can be done about it?"

She cocked her head. For the first time since he'd entered her office, she looked unsure of herself.

"As I said when we began our conversation, I'm seeing you as a favour to your GP. I can put you on a list for therapy sessions with the hospital, but it could take years to get you into a program unless your problems stem from sexual abuse. Rape, for instance."

"What about other hospitals?"

She shook her head.

"You will have a hard time getting a referral anywhere in the city, simply because most trauma programs are set up for survivors of sexual abuse." She paused. "I am pretty sure you have CPTSD, but I can't recommend we take you on if your problems don't stem from sexual trauma of some sort. You would have been better off if you'd been in the military. Then you could apply on grounds of battle fatigue."

Dan felt panic grip him. Now that he had a name for what he was suffering, it seemed as though someone should be able to help. He flashed on all the stories of Gulf War veterans coming back home and the high suicide rate they suffered upon their return.

"There must be someone who could take me on."

She tapped her pencil on the pad.

"I can offer you private counselling services, but my rates are very high."

"How high?" he asked, feeling desperate.

"Three hundred dollars an hour."

He swallowed. "And how … how many sessions would it take?"

She looked uncertain. "It's hard to say. A year at the very least, but probably more. You would have to agree to at least one session a week and be consistent about the effort."

Dan sat back. One year at that rate would almost wipe out the little he'd managed to save to help Ked through university, a sum his son would soon be needing.

"That's not possible," he said. "Not on what I make."

She nodded. "I understand. Most people have the same reaction."

He felt dazed. It was as though he'd just realized the hole he was in was much deeper than he'd thought, leaving him unable to scramble back up to the top.

"My advice to you, if you can't do anything else, is to change your profession."

"Change my profession?"

"Yes. To something kinder, gentler, as they say."

Doctor Chranos stood.

"I'm afraid that's all the time I can give you at present. If you decide to go through with the program, give me a call."

She handed him a card from a holder on her desk. Her businesslike demeanour had returned.

Dan turned to the door then stopped and looked back.

"Do you have a family, Doctor Chranos?"

She looked startled. "I ...?"

"Do you have any kids?"

She stared at him.

Dan waited. "I'm sorry, I'd just like to know."

"No," she said in a taut whisper, as though he'd punched her in the stomach. "I ... no." She shook her head.

Dan nodded. "Thank you," he said, and turned and went out the door.

Eight

No Woman, No Cry

They arrived at the Panorama Lounge at sunset. From the outer deck, the city lights spread below in all directions. This was Toronto's most impressive view, affording a kind of quiet magnificence it often lacked from the ground.

Inside, the atmosphere was subdued and comfortable, the lounge filled with an affluent younger set. Ren wore black trousers and a turquoise silk shirt that contoured his chest. He glowed. Dan, uncharacteristically, had dressed up as well, donning a red linen shirt and grey jacket. Judging by the heads that turned to watch, he knew they made a good-looking pair.

Their waiter fussed over them as if putting them to bed for the night, flourishing napkins across their knees and laying the cutlery as though unveiling treasure. Dan ate crab cakes and drank soda water, mindful of Ked's approbation should he come home looking hungover again.

He hadn't decided where or how far to take things from their current state, yet he was keenly aware of the desire he felt for the man seated across from him sipping from a tall stein of Sapporo. He'd made a few inquiries into Ren's sister and come up with nothing. If she was alive, the likeliest bet was that she was living under another name, as Ren had suggested, or as an illegal alien flying under the radar. Dan knew through various organizations tracking refugees that there were upwards of a quarter million suspected illegals in the city. Many worked for abysmal wages just to stay in Canada, preferring a life of anonymous penury to the scenarios of violence, war, or starvation they faced at home.

Ren wasn't fazed by Dan's lack of progress. If anything, it seemed to make him more adamant that Dan find her. Money wasn't an object, he repeated. He suggested a number of possible aliases she might have assumed. Dan made note of these and left it at that.

The conversation turned to Dan. Ren was intrigued to learn he had a son and that he lived in a house with a dog and a backyard. A rather typical Canadian existence, apart from a few pertinent details proscribed by Dan's sexuality. It struck Dan that he seldom discussed his personal life with a client. As they talked, their legs occasionally brushed together under the table. Each time, Ren looked over with a smile as though they were engaged in an amusing game.

A burst of hilarity from the far end of the bar reminded them they weren't alone. By the time the meal was over, Dan was decided. He would continue seeing Ren privately, even if he took the case. He was a man in the middle of life and experiencing very human needs. Differences of lifestyle and outlook aside, in many ways Ren seemed the answer to a number of them.

Knowing Ked was at his mother's for the weekend made his next decision easier. Ren silently nodded when Dan suggested going back to his house.

Ralph gave Dan a knowing look when the two men showed up at the door. He reminded Dan of the concierge at the Saint-Germain. He shook a box of dog biscuits and gave one to Ren, who then held it out to Ralph. After a bit of inquisitive sniffing, Ralph gruffly accepted the treat and a pat on the head before returning to his bed. Friends for life.

Ren refused Dan's offer of a drink. Apart from his elaborate manners and occasional compliments on Dan's abode, he seemed to prefer to dispense with superfluities. What they both wanted was sex. Once again the experience was vigorous, though perhaps as an unspoken acknowledgement on Ren's part that they were on Dan's turf, the encounter stopped short of outright aggression.

Afterward, they lay sprawled on the bed, limbs entwined.

"Do you ever just have easy-going sex?" Dan asked, his chest heaving with spent effort.

Ren shot him an odd look. "What is the point?"

Dan nodded, thinking back to Donny's question as regards the pursuit of love. "I'm not sure," he said.

"How many men do you sleep with?"

"Usually, just one at a time."

Ren turned to regard him with a curious expression. "If you mean in total, I can't say."

"Why not? Is it not allowed by your government?"

Dan restrained himself from laughing. "No, I mean I can't recall. I don't keep count."

Dan wasn't anxious to reveal he'd spent time on the street, making his life sound more sordid than necessary, but those few months as a teenage runaway had given him valuable survival skills.

"And you? How many men have you slept with?"

"Three."

Dan wondered if he'd heard correctly or whether Ren had misunderstood his question. "Only three men? In your entire life?"

A nod. "You are number three."

"I'm honoured. But you don't seem like a beginner. How did you get to be such an experienced lover?"

"I practised with a woman."

This time Dan was unable to suppress the urge to laugh.

"Why is this humorous?" Ren asked.

"It's just …" Dan waved it off. "I don't know. It just sounds funny. How many women did you sleep with?"

"Just one."

Ren's face remained almost comically serious. He looked away, perhaps in embarrassment. Dan resolved not to laugh again, if he could help it. It proved a challenge.

"Do you still sleep with her now?" he asked, not entirely having divested Ren of the visiting business-man image.

"No, I don't need woman since I became gay."

"Since you became gay?" Dan asked, incredu-lous. "When did that happen? When you crossed the International Date Line?"

Ren shook his head.

"No, it happened when I left China and learned there was such a thing. How many women did you sleep with?"

"Also just one. The mother of my son."

"I saw his picture downstairs. The resemblance is striking."

"Do you think so? Everyone says Ked looks like his mother. She's Syrian."

"No, it is there. In the chin, in the eyes. A very good-looking boy. He will make you proud."

"Thank you. I believe so, too. Who do you look like?"

"Also my father. My sister looks like my mother."

"Tell me more about your sister."

Ren looked off for a moment, as though recon-structing her features from the distance of time.

"Ling and I were very close when we grew up. There were not many other children around us. As I mentioned previously, we were very poor. Often we went to bed hungry, in fact almost every night. In China when we were growing up, even the most basic food was scarce. There was no meat except on festival days, and then only just a taste for something special. Sometimes, when my parents were away, Ling and I would play a game called Going to Kowloon Café. We would write up an elaborate menu with many expensive items on it. Then she and I would take turns pretending to be the guest. If she was the waiter and I the guest, she would make an elaborate charade of spreading a napkin and laying out the table for me. I would go over the menu, asking her to describe each dish in detail. Finally, when she had done so she would ask me to select three items for my meal."

Dan watched Ren's face as he spoke. He seemed haunted by the memory.

"Always, I would tell her to make the meal for two, as I was expecting my fiancée. Afterward, Ling would retire to the kitchen as if to prepare the dishes. When she emerged holding a tray, she would bring it to the table and lay the meal before me, very slowly and carefully. I would wait till she had finished, then I would pretend to be about to cut into the dish, very selfishly. At the last moment I would look up at her and say that as I had unexpectedly found myself alone she was welcome to join me in the meal."

Dan smiled. "And did she?"

"Always. Then she would sit and we would eat our imaginary meal together."

"But you still went to bed hungry."

"Yes, sadly."

The wind blew outside. A branch scratched at the bedroom window as though it had been moved by Ren's story and wanted to reassure him. Dan waited a beat.

"Why do you think Ling might have ended up here without trying to contact you?"

A shadow crossed Ren's face. "To protect me from my government."

Dan cocked his head. "Why? Your government trusts you, obviously, or they wouldn't have let you come here."

"If they knew Ling was here, I would never be allowed to leave China. I believe that is why she may be using a false name. They would think it might lead to a risk of defection and would never allow that to happen."

"Even so, that's only recent. Why wouldn't she have tried to get in touch with you before now?"

Ren's expression grew hard.

"After Tiananmen, my mother and father were put in jail and tortured. At the trial, the court said they helped my sister escape justice. They said she was part of a student uprising that started the riots. When we said she was dead and we did not know anything about these student activities, they did not believe us. I think now the government officials knew something. I believe my parents helped Ling to escape."

"They never said anything about this?"

Ren gave him a long, hard look. "Only once,

before he died, my father said he would like to see Ling again. At the time, I did not think anything of this. I thought he was becoming a senile old man and did not remember she was already dead."

"But now you think he may have been telling the truth?"

Ren nodded. "Life in China is often difficult. People are not allowed free expression of opinions. It is possible she was a student rebel, as you say over here. I believe my sister may have developed such progressive thoughts that led to the Tiananmen protests."

"You think she was involved in radical politics?"

"Many students disappeared in the fighting. That is when we began to hear the reports. Another student told me that Ling was part of a group that met in secret to discuss ways to protest. I did not believe this at the time, but later I found a book in her room about student politics. I was very surprised, as it was forbidden. I burned it."

Dan gave him a searching look.

"There are not so many freedoms in China as there are here. Here in your country, people say what they think. In China, sometimes it is forbidden to say what we feel."

"So you think — somehow — she made it to Canada and has been hiding out ever since?"

Ren shrugged. "I believe she would not dare to return to China and jeopardize her family's safety back home. Perhaps she remained unaware that this had already happened because of her disappearance."

"And now you want to find her?"

A look of urgency spread over Ren's features. "I want to give her a better life. My family is all dead now. It is just me and Ling. I would like to know my sister again, if it is possible." Ren paused, his expression wistful.

"I'll see what I can do." Dan squeezed Ren's shoulder. "I'll need you to show me the website where you found her picture and point out your sister for me. If she looks like you, she must be very beautiful."

Ren smiled. "This is a word for a man? Beautiful?"

"For a man like you, it is."

He nodded appreciatively. "If I may ask, what is your rate?"

"Never ask that of a man while you're in bed with him."

Ren gave him a quizzical look.

"Just a joke. Never mind."

"I do not understand your Western humour."

Dan named a price. Ren seemed to be thinking it over.

"I would like this to be your priority, if possible. I am willing to pay for this privilege. I wish for you to put everything on hold until you find my sister. I do not know how long I can stay in the country and I would like to make sure this happens before I leave."

"I can't just drop everything," Dan said, thinking of his promise to Ian Cunningham to find his daughter.

Ren suggested a fee that was much greater than Dan's usual rate.

"You don't need to overpay me. I'll do whatever I can for you," Dan said.

He got up and offered Ren a spare bathrobe. It looked comically large on his frame. They went to the sitting room and relaxed in front of the fireplace.

Dan brought out his laptop. Ren quickly ran through a selection of sites hosting Chinatown restaurants until he found the one he was looking for.

"Here," he said excitedly. "That is my sister. I am sure."

Over Ren's shoulder, Dan saw a contented-looking woman sitting casually at a café table. Nothing about her suggested she was in hiding from anyone or anything. Nor did anything hint at a past of penury or deprivation. She was beautiful, as Dan expected. In fact, she looked much more like a movie star than the frail, ghostly girl she had been in Ren's family photograph.

Nine

The Good China

Silence ruled the airwaves. Dan had Ked in the car with him. They were headed across the Bloor viaduct on the way to pay a Mother's Day visit to Kendra. His normally talkative son, once the best of company, had become more and more reticent over the past year. Dan looked over, noted the recent acne disruptions, the faint outline of hair shadowing his features. Yup, he was a teenager, all right.

They pulled up before a stone house stuccoed over greenly with ivy. When Kendra came to Canada as an exchange student, the Annex was the first neighbourhood she'd known. It proved to be her choice when choosing a permanent home as well. Dan wasn't surprised that she chose to remain in Canada rather than return to Syria. Besides the obvious determinant she had in their son, she'd also proved herself a modern woman and a fan of the greater freedoms Canada offered, unlike her tradition-minded brother whom Dan had once fancied.

Kendra greeted them at the door. Her hair was done to perfection, her eyes softly lidded with make-up, which she seldom wore. The overall effect was arresting.

The dining room seemed unusually formal. The good china. The best crystal. The polished silverware. Candles stuttered in anticipation, but of what it was impossible to tell. *Just wait and see*, they seemed to say as they danced around. The arrangement would have cheered Donny at seeing someone else meeting his exacting standards. Dan wondered whether to ask Kendra why all the fuss she was making over a day she normally forgot was even approaching.

Ked kissed her cheek and presented her with a small package.

"Happy Mother's Day."

She took the gift. "Thank you, sweetheart."

"You went to a lot of trouble," Dan told her. "We could have taken you out."

"I prefer to have you here. It's my Mother's Day gift to you." She smiled mysteriously, the sphinx unbound. "Besides, I've got a surprise."

"Really? What might that be?"

"You'll see soon enough."

She seemed animated. Dan suspected it must be something special.

"What's new with you?" she asked, unwrapping Ked's present with elaborate care. "How are Donny and Lester?"

"Donny's good. Lester's been doing well at school. I think I told you they decided not to hold him back because of the year he missed. They felt he was mature enough. School curricula are so varied, what he studied in Oshawa was different enough that they didn't feel it mattered."

Kendra held up a turquoise pendant as Ked watched. He seemed almost fearful of her reaction, Dan thought.

"It's beautiful," she said, holding it against her chest. "Thank you."

Ked nodded, as though it didn't matter one way or the other whether she liked it or not.

Kendra placed it carefully back in the box and looked thoughtfully at her son.

"And you, good sir? How are your studies holding up?"

Ked shrugged, a habitual gesture with him these days. "Same," he said.

He looked at the two adults staring at him.

"What? I'm fine," he said. "School's fine. Can't get enough of it."

He turned and went into the kitchen.

"Pop's in the fridge. Help yourself," Kendra called after him. She turned to Dan. "What do you make of that?"

"Girl trouble," Dan said. "He doesn't like talking about it much."

"Ah!" She gave a knowing nod and fussed with a flower arrangement on the table.

Dan tilted his head quizzically. "So what's the surprise?"

Before Kendra could answer, there was a knock at the door. The look on her face flashed so quickly Dan couldn't read it. Part pleasure, part trepidation. Maybe something more. She was a sphinx, after all.

Noises in the front hall, followed by exclamations of delight. What sounded like a chaste kiss. She returned leading a man by the hand. But not just any man, Dan noted. This was quite a man. Dark hair, dark skin. One solid eyebrow like a horizontal exclamation mark. Square-jawed and broad-chested, he was a Middle Eastern Superman. He looked as though a jaunty run would be his favoured speed. A lone cheetah penned and chained by this lovely woman — Dan had forgot just how beautiful she was — who held his paw in one hand and an invisible leash in the other.

"This is Ali," she said. "And this is Dan."

Teeth flashed into a glare. Ali extended his hand, shook Dan's briskly, and nodded.

Ked's head popped out from the kitchen, curiosity written all over his features.

"Hi," he said quietly.

"That's our son, Kedrick," Kendra said, causing Dan that jolt of unfamiliarity he always felt at being included in the equation.

Ali walked over to Ked, who seemed glued to the doorway, whether in wariness or shyness it was difficult to say.

"I have heard much about you, Kedrick," Ali told

him. "I am very glad to meet the young man of the family."

Ked's face was blank. Obviously, he hadn't heard much about Ali, if anything. Dan regarded the curly hair and Semitic slope of nose he'd inherited from his mother. *Semitic.* It was a word Dan had seldom heard before meeting Kendra. When they were expecting Ked, he'd looked it up. Derived from Noah's son, Shem, it included not just Jews, but all users of languages created in the Middle East. Babel's sons and daughters. Dan's own features had morphed and softened in this boy he'd fathered nearly sixteen years ago. But at a certain angle, he thought, Ked might have been mistaken for Ali's son rather than his own.

"Food's almost ready. We can move into the dining room," Kendra said.

The three men followed her. She opened a bottle of wine and poured. A toast to mothers proceeded. Ali drank without hesitation, Dan noted. If he was a practising Muslim, he wasn't strict. If so, then he and Kendra might be a good match. They made small talk for several minutes before Kendra went out to the kitchen, leaving them alone.

Ali turned to Dan. He mentioned his early upbringing in Iran, as though to dispel any doubts Dan might have about his background.

"My family left when the Shah was deposed. I was four years old. I don't really remember much of my homeland. People don't realize it, but he was a good man, the Shah."

Not by a long shot, Dan thought.

"Your country has an interesting history," he said. "I believe the Shah was a favourite of the Americans because he offered them access to the oil reserves."

"Yes, this is true," Ali said. "He was a very enterprising man."

"By all accounts a very enterprising man," Dan said. "I believe he was put in power by the U.S. after they arrested his predecessor, a democratically elected ruler who nationalized the oil industry in your country. It seems he'd upset both the British and Americans, who conspired against him."

Ali's eyebrows rose. "Yes, that was Prime Minister Mossadeq. I see you know about my country's history."

Ked's eyes travelled back and forth between them.

"That was Kendra's doing," Dan said. "She comes from a part of the world I knew little about, but with Ked's birth she encouraged me to learn more."

"Still, do you not agree that the Shah would be preferable to the current leader of Iran? A man who threatens the world with nuclear war and bloodshed?"

"I couldn't say which of them I'd prefer," Dan said. "A man who abused his own people or a man who threatens war with his neighbours. To me, neither one is preferable. As for Ahmadinejad, it seems to me the Americans are indirectly responsible for his rise to power after deposing Mossadeq. I'm not sure they should complain so loudly in public when he annoys them."

Ali smiled. "Ah, well spoken. A diplomatic answer."

"And a truthful one, I believe," Dan said.

Kendra returned with a tray, setting it on the table, and uncovering the steaming bowls of food.

"Do I hear international politics?" she asked.

"History mostly," Dan said.

"International relations," Ali said.

"Well, as long as we keep to civil topics," Kendra said. She flashed a generous smile at them. "This is my day, after all."

"Dad's dating a guy from China," Ked spoke up, having kept silent till then.

Dan threw his son a look. This was the first he'd heard that Ked knew of his involvement with Ren. He wondered if this came of his son's trying to keep tabs on his drinking or on his dating.

"What?" Ked asked. "I heard you talking to Uncle Donny about it."

"I see."

Ked shrugged. "You said we had no secrets, right?"

"I didn't realize that gave you carte blanche to listen in on my phone conversations."

Ked sighed and looked across the table. "Pass the couscous, please."

Kendra lifted the bowl and offered it to her son, trying to disguise her smile. She looked over at Dan.

"So, now that the cat's out of the bag …"

Dan shrugged. "Yes, I've been seeing a Chinese national named Ren. As Ked can no doubt tell you" — he shot another quick glance at his son — "we met one night while I was out with Uncle Donny."

"Is it serious?" Kendra asked. "You should have invited him to dinner."

Dan caught his breath. He recalled the feelings Ren aroused in him, the sense of urgency and of being alive in every nerve ending when they were together. But in truth, they hardly knew each other.

"It's too soon, really. I guess it's as serious as it can be when you meet someone from halfway across the world. I don't even know how long he plans to stay in Canada."

"Is he hoping to move here?" Kendra asked.

"I don't think there's any question of immediate immigration, because of China's strict policy on such things. All I know is that I like his company."

Dan picked up a dish and helped himself to lamb *tagine*.

"Dad's been lonely," Ked chimed in. "This is his first date since before Christmas."

Dan turned a surprised look to Ked. "I didn't know you kept track."

"Well, I do."

"You'll have to invite him over next time," Kendra said.

"I'd like that."

Ali had remained silent throughout the exchange, his eyes moving from Dan to Kendra and Ked then back again, as though observing the antics of a peculiar species of animals in their native habitat.

"This is a most unorthodox arrangement," he said at last with the trace of a smile.

Dan wondered how much Kendra had told him about their family dynamics, wondering if he heard a judgment there or if he was just being overly sensitive.

"We're a family like any other," he said. "As for me, I'm anything but orthodox in my ways."

"The world is changing quickly," Ali said, but whether he liked the fact or not was unclear.

After the meal they retreated to the sitting room. It had been richly coloured and decorated with taste: brocaded rugs, elaborate paintings and sculptures. Kendra had a collector's eye for art. They'd been seated for a few minutes when she motioned for Dan to follow her to the kitchen. She turned to him, her face uncharacteristically serious.

"What do you think?"

"Handsome guy. Should I be jealous?"

She twinkled, her expression turning mysterious again. "Of him or me?"

"That depends. I assume he's straight and somewhat of a romantic interest."

She just smiled.

He stared at her. "Tell me you're not setting him up with me."

She swatted him with her hand. "No, silly. He's *my* date."

"Then I reserve the right to be slightly jealous. Of both of you. He's very attractive. How long have you known him?"

"We've been dating casually for four months."

"You keep a secret well."

She smiled flirtatiously. "You should know that by now."

She picked up a bottle and handed Dan four small glasses. They went back out together.

"Dessert is coming. Who would like some port? Kedrick?"

Ked glanced at his mother then looked to his father. "Is it all right?"

Dan smiled. "It's all right with me. You're turning sixteen this year. It won't hurt you to try."

Kendra poured a small glass for him, watched as he brought it to his nose and sniffed.

He took a tentative sip then put the glass down.

"It's all right," he said. "I wouldn't go crazy for it."

Ali made a show of savouring his drink as though to say that he, a practising Muslim, was also anything but orthodox in his habits.

He turned to Ked. "How do you like your school?"

"It's all right," Ked said, sounding a trifle detached.

"What do you want to be?"

Again, Ked looked to his father. "Dad says I have 'people' skills. I don't know yet. Maybe something in human resources."

"You also have good math skills," Dan said.

"You have Islamic blood," Ali said to Ked. "So you should be good with numbers. Maybe something in a bank then? I work in a bank."

"I don't think so," Ked replied. "It sounds stuffy."

Ali smiled. "You will figure it out," he said with a

wink, as though trying to win points in some abstract game.

The evening went quickly. Dan made motions to leave so that Kendra and Ali could have time alone. As they said goodbye, Ali stopped Ked at the door.

"Perhaps you will allow me the pleasure of getting to know you better in the future, Kedrick."

Ked looked like he was about to shrug, which would have annoyed Dan to no end, but instead he said simply, "We'll see. School's pretty intense right now. It's almost the end of the term."

They got in the car and headed home. Dan said nothing while Ked fiddled with the radio till he found a station that suited his mood and sat back. Dan could tell he was feeling unsettled about something.

"Did you like Ali?"

"Not really."

"Why?"

"I don't know. I just didn't." He looked out the window then back to Dan. "Is that okay?"

"You don't have to like everyone."

"Good. Because I don't."

Dan nodded. "That's fine."

Ked sat silently for another minute then said, "Why did he say I have Islamic blood?"

"Well, you do. Your mother is Muslim. Does that bother you?"

"No, I love Mom. I just don't think he should mention things like that. It's none of his business."

Dan smiled. "That's your WASP side. You get that

from me. Just remember he's your mother's boyfriend, so he could become a significant force in the family."

Ked turned to his father with a surprised look. "Really?"

Dan saw it hadn't occurred to him that his mother might one day find a permanent love interest.

"You said you didn't want me to be alone all my life. Why wish that for your mother?"

Ked sat silently for a while as the car slid over the Queen Street bridge and approached Broadview.

"I don't think she needs anyone the way you do," he said at last.

"Your mother may seem independent, but I still think she would like to find a husband who suits her needs and lifestyle."

They stopped at a light. Dan looked over.

"I'm sorry if I was impatient when you mentioned the man I'm dating. Would you like to know more about him?"

Ked pondered this.

"Not unless I meet him, I guess."

"Fair enough. But you can ask me anytime, if you change your mind."

"Okay, but I doubt I will."

Dan waited a beat then said, "Does it bother you that your parents are dating?"

"No."

"Okay."

The light turned. The shops and restaurants on either side of them began to whiz by again.

"Dad, is China a bad place?"

Dan thought about it.

"I don't know how to answer that. It's a communist country, but that doesn't make it a bad place. It also seems to be turning to a capitalist economy. And that doesn't make it good, either. What people object to about China is how hard it is to voice your disapproval of the government. There are a lot of restrictions on what you can and can't say." He thought of Ren and his sister. "Here, in Canada, we can say anything we want. In China, you have to be careful about expressing views that criticize or oppose the ruling regime."

"Or what?"

"Or you might be put in jail. Worse, you might be tortured or killed and your family threatened."

"Really?"

"It happens," Dan said. "Twenty years ago there were country-wide protests over the strictness of government rules. Eventually, the army came in and a lot of people were killed. Others went to jail. Still others vanished and were never heard from again."

"Maybe you should go to China and work there," Ked said. "Then you'd always have a job."

"What, you don't think I work hard enough now?"

"I'm just saying there'd be lots of people for you to track down."

"And I might end up in jail for trying to find them," Dan said.

"Wow!"

Dan turned onto their street and continued down the tree-lined avenue.

"Total freedom is still a very rare thing. There are not a lot of countries that respect its citizens' rights in that regard. You should be very thankful you live in Canada."

"Even if it's boring here sometimes?"

Dan smiled.

"Especially if it's boring. That's how you know you live in a safe country."

Ten

The Scent of Almonds

The jarring reds and yellows fluttered above his head in banners and business signs. They were China's "lucky" colours. Dan always felt a slight unease in Chinatown. The noise and congestion unsettled his WASP sense of propriety and personal space constraints, while the street markets plagued him with hygiene concerns. Then his nose picked up the scent of good cooking and he forgot his worries.

The community had grown out of a period of racial "unrest" — meaning outright violence perpetrated against racial minorities in Depression-era America. Where the Brits drove the French out of Canada in the mid-1700s, giving their southern neighbour New Orleans with its attendant Cajun culture, the Americans returned the favour nearly two centuries later by sending north a generation of Chinese workers who settled in Toronto and other urban centres. Tit for tat. International relations made easy.

The Kowloon Bakery sat a few doors east of the corner at Cecil Street and Spadina Avenue. Dan made his way through a caravan of produce stands — vegetables, fruit, mysterious-looking herbs and spices, even some exotic seafood that had him guessing. He had just passed Got Dumpling and Golden Pineapple, the latter's ceramic lions covered in a swath of black spray paint, when he caught the telltale scent of almond. It was the Kowloon's specialty, he remembered. He loved the big crumbly yellow biscuits with their cracked-earth appearance, which actually took more than four bites to consume, unlike the more refined confections churned out by brand-name bakeries.

He turned the corner and suddenly there it was: a Victorian red-brick building towering over the neighbourhood like someone's gaunt aunt. Dan's memories hearkened back to when he was a fledgling university student. The neighbouring addresses on either side had been variously a used-clothing outlet, a shoe store, and a teahouse, but the bakery remained, like a landmark surviving the assaults of style and time.

He pushed the door open and heads turned to stare. Even in the heart of Toronto, a white face in a Chinese bakery could still seem a novelty. Especially on a man with a six-foot-three-inch frame, grey eyes, and a scar running down the side of his face. His features might make anyone nervous. An indemnity policy, was how Dan looked at it.

He sauntered down the long, narrow aisles flanked by shelves of baked goods and made his way to the counter. The youngest of three clerks nodded shyly at him. Seventeen or eighteen at best, she had a worse case of acne than Ked. Her bangs hung long at the sides of her face and her teeth were bad. The girl's English was minimal, her pronunciation atrocious, but her willingness to serve a customer beat the hell out of what most Canadian kids her age would have attempted. Dan wondered how long someone had saved and slaved to put together the relative fortune it had taken to get her on a boat heading for the New World. Perhaps she was the niece of the café owner, in which case it would have been his dime she'd come over on. Meaning she would have to work to pay him back for who knew how many years.

"Nice café," he said.

She looked at him with a concerned expression. "Yes, please?"

Obviously compliments were not the usual order of the day.

"I like your café." He indicated the establishment with a wave of his arms.

"Ah, yes! Thank you!"

Recognition brought a smile of relief. He wasn't asking for something she couldn't offer. A sale was still possible.

"You would like please?"

Dan looked up at the sign posted overhead then down at the display of food behind the counter: LUNCH

SPECIAL $4.50 WITH BEST RISE AND TWO SPECIAL CHOICE. He assumed the "best rise" referred to the glutinous mound heaped on one side of the display. He glanced at what constituted the specials. One of the pans carried some sort of enigmatic stir fry with eggplant. The others were open for guesses.

"Which one is the best?" he asked.

"I don't know. We don't allow eat here." Her eyes darted nervously. "Customer like this." She pointed to a pan containing a concoction of light brown wedges and cubes.

"What is it?"

"Chick-an-potao," she said hopefully, running it all together.

Dan hoped "chick-an-potao" wasn't some sort of flora-to-fauna genetic modification. You never knew these days. He couldn't make out anything that looked even vaguely bird-like. He nodded. "I'll take it. And the eggplant," he said, thinking he could manage that if the other turned out to be inedible.

She scooped a generous portion of rice into a Styrofoam tray and a meagre mound of the mysterious cubes into one of the neighbouring troughs, followed by some of the eggplant. She placed it on the counter and pushed it forward. Dan could already tell he wasn't going to be back for seconds. The girl ran his debit card through the machine and handed it back. He added a three-dollar tip. She beamed as though he were the Buddha conferring a blessing on her.

At the last second, he flashed the photograph at her.

"Do you know this lady?"

Her face took on the look of someone just informed of the death of a close friend.

"I'm not a police officer," Dan said quietly.

Far from reassuring her, the declaration set off some sort of seismic tremor in her limbs. She nearly dropped the debit machine and shook her head frenziedly without looking up.

Dan took up his tray and left her to her terrors. He met with less success when he approached a table of older women seated with their shopping bundled on the floor around them. Each wore a different coloured hat and a pair of stylish sunglasses.

They turned blank faces to him when he held out the photograph. None of them admitted to speaking any English. He thanked them and sat at a table a short distance away. The women scowled at him all through his meal. Whatever he represented, they wanted none of it.

So far, Dan's quest for information had come up empty-handed. Usually a search turned up something, no matter how trivial, but finding a possible refugee who may or may not be using her real name in an urban centre of nearly six million was proving a challenge. Maybe a challenge that Dan wasn't up to meeting. Ren's sister, or whoever she was, had vanished, if indeed she'd ever lived in Canada. Though according to her brother, she once sat and posed for a photograph in this very café.

Dan turned his head and looked over at the corner

table next to the window. That was where she'd sat. He tried to visualize the woman waiting quietly while photographers and make-up artists buzzed around her. Or possibly it had been an impromptu shot, taken on the fly, just a slice of life in real time. A face photographed anonymously, to be gazed on years from now whenever someone wanted a capsule of life in twenty-first-century Chinatown in Toronto.

He ate his meal with a plastic fork, unwilling to risk stabbing through the thin Styrofoam with chopsticks, though it wouldn't have been a loss if the food ended up on the floor. The "chick-an-potao" consisted of undercooked potato cubes covering two gluey pieces of what might once have been tiny wings, but could also have been something else entirely. The jokes about cats and Chinese food came to mind, but this clearly did not look like cat. Rat possibly. He had a bite or two and pushed it aside. The eggplant was passable, while the rice was inoffensive at best. He wished he'd stuck with the almond cookies.

As he ate, he noticed a steady stream of men who wandered into the café, looked around briefly, then made their way quickly and casually down a flight of stairs. In Chinatown, the washrooms were invariably housed in basements and accessed by passing through a maze of dungeon-like passages. Often lacking in hand towels or even toilet paper, they frequently became a repository for all manner of disreputable things. Dan had learned not to judge the quality of a restaurant's food by the condition of its restrooms, though he wondered how safe it was to eat in a place where you were afraid to take a leak. Still, he thought it odd how the number of men going down did not equal the occasional face that resurfaced. It occurred to him there must be some sort of gambling operation in effect below. No wonder the cashier had been nervous when he mentioned the police.

He stood and casually made his way down to a long, narrow hallway lined with stained yellow tiles. There were three doors, one marked LADIES and another marked GENTLEMEN. A third was marked PRIVATE. That would be the one. He put his ear to the door and heard mumbling and shuffling feet, followed by something that sounded like dice being shaken in a cup. Mahjong? It was none of his business, so he let it pass and entered the washroom instead. A quick look told him that if he touched anything here he risked leaving dirtier than when he went in. He left without washing his hands.

Upstairs, an old man caught his eye from behind the counter. Dan made his way over.

"You are looking for someone?" the man asked politely.

"Yes," Dan said, retrieving the photograph.

The man pulled out a pair of fold-up spectacles to scrutinize it. He made a show of trying to focus, gazed at the photograph, then handed it back with a mask of polite interest.

"It is my bakery in the photograph," he said. "But this woman I do not know."

His face expressed sympathy for Dan and whatever reason he had for wanting to find the woman. A runaway bride, perhaps, or maybe a poor investment he was calling home.

"I am very sorry," he said, shaking his head.

"So am I," Dan told him. "Her family is trying to find her. I may have to take the matter to the police. I'd prefer to find her myself, if at all possible. It would save a lot of bother."

The man's expression changed at once. He turned to the young woman who had served Dan and barked a few words. She scurried off to the back of the bakery with a terrified expression.

"One moment, please," the man said.

When the girl returned, she carried a wall calendar. She offered it to the man, who turned to the back page and held it out to Dan.

"Ask this man," he said, pointing to a photographer's credit in small print.

Dan took it and flipped through the pages. Ren's sister was in two other photographs, her face mysterious and inexpressive, as though the photographer had been trying to capture an Edward Hopper moment.

"May I keep this?"

The man made a show of courtesy.

"It is yours. You may take it."

"Thank you," Dan said, then made his way out to the street.

Only when he had gone a little way did he turn to look back at the bakery. The owner and his young helper were staring at him, one suspicious, the other mournful, perhaps trying to ascertain what he'd really been hoping to find and whether or not they could expect a visit from the police later that evening. He smiled and waved.

Let them wonder, he told himself.

Eleven

The Naked Eye

Dan located the photographer's studio in the film district, less than a kilometre from his own office. The building had seen better days: corrugated tin covered one side of the edifice. He'd seldom seen corrugated metal used on buildings outside of developing countries and the occasional rural construction meant to contain pigs and goats.

As the city's profile had risen with international investors over the past decade, it became harder for up-and-coming artists to find a low-rent neighbourhood in which to live and work. Leslieville was one of the last in the downtown core, but even that had been hard hit with developers squirreling away property as everyone rushed to cash in on the boom.

The studio was sandwiched between a BMW showcase overlooking the Don Valley on one side and train tracks on the other. As far as cost went, Dan figured it probably lay somewhere between off-market retail and a low-end condo. Still, it looked like the sort of slum any self-respecting bohemians would have been glad to call home, even if they had to hustle a bit for this meagre option.

The lobby was littered with rubbish. Cast-off fly-ers, chocolate bar wrappers, and a rusty bicycle miss-ing a seat were the current contenders for unwanted debris. Dan checked a row of mailboxes. Most of the residents appeared to be wholesale enterprises of a spu-rious nature: Mongolian Adventure Tours Inc., Heavy Metal Thunder Sound Systems, and Easy Wedding Rentals! The only exception was a gold-scripted sign for Matt Parks, Photographer.

Over the entry phone, someone had spray-painted GET LOST! in vivid purple lettering. Dan pressed the buzzer, feeling like a door-to-door salesman drilled never to take *no* for an answer. The buzzer had other thoughts, apparently. There was no response. Just as he was about to turn away, the door opened and a teenage girl with white dreadlocks came out counting a fistful of twenties. Dan caught her eye. She stuffed the bills into her pocket and stepped quickly outside.

He grabbed the door handle and made his way up a flight of stairs where some enterprising graffiti artist had spent a good deal of time decorating the space for the tenants. There were only two doors on the second floor. The first was labelled MATT PARKS, RESIDENT GENIUS.

Dan knocked and waited as footsteps approached and the door opened wide. He disliked the face of the genius at first sight; he was pretty sure he wouldn't like it if he saw it a thousand times more. Parks's dominant feature was a disdainful scowl. He had long stringy hair that begged for a comb and teeth that looked as though they'd been gnawing on raw bones for some time. He had probably once been faintly handsome before whatever drug he subscribed to took its toll.

"Yeh?"

On the wall behind him, a series of blow-ups featured a variety of young women in different states of undress, all attempting to strike alluring poses while appearing natural at the same time. They weren't particularly successful. Nor was it clear if the suggestiveness was meant to have pretensions of artistic merit or otherwise.

Dan smiled. He held up the calendar. "You Matt Parks?"

The man's expression notched up one degree of friendliness in anticipation of a possible compliment or calendar sale. It still rated three on a scale of a thousand, as far as Dan was concerned.

"Yeh, that's me. What can I do for you?"

Dan flipped to a shot of the bakery's interior with Ling's face clearly lit.

"I'm a private investigator. I'm interested to know if this woman is one of your models."

The scowl turned to a snarl.

"Man, I do so many chicks. I can't keep track of them all."

Dan wondered if he was speaking professionally or personally.

"Was she just a customer in the café then? Otherwise, you'd have to have a model release form, wouldn't you?"

"I wouldn't know about that."

Dan continued to smile. "You're a photographer and you wouldn't know about a model release form?"

Parks glanced at the calendar in Dan's hands and shrugged.

"It's not a commercial release, just some shit calendar I shot for a shit café."

Dan nodded. "Some of the images made it onto the Internet. There was a complaint lodged about copyright exploitation."

The photographer gave him a smug look. "Really? I'd be happy to look into it once I see it on paper."

"Wouldn't it be easier just to check to see if you had a model release form?"

"No, it wouldn't. Because it wouldn't be my problem, would it? It was freelance work. I had nothing to do with putting it on the Net. You'd have to talk to the owners of that dump."

Obviously, Matt Parks was not going to be as easily intimidated as the owner of the Kowloon Bakery.

"Maybe you could just give me a little friendly information, then."

Dan pulled out his wallet and removed a fifty. The photographer pushed it away when Dan held it out to him.

"Fuck off," he said. "Get out of my studio."

He shut the door in Dan's face.

Dan stood there for a moment then pulled his card from his wallet and knocked on the door.

"I'm leaving my card," he said loudly. "If you think of anything, call me. It might save you some trouble later on."

Dan slid the card under the door. As he stood up, he heard a mocking laugh. Chances were that he would not be hearing from Mr. Matt Parks, Resident Genius, in the near future.

Dan got back in his car and drove to his office. He slid into his chair and glanced over at his files. Some days he spent an inordinate amount of time fiddling with note pads, trying to stretch what he merely suspected might be true into something solid, something he could prove. Something that would lead him to the person he was searching for. He checked his phone. There were no messages waiting for him. Then he saw the envelope on the corner of his desk. It was from Ian Cunningham, the police officer who'd asked him to keep an eye open for his daughter. He tore it at the seams; a photograph slid out and lay staring up at him. A girl with a pretty face and a sneaky glint in her eye. But more than that. She had white dreadlocks.

A good girl gone bad indeed.

Dan recalled the fistful of twenties he'd watched the same girl stuff into her pocket half an hour earlier. What were the chances she'd been coming from

Matt Parks's studios? Why did kids do the things they did? Ah, right — to get at their parents. Want some affection from an overworked dad? Great, here's how to do it: first, twist your hair into a snaky mess, then throw in a nose ring and a well-placed tattoo or three. Finally, have some erotic photographs shot by a sleazy photographer in the wrong end of town. And *bingo!* Instant attention. Only problem is, it will invariably be of the negative variety, guaranteed to garner more of the same over time till a cry for affection becomes a full-fledged rebellion in the eyes of a man trained to deal gruffly with dissent. No discussion. No compromise. Simply a hands-down decree: *Clean up your act or clear out!*

He phoned Ian to say his daughter was alive, at least, and to ask a few more questions about their faltering relationship, which elicited the expected answer: obviously not good at the best of times. Then he packed up for the day and went home.

A man never gets to spend enough time with his dog. Dan sat on his back patio, scratching Ralph behind the ears with one hand and sipping from a mineral water with the other hand. It was a good balancing act.

At five, Ralph's ears pricked up. Dan heard the front door open and close. Ralph stayed where he was. Ked came in and sloughed his knapsack onto the banister, as he usually did. He did not, however, call out a greeting, as he had for nearly every day of his life since

Dan could recall. His fun-loving, light-hearted son had turned into a silent, truculent young man.

No accounting for hormones, Dan told himself.

A few minutes later, he heard his son, apparently talking to himself, in the front room.

"Problem?" Dan called out.

"How do you know Trace?"

Dan walked out to the hall. "Who?"

Ked nodded to the file on the table. It was opened to the photograph of Tracy Cunningham. Ked was wearing his the-world-is-a-terrible-place-so-don't-joke-with-me expression.

"Right there," he said. "That's Trace Cunningham."

Dan nodded. "You know her?"

"Of course. She goes to school with me."

The things a father doesn't know, Dan thought. "Was she at school today?" he asked.

Ked's eyes looked away then back to Dan's face. "No."

"Are you sure?"

"Yeah."

"When was the last time you saw Tracy?"

"Why?"

"Ked — just answer the question."

Ked's cheeks expanded and expelled an impatient breath. He shrugged. Dan was starting to feel impatient himself.

"Think!"

Ked suddenly looked concerned.

"I don't know. Last week, probably."

Something suddenly occurred to Dan.

"Is this …" He didn't know how to phrase it. "Is this the girl you were asking about at school? The one you feel awkward in front of?"

Ked shook his head with that look of scorn Dan hated. "No."

"But you know her?"

A nod. "Yeah."

"How well do you know her?"

"So-so. She's Lester's friend, actually."

"Lester?"

"Yeah. What's wrong with —?"

Dan was tired of this cat-and-mouse game.

"Would you please stop answering like every question I ask is either stupid or incomprehensible?"

Ked sighed and looked away. "All right," he said softly.

"Thank you. This is important or I wouldn't be prying into your personal life."

Dan could see the debate passing over his son's face, the dilemma of answering his father's questions balanced against the teenage credo of not ratting on one's friends.

"What's Trace done?" Ked asked.

"She disappeared some time last week."

Ked's mouth hung open. "Then that's why she hasn't been at school …" He looked down at the floor. "Is she in trouble?"

"No. Listen to me. It's very important. She's not in trouble with the law, but something bad could happen to her. I need you to let me know if you see her again. Call me right away. Don't wait till you get home to tell me. Can you do that for me?"

"Yes."

"Good."

The phone rang. It was Ian Cunningham again. He sounded panicked.

"I ran a check on the photographer you named. I don't like what I found."

Alarm bells were going off in Dan's head. He shouldn't have given him Matt Parks's name. Normally, he wouldn't have offered such information to a client, but this was simply a favour he was doing for a father who also happened to be a police officer. Dan had thought it merited a little more openness. He hoped he wouldn't end up being sorry for having revealed Parks's identity.

"The guy's a fucking pornographer. There's even the possibility that he runs an escort service."

Dan felt his blood curdle. All he needed was a renegade cop getting worked up about his runaway daughter. He did his best to calm him down, but he could tell he wasn't getting very far.

"Send me whatever you found, Ian. I'll go back and put some pressure on him. For now, just promise me you'll stay out of the way and let me handle things my way."

"The fuck I will! I'm not promising anything," Cunningham said in a menacing way that made Dan nervous.

The phone went dead.

Dan turned on his computer and Googled Matt Parks. His photo showed up in the background of a couple of recent arts fundraisers. Apparently he'd had a reputation as an *avant-garde* photographer a decade earlier. Since then, he seemed to have become more *derriere-garde*, little more than a celebrity on the fringes of Toronto's arts scene. He didn't even have a website, which was odd for a commercial photographer.

Dan checked his watch. He had a dinner date with a very attractive Asian man in an hour. A man who also happened to be his client. For now, he just had time for a shave and shower.

Twelve

Cooking for Two

Ren stood at the counter, a blade in one hand and pressing down on the butcher's block with the other. He sliced into something that might have been glass noodles, plucking the long, glycerine strands from a bowl of grey-blue water. The suites at Le Saint-Germain came equipped with cooking facilities and he'd promised Dan a full-on traditional Chinese meal. No General Tao's Chicken, no mushy egg rolls, no sweet-and-sour anything. Dan was already dazzled by the array of ingredients set out on the counter.

Ren's fingers moved like a thresher, nimbly pushing things about and chopping them into smaller and smaller piles. The knife looked professional, with deep ridges running along the blade and a rich patina flashing as it worked. In Ren's hands it seemed more like a surgical instrument wielded with precision rather than a cooking tool.

Dan watched him at work, his face mute with concentration. He found Ren's looks impossible to describe. Something about the angle of the eyes set in the hollow of his cheekbones, the fine brows overarching them, the pure skin the colour of almond. Dan felt a sense of annihilation, of losing himself in another man's appearance. Maybe Donny was right — he was a relationship junkie with a sex addiction — because just being with Ren left him tingling all over. In all probability it was simply an over-excitation of hormones, but he felt stirred to his depths. He had an urge to tear Ren's clothes off and drag him to bed, as though his hunger could be satiated only by total immersion in his physical beauty.

Snap out of it, buddy, he told himself. *You're sounding like a love-obsessed teenager*.

He couldn't afford to forget that Ren was also his client. In all his years as an investigator, he'd never fallen for a client. It wasn't the kind of relationship that made for a happy ending. He had to do his job dispassionately, with no agenda other than finding the missing person.

While Ren chopped, Dan related the details of his visit to the Kowloon Bakery, explaining how he'd gone to see the photographer afterward, but with no luck. All the while he spoke, he was aware of an urge to please Ren. Normally, he just did his job and walked away with his feelings intact. This was different.

Something had changed. Something had happened to him.

Ren said little during Dan's recitation of his adventures. He listened in silence then, as if what he'd heard didn't matter in the least, as he carried a bowl over to the table and set it on a bamboo mat. Opaque purple glass, filled with every variation on green: bean sprouts, Chinese cabbage, green onions, and finally the chopped noodles. The scent of warm sesame and soy wafted upward.

Ren turned to Dan and nodded to the bowl, chopsticks laid out on either side.

"You can use these?" he asked, holding up the sticks.

"I'm capable enough," Dan assured him.

He fished a quantity of the salad onto Dan's plate then turned his attention to his own.

"Jellyfish salad," Ren said, seating himself across from Dan.

"Interesting," Dan said, feeling a queasy sensation set in.

He'd already assured Ren that he ate everything; he wasn't going back on his word. Dan picked up his chopsticks, positioned them between his fingers and deftly scissored what he had earlier assumed was some sort of noodle. *Go for the worst and get it over with*, he told himself. He bit into it. It had a slightly crunchy texture. The flavour was subtle, nothing repulsive about it at all. The dressing made it slightly sweet, slightly salty.

Ren was watching him. "Do you like it?"

"It's very good," Dan told him. "Nice flavour. Slightly crunchy and very tasty."

"Like you."

Dan stared at him. "I think you just made a joke."

Ren smiled.

Dan slipped more of the salad into his mouth, assessing the taste. "Delicious," he concluded.

"Thank you."

"Anyway," he said. "I still haven't decided what my next angle is going to be. I learned something interesting, though. I've been keeping my eyes open for a girl who ran away from home. A friend of my son's. She might have a connection with the photographer who took your sister's picture."

Ren's eyebrows rose, but he said nothing.

"It might be nothing," Dan said. "On the other hand, they could have something in common. I'm not sure what that is yet." He hesitated, unsure how to proceed. Some things needed to be treated with great delicacy. This was one of them. "Can you think of any reason your sister might know a photographer who is involved in pornography?"

Ren glanced up, an inquisitive look on his face.

"Sex trade," Dan explained.

"Yes, I understand what this means." He shook his head and looked off. "Perhaps my sister has changed a great deal more than I anticipated," he said at last, with something like resounding finality.

"I'm not saying she's involved in the sex trade," Dan hastened to assure him. "I'm just trying to figure out what connection she may have had with this photographer. Because clearly she did."

Ren nodded. "We will speak of this more."

They finished the salad in silence. Ren stood and gathered the bowls, bringing them to the counter. When he returned, he brought a platter of finely chopped meat and fried vegetables. The air was filled with an aromatic scent.

"Lamb with cumin," he said.

"You're quite a chef," Dan said.

Ren smiled. "Growing up poor, food takes on a different meaning. When I began to travel, I enrolled in cooking classes to understand all I had been missing."

He went back to the stove and returned with a ceramic bowl brimming with rice. He waited till Dan helped himself, watching as he raised his chopsticks and tasted.

"It's great," Dan told him, savouring the flavours. "You're a terrific cook."

"I am glad you enjoy it."

When they had eaten, Ren cleared the table. He returned and stood behind Dan with his hands on his shoulders. Dan leaned his head against Ren's abdomen, breathing in deeply.

"You smell good," he said.

Ren ran his fingers through Dan's hair.

"Now you will tell me more about my sister, please."

"The picture you showed me was part of a wall calendar. I asked the photographer if he had a model release. Something to give him permission to use the subject's photograph. He wouldn't answer. I was hoping it might show an address for the woman you think is your sister."

Ren nodded. "I understand. This is how you will find her."

"I'm doing my best," Dan said. "I just hope for your sake that when I do, it turns out to be her."

"Yes, of course. There is this, too. As you said once before."

His fingers slipped inside Dan's shirt, toying with the hair on his chest. "And now perhaps for the other? If it is not asking too much."

Dan gripped Ren's wrists. "It's not asking too much."

Ren reached out and pressed a button. The room lights lowered as the automatic blinds shimmied open, revealing their dramatic view of the harbour.

Lips met, clothing was shed. Once again Dan experienced a feeling of annihilation, giving in to a spell of searing intimacy. He was expecting another struggle, but Ren's touch was unexpectedly mild. This was another side to his lovemaking, as though off-setting his partner's expectations intensified the game for him.

As if reading Dan's thoughts, Ren said, "Perhaps we will try the gentle tonight, if you prefer?"

"Why not?"

Afterward, Dan lay in bed caressing Ren's skin and studying his face as though it might yield up the secret of his desire. There was something irresistible about his features, some attraction that got under his skin.

He ran his fingers down Ren's ribs, feeling the bones beneath. His eyes became X-rays, tracing where liver linked to spleen linked to gall bladder linked to pancreas, the body beneath his hands turning into an anatomy model. Skin, bones, flesh, organs, fluids. All the vital components making up a human being. The hip bone connected to the thigh bone connected to the shin bone. Was that all attraction was, simply a physical preference for this skin tone or that eye colour, for a particular hairline or a certain muscle grouping?

Or was he falling in love again? He hadn't thought it possible.

"What were your sexual experiences like with men in China?"

Ren gave him a curious look.

"I did not have any. Only later, when Chinese government sent me to different countries, I discovered what it was like."

"All your sexual experiences were abroad? Didn't you meet anyone gay when you were growing up?"

"In China there are no homosexuals."

"You don't really believe that?"

"It doesn't matter what I believe. It is what Mao told the people and the people believed him. I did not even know what this feeling was. It was not something I heard anyone speak of." He looked off for a moment. "When I was in school, there was one boy I liked very much. Sometimes we would sneak out to share a cigarette. He was popular with the other students because he was a very good artist. He could draw anything.

One day he gave me a piece of paper with my portrait that he had drawn in secret. I did not know what to say. I could not speak to him for several days. He was very shy afterward. I believe he thought I was angry with him for his conduct."

"Do you think he was gay?"

"Now I think maybe he was in love with me. Perhaps I would be in love with him had I known such things were possible."

"Did you keep in touch with him?"

Ren shook his head. "No. This is not a common practice. When Chinese students graduate, we go to different parts of the country to take jobs. We just say goodbye and then we leave. There is not this need for emotional ties as there is in your culture. It is not encouraged. I do not know if I understand it."

He looked questioningly at Dan, as though waiting for a judgment.

"It is like religion. Sometimes when people try to tell me about God, I say I do not know what it is. I did not grow up with this knowledge, so how can I understand it? Is it somewhere inside me? Is God somewhere up in the sky? I do not know. If God exists, why can't I feel it?"

"That's a good Existentialist question. I don't have the answer to it."

"Existentist?"

"Existentialist. It means that only the individual can give meaning to his or her own life, regardless of what they have been told."

"But the individual is not important." Ren smiled quickly. "At least, that is what I was taught to believe."

"I can't help you there," Dan told him. "But obviously your homosexuality was inside you, because you found that."

"Yes, though not until I came to North America." Ren frowned. "But when I go back, I must be normal again ...."

Dan shook his head. "We don't call it *normal*. We call it *heterosexual*. It's only one aspect of sexuality, no more normal than any other. And nobody gets to choose what they are."

"In China it is hard to be gay."

"Have you thought of staying here?"

Ren nodded. "It occurs to me. In fact, I think of it many times. Maybe when you find my sister, she will help me."

"It's easier when you have family to sponsor you."

Ren smiled. "I know this already."

"I've got to go," Dan said, rising. "I have a long day tomorrow. Do you want some help with the dishes before I leave?"

"No, tough man. It is my pleasure to cook for you."

They kissed. This time it felt genuine, not just a sexual expediency.

"When will I see you again?" Dan asked.

Ren's expression changed. "I must leave the city for a short duration," he said. "I learned this today. It was unexpected, but my government requires my expertise elsewhere."

Dan looked at him in surprise. "Where are you going?"

"To Berlin," Ren said. "It is an important trade mission. Someone has fallen ill and I must substitute for him."

Dan smiled. "You must be an important person if you can take over for others at a moment's notice."

"I must do as required. I cannot always choose what I do." He hesitated, glancing around the room. "Perhaps when I return you will stay the night with me. There is no one to know about it, so there will be no shame."

Dan stood with his back to the door. "I don't care if anyone knows or not. In the meantime, I will continue trying to find your sister. But what if she won't meet with you? Have you thought about that?"

Ren was silent for a moment. "Then I should like to have something returned to me," he said at last in a decisive tone. "A jade butterfly. It is a family heirloom."

That, in Dan's experience, had as often as not proved to be the reason many relatives "missed" their loved ones — for the valuables they relieved them of in their haste to get away. Artwork, signed first editions, jewellery, heirlooms. In Dan's estimation, however, Ren was quite well off for a Chinese citizen, so why would he want a simple piece of jade returned to him?

"I take it this object is of considerable value?"

Ren hesitated, as though trying to get the words exactly right.

"If I tell you it has more symbolic value than monetary worth, you might find it hard to believe, but this is so. The butterfly has a certain value as a piece of art, of course, but it is nothing extraordinary. I thought it was lost during the Cultural Revolution, destroyed as a symbol of old-style capitalist decadence. Later, I discovered my family hid it beneath the floorboards of our house. I found it and gave it to Ling the summer she disappeared. If she does not want to see me, I would like to have it back." He paused and turned to Dan. "Can you understand this?"

"Yes, I think I can."

Thirteen

Stiff

With Ren away, Dan had more time to follow up on finding his sister. He'd already done an official search and come away empty-handed. If she lived in Canada, then she was definitely not here legally or else had changed her name and was untraceable. So far, the only tangible lead he'd come up with was her connection to Matt Parks. There was nothing to do but follow and see where it led.

The next night found Dan parked across the street from the photographer's studio. He turned off the car and checked his watch: a little past eleven. Not that late, as things went. He scanned the roadway, but there was no one about. An occasional car zoomed past, but the neighbourhood was deserted. Even taxis didn't slow down in that dark, gloomy strip on the outskirts of the film district.

Somehow, in his head Dan had entwined his future

with finding Ren's sister. If he could track Ling down then maybe, just maybe, he might convince Ren to immigrate to Canada with her sponsorship. Of course, the other option was for Dan to marry him, though he wasn't sure it was a practical idea. For one thing, they'd only met. Immigration authorities would not look kindly on that. For another, their cultures and upbringings were immeasurably different. He wasn't sure Ren could conceive of anything as radical as gay marriage.

In the meantime, he had a plan.

On his previous visit to the studio, he saw the building was not highly secured. There were no alarms, no cameras in the lobby. Nor were there guards, human or canine, to watch for. If he looked, there might be a window he could shimmy up to and slip inside, though he'd far prefer to pick a lock if it came to that. Assuming he wanted to do anything so risky and stupid, of course. On the other hand, it was a chal-lenge and he'd been feeling under-challenged lately.

At a quarter to twelve, he got out of his car and walked across to the building. With a glance over his shoulder, he turned and slipped down a side alley. The shadowy outlines of industrial garbage bins hunkered at the far end like elephants frozen at Pompei. He turned his gaze to the second floor. No lights on. There was also no easy access via an emergency escape. A fire might prove highly detrimental to anyone on the higher floors. In any case, he wouldn't be able to reach the windows to see if any were unlocked.

He stepped out of the shadows and entered the lobby. The graffiti lingered on the walls and over the mailboxes. Rubbish still littered the stairwell. Thankfully, someone had put it to use: a flyer protruded from the catch, freezing the lock. A late delivery or a late-night tryst? No matter — whoever it was intended for hadn't arrived yet. Dan let himself in and made his way up to the second floor. Once again, there were no cameras on the landing or in the corridors. If he'd thought about it, he might have realized it wasn't supposed to be that easy.

The lock on the studio was stiff at first, but with a little jiggling it lifted freely. Dan would regret that later, but for now he let himself in and stood there getting adjusted to the dark, composing himself for the task ahead. There was an eerie tone hanging in the air, different from what you feel coming home to a silent house an hour before everyone else arrives. This particular silence, this emptiness, was inert, unexpectant, and dead.

He took a step. The planks creaked beneath his tread. Immediately, it was as though the place had come alive. He stopped and held his breath. Outside, the wind rose half a degree then subsided again. Dan was pretty sure there wasn't another living soul in the building, but if he got caught he had a few friends on the police force. If it came to that, of course, which he sincerely hoped it would not. He had never pushed his luck that far and was pretty sure that one "Get Out of Jail Free" card was all he could manage. Better never to have to ask at all.

He snapped on his Maglite, training the beam on the ground like a poacher checking for prey in his traps. Above, the models were stuck in their seductive poses. They glared down at him from the shadows, as though they disapproved of late-night visitors. Perhaps they were Matt Parks's security. They seemed to Dan to be waiting for something. Personal references, date requests, possibly. Maybe his business there at half past midnight. Or maybe they were just trying to tell him something like, *Get Lost!* That was more likely, he thought.

He located a file cabinet near the back of the room. If Parks kept anything as proper as a model release, it would be in there. He slipped on his latex gloves and went to work. Inside was a mishmash of job orders and receipts for everything from cab rides to groceries and cellphone records. There seemed to be little organization or thematic continuity.

He'd been rifling through the files a short time when he realized everything was grouped loosely according to date rather than alphabetically. Not that Ren's sister would have used her real name if she'd modelled for him. If she didn't want to be found, she would have falsified her identity completely. In that case, he would have a lot of sifting to do.

The files seemed to go back years. He thought for a moment: roughly how long before a calendar was released would you have to start to work on it? Six months? A year? He pulled out a sheaf of papers and began to thumb through it. Luck seemed to be with him. He found an order for the Kowloon Bakery and then, miraculously, a note from Matt Parks to a local printer with a delivery date of November 30 for a calendar ordered August 23. Clipped to this were various pieces of paper, including a list of names: Ling Siu was third on the list. It was one of the aliases Ren had suggested his sister might use. Nothing else. No phone number, address, or contact info. But here, at least, was confirmation of what he'd been looking for.

He dug around a bit more. There was nothing further to connect Matt Parks to either Ren's sister or the café. He was about to return the papers to the folder and replace them in the drawer when he saw something else, a file at the far end that seemed to have been slipped in among several others.

Dan pulled it out. Had he not been searching for something unusual, he might have overlooked it. In fact, the only thing unusual about the file was the lack of date or any sort of numerical reference. Inside, it contained what appeared to be model release forms, signatures sprouting at the bottom. But there was more: photographs of women, both dressed and undressed, in various poses meant to suggest some sort of fetish, from the slightly risqué to the injudicious. Chains, whips, leather, and rubber, all very ordinary. Alongside these were smaller photographs, each about the size of a passport photo, labelled with a numbered code.

The file was voluminous. He could be there all night, Dan thought, and he presumed he didn't have that long. He pulled out a sheet and looked it over. The woman gaped at him, as though she wanted him to crawl into the photograph with her. There was a name along with an address. He flipped opened his cell to look it up on Google Maps. It didn't exist. He went to the next file. The same thing. So if the addresses were faked then it was just as likely the models' names had similarly been fabricated. But why encrypt them? Escort services were nothing new. These days, even pandering to sexual fetishes was nominally legal when they were rendered as a skill or trade. Was it just to obscure the identities of the women or was there something more to it?

Dan remembered Ian Cunningham's allegations that Matt Parks was involved in the flesh trade. Perhaps this was what he had stumbled onto. But these women did not look drugged and coerced into posing, as he might have expected had it been some third-world agency offering women for exploitation. Rather, they looked as though they enjoyed what they were doing because they were very, very good at it. He dug deeper. There were other photographs, these not so ordinary. One showed a man and a woman, both naked. The woman stood behind the man, head shaved, breasts full, her red bush outlined by the light. She was smiling cruelly. Her left hand gripped an instrument that might have been a surgical tool. The man's mouth was gagged, rendering him unable to speak or cry out. His eyes were closed in pain or possibly ecstasy, testicles trussed and bleeding down his thighs. Another showed a masked woman brandishing an ordinary kitchen knife. The man at her side had as yet been untouched, but his face showed fear glazed over with something like erotic expectation, eyes focused on the blade held directly beneath his scrotum.

Dan turned over the page and found an even more disturbing presentation: the naked body of a man lay prone on a table. His arms and legs were strapped down with leather thongs. Jagged gashes crisscrossed his chest and abdomen, while his face was obscured by a blood-stained towel. There was no way of telling whether the man was dead or alive. It might have been a vivisection performed by some warped medical student or it could have been the end results of a snuff session. The woman in the picture — a dark-haired dwarf — looked directly into the camera, posing with what looked like pinking shears. This was a highly-specialized fantasy scenario, if indeed it were fantasy. Dan wondered about the propriety of such photographs. Were they legal, even as fetishist props? Of course, the other option was far more disturbing. He'd heard the stories of online transactions: people searching for their own killers, victims who fantasized about being cannibalized, and the individuals who were willing to make their dreams come true, such as they were. It was no wonder *Matt Parks, Resident Genius* did not have a website with a welcome page on it.

Dan felt stiffness creeping into his arms. He'd been holding the files in fascination for a considerable time. He was about to place them on top of the filing cabinet and give his arms a shake when something sounded far off. A distant footstep, soft as a night breeze. Just the rumour of a whisper. But he heard it. Coming up the stairs.

His watch read 12:23. He'd been there nearly thirty minutes.

It felt like hours.

He closed the drawer and snapped off the gloves, stuffing them into his pocket. He flexed his fingers and rubbed the sweat off the backs of his hands. Only now did it occur to him what a reckless thing he'd done. As far as finding Ling was concerned, it had largely been a waste of time and he'd jeopardized himself by trying a very stupid stunt. Who had he been trying to impress — Ren or himself?

Footsteps reached the second-floor landing and stopped. Dan looked around. Two doors led off from the studio. One was probably a changing room for the models, the other a bathroom. He tried the first door. Locked. Why would you lock a makeup room? Maybe lipstick was expensive. No time to wonder, he decided. He reached for the second door handle.

It turned without effort. The last thing he expected was to find the bathroom occupied. Less so by a corpse. But there was Matt Parks, caught in the flashlight's silvery beam. The photographer was propped on the toilet and facing the wall ahead, looking for all the world as though he were contemplating his balls, which had been strung up across from him. The *coup de grâce* had obviously been the bright red necklace marking his throat, darkened to the colour of brandy where the blood had started a slow roll downward before the residue dried and stuck. Definitely not a fantasy scenario, but any accompanying photograph would have been right at home in the file Dan had just perused.

His first thoughts were not sympathetic, but tactical: *What have I touched without gloves?* He tried to recall his movements. *A door handle only.* Good, that part was easy. He would attend to it on the way out. Well … he would so long as the person moving about on the landing didn't stop him.

He turned off his flashlight and concentrated on listening. At first, there was no sound. Then he heard the slow, furtive movements of someone trying the handle. An entire scenario went through his head: the police had received a tipoff about the murder and were about to burst in and capture the prime suspect on the spot. He would have a hard time making them believe his story at first, but eventually they'd realize he wasn't carrying the murder weapon. There was nothing inside the studio with his fingerprints on it. Then again, he had gloves with him and he'd broken in. But, judging by the congealed blood, the body had been there for some time and, once it was established that he'd been there less than half an hour, things would begin to lighten up. A little. He hoped. Until then he would be arrested and held without bail.

He heard a slight scraping. Someone was picking the lock, exactly as he had done. The pins twisted, the latch lifted, the handle turned. Not the police, then.

Which left him with the worst-case scenario: the return of the perpetrator.

His flashlight was too small to use as a weapon. He turned it back on. Over in one corner stood a toilet roll holder with a long metal handle and a solid bottom, one of those jokey things with Brian Mulroney's face on it. *Ah, the days gone by! That would do*, Dan thought. Avoiding looking at Matt Parks's mortal remains, he gripped the holder as though it were a crowbar, prepared to crush any skull that belonged to a murderer.

Better him than me, Dan thought.

He waited. For a moment nothing happened. The studio door opened slowly and held. The hall light cast long shadows around the room. Someone was standing outside listening.

The door opened wider. A figure slipped in and froze. Dan tensed, gripping the metal tube. A sudden flashlight beam blinded him. Before he could move, the figure slipped back out, leaving the door open and the light streaming in.

He heard a ragged, wheezing intake. It seemed to come from several places at once. It scared him until he realized it was his own breathing. Then he heard footsteps racing down the stairs and understood that he was the one presumed to have the advantage under the current circumstances.

He ran to the door, making no attempt to keep quiet. Out in the hall, he hesitated before glancing quickly over the balustrade. At the bottom, a hooded figure raced through the lobby. The front door swung open and shut again. He was alone. Turning back to the studio, it took Dan three seconds to wipe the handle clean. Then he closed the door and walked downstairs as though it were the most natural thing in the world.

He stepped out into the night, accompanied by the sound of his thumping heart and punctuated breathing. He didn't stop moving till he got to his car and turned the key.

Somewhere there was home. There was safety and a son he loved more than anything. A son who would be waiting for his father to return and get into bed and go to sleep and have dreams — good ones, bad ones, it hardly mattered at this point. A son who needed his help to grow up to lead a normal, happy life. Whatever that was.

Sure. Easy.

So why not try it?

Fourteen

A Model of Release

His first stop upon leaving the studio was to find a phone booth. From there, he called in the murder without leaving his name. It wasn't, strictly speaking, his responsibility. He hadn't, strictly speaking, called in a murder but rather a suspected break-in. Just a neighbour out walking a dog who saw someone running from the premises of a building that was normally closed after-hours. He gave the description of an Asian woman, but stopped short of voicing his suspicions — that it was Ren Hao's sister-in-hiding he'd seen running from the scene. After all, he might have been wrong. And after all yet again, he still wasn't positive Ren had been right about the woman he claimed to be his sister.

At least that was his reasoning at the time.

He got home just before one, washed his face at the bathroom sink, and stared at himself in the mirror.

His mind was doing whirligigs as he contemplated his possible best next move. He'd upset his son by waking him and grilling him about his missing classmate, but without divulging anything in return that might let Ked go back to sleep in peace. The hallmarks of their father-son relationship had always been honesty and trust, but suddenly Dan was the one making excuses and withholding information.

In the midst of their third-degree session, Ked let slip that Tracy had posted questionable photographs on her Facebook site the previous month. Dan's patience wore thin. He yelled at his son for not divulging the information earlier. Ked returned to bed looking more than a little resentful. Dan's world seemed to be turning backflips.

Now, he chanced calling the one person who would understand and accept what he'd done without too much admonishing. Or so he hoped.

He answered on the second ring. Which meant he was still up. Which meant he would be coherent. Otherwise he would have grabbed the bedside phone in a panic on the first ring.

"I need your advice."

"I wouldn't mind giving it if you didn't ignore it so often," replied the cool voice in soft undertones without a perceptible pause for reflection.

"I'm working on that. Got time for a late-night visit?"

"For you, of course."

"I'm flying."

* * * *

"So let me get this straight." Donny exhaled his signa-
ture blend of cigarette smoke and disapproval, aiming
it out over his balcony, across the neighbourhood, and
beyond the city lights stretching to the far reaches of
infinity. His aim was true, if occasionally a bit wide.
"You broke into some photographer's studio to ransack
his files, which happened to contain some dicey material of questionable taste, and also ended up in the
bathroom with a stiff."

"I didn't check to see if he was actually stiff, but
yes, that's more or less the scenario."

"And you made sure to wipe off your fingerprints
from anything you may have touched before you actually scrammed and called the police?"

"I hope so. God, I hope so."

"A bit late now, if you didn't. Nevertheless, we'll
give you credit for using a small but significant portion
of the brains you were born with." He stopped to consider. "You also think a friend of Ked and Lester's has
something to do with this dead photographer?"

"I saw her coming down the stairs with a handful
of bills the first time I went by."

"And her father's a cop?"

Dan nodded.

"Boy, that's a good one."

Donny waited a moment, exhaled even more
expressively, then said, "You don't think the boys are
involved in any way with whatever's going on here?"

"Ked swears not. But these days, I don't know what to make of him. He didn't tell me things about the girl when I asked earlier."

"Maybe you didn't ask the right questions."

"That's what he said."

"That's good enough for me. Your son wouldn't lie to you. Nor would Lester to me, because he spent enough time on the street to have the smarts about things that could lead to trouble. He doesn't want any more in his life, so that's why I know he wouldn't lie to me."

"This isn't about the kids. I don't question their story. I'm concerned that a schoolmate of theirs would have her photograph taken by someone who runs a very specialized escort agency and ends up murdered."

"Coincidence, possibly."

"Maybe. But if you saw some of those photographs, you would have shivered. Extreme stuff. Violence, fetishes. I'm not surprised he ended up dead, considering what I saw in those files."

"Still, we can't jump to conclusions." Donny held up a hand to indicate a shift in his train of thought. "I hope you won't mind if I back you up a bit to add my two-cents' worth about men who go breaking into places in the middle of the night, risking a heavy jail sentence and — clearly, with hindsight — their lives as well?"

"I guess not."

"Good, because we shouldn't overlook that little misstep in your otherwise almost reasonable story." A pause with a meaningful glance. "I'm assuming there was a reason?"

"It's client-related. I shouldn't really say anything."

Donny cocked an eyebrow at him.

"Yet you don't mind telling me you committed a felony in pursuit of said client-related matters."

Dan sighed.

"It's Ren."

"Ren? As in the S-and-M Taiwanese businessman from Slam last weekend? You didn't mention him again. I thought you said he was a tourist frolicking through the city on his way back to wife and kiddies."

"I assumed he was —"

"Yes, let's see you dig your way out of this one."

Dan stopped to gather his wits. "I've been seeing him. He … he cooked supper for me."

"Do tell."

"He made a jellyfish salad to die for."

Donny shook his head. "Spare me the menu. We'll save it for polite cocktail banter one day in the old folks' home when we're really bored. What else?"

"He hired me."

Here, Donny's face assumed an expression of utter chagrin. "In what capacity? If it's not too much to ask."

"To find his sister who died." Dan stopped to rethink that one. "Or who went missing in the Tiananmen massacre."

"Which?"

"What?" Dan looked startled.

"His sister who died or went missing? Or both?"

"We don't know yet. Ren thought she was dead till he found her on the Internet. Now he thinks she might be living somewhere in Toronto."

Donny shook his head.

"And that's why you broke into a photographer's studio in the middle of the night for a client you're sleeping with?"

"It was midnight."

"A trifle, but go on."

"So anyway, I found the photographer's address and went to his studio —"

"To break in."

"No. Well, not at first. I just went to see what he could tell me about the woman Ren thinks is his sister. I was hoping he could tell me her address."

"Whoa, whoa, whoa!" Donny waved his arms about. "How did this photographer come to have her address?"

"Well, he didn't. I mean, if he does ... or *did* ... he didn't give it to me. Obviously."

Donny's eyes were glazing over.

Dan sighed. "I'm not telling this very coherently, am I?"

"You wouldn't pass the police lineup audition, I can tell you that."

The cigarette was quietly stabbed out in a pot of hibiscus, smoke dwindling away with each deft jab.

Donny eyed him squarely "Start again. This time tell it to me as though I'm five."

Dan took a breath before continuing. "Ren did

some research before coming to Toronto. He found an online picture of a woman he believes is his sister who disappeared during the Tiananmen riots twenty years ago and was presumed dead."

"Better. So far, I'm with you."

"The photograph on the website led me to a bakery in Chinatown. From there, I obtained the name of the photographer who took the pictures for their calendar. I visited his studio, but he wasn't very forthcoming. About anything, really. Not even when I tried to bribe him."

Donny grimaced. "Classy."

"I detect sarcasm."

"You were expecting praise?"

"I guess not. Anyway, I went back tonight to see what I could come up with in terms of an address — maybe a model release, that sort of thing."

"And instead you found a model of release."

Dan shot Donny a quizzical look.

"A joke. Inappropriate, I'm sure."

"Ah. Yes, I see."

"So that brings us up to date, then? That's why you called me at one in the morning?"

"More or less."

"What exactly do you want my advice on? Where to hide the body?"

Dan shrugged. "You know what they say — a friend will help you move, but a good friend will help you move a body."

Donny gave him another withering look. "And god knows I'm the best friend you have."

"I won't argue that." Dan considered the question. "I guess I just needed consolation —"

"I'm out of consolation coupons again."

"— and to know that someone besides me knows the stupid things I've done."

"Not a word of a lie."

"And that you still accept me as a friend after all that."

"Without question."

"Thank you."

Donny shook his head. "But I surely hope to God you didn't leave any fingerprints around that studio."

"If I did, I could claim it was from my visit the other day."

Donny nodded. "You're a clever boy, I'll give you that. By the way, would you like a drink?"

Dan shook his head.

"You're right, it's a bit late and I shouldn't tempt you off the wagon."

Donny stood and looked over his shoulder.

"Let's have a moment of practicality." He went over to a door and knocked lightly. A boyish voice called from within. "Sorry to disturb you, Lester. Would you come out here, please? Your Uncle Dan wants to ask you something."

After a moment, the door opened and a sleepy teenager looked groggily out. Dark hair, dishevelled. Pajama bottoms and wrinkly T-shirt.

"Hi, Uncle Dan."

"Sorry for waking you, Lester. I was wondering if you could help me out with something."

"Sure. If I can."

"You know a girl from school named Tracy Cunningham?"

"Uh, yeah."

"Have you seen her lately?"

Lester fidgeted.

"No." He shrugged. "Not for a couple weeks, at least."

"Do you know where she might be?"

"No."

"Do you know why she might have gone away?"

"Well …"

He glanced at Donny.

"It's cool. Just tell Uncle Dan what you know."

He nodded. "She was pissed off with her dad. He's a cop."

"I know."

"He was kind of strict with her. Cheap, I mean. She said she found a way to make money. I asked if it was drugs, but she said it wasn't."

"Do you know what she was doing?"

"No. She didn't tell me." He hesitated. "She kind of knew about my time on the streets, so I think she was curious. I told her she could talk to me if she wanted to, but she didn't."

Dan nodded. "Do you think maybe she might have been talking about joining an escort agency or anything like that?"

"She didn't say so."

"Did you get the feeling she might be in trouble?"

Lester's mouth hung open. "Uh, no. She seemed okay, whatever it was. She looked kinda happy."

"Okay, thanks," Dan said. "I've already asked Ked to let me know if he sees or hears from her. Will you do the same for me, please?"

"Sure."

"Thanks, Lester. Go back to bed. Sorry for disturbing you."

The boy nodded.

"Good night."

"See you in the morning," Donny said.

The door closed.

Dan looked at Donny and nodded. "Sounds straight-up."

"You think this girl is one of his kinky escorts?"

"Hard to say. I wondered if that was why I saw Tracy leaving his building with money."

"It's possible, I guess." Donny looked off. Dan saw the urge for a cigarette come and go in his eyes. "Did you ask why your client wants to find his sister?"

"He wants to reunite with her. He says she's the only family he has left. And of course, my question was why she hadn't contacted him before now. He didn't have an answer, other than that it was to protect him and his family from government reprisals back home."

"What do you think?"

"My guess is that he's wrong about who he found on the Internet. I think he wants his sister to be alive so badly that he's mistaken someone else for her. After all, it's been twenty years since he's seen her. Would you recognize a sibling you hadn't seen in twenty years?"

"People change, it's true, but if he's convinced it's her then it's possible."

"If it is, I hope she's still the person he remembers. Alarm bells went off in my head when I realized the photographer was involved in the sex trade. And now that he's dead, it suggests a whole lot more. A woman who vanished twenty years ago as a teenager could have got herself involved in a lot of things since then."

Donny appeared to be taking this in. "That's true, of course. What would a brother really know of a teenage sister who disappeared and returned more than half a lifetime later? She could be anybody now."

Dan nodded. "Exactly. I just hope he's not devastated if I find her and she's not the nice sister he remembers growing up with. Or worse, if it turns out she's the killer."

Lester's door reopened. He came out. "Weird, I just checked Tracy's Facebook page. It has a picture of her with some guy named Marlon in Hamilton."

"Why weird?"

"She hates Hamilton. Said it's where you go if you're not cool enough for Toronto."

On the run, Dan decided. Thoughts ran fleetingly through his head. Had she known about Matt Parks's untimely end? And if so, who tipped her off? He was pretty certain that it was a woman he'd seen running from the premises earlier. He was less certain that she was Asian. How hard would it be to hide white dreadlocks under a hoodie?

"Can you find an address for her?"

Lester smiled. "I'll work on it. I could probably have something for you tomorrow."

"You're a smart cookie, Lester. Thanks for this."

Fifteen

Steeltown

There was nothing in the morning papers about a murdered photographer. Dan waited till the afternoon edition, but it simply brought more of the same. He kept one eye on the television, but news of the death seemed to have passed under the radar. *Odd*, he thought. It left him wondering if his call to 911 had gone unheeded. Or perhaps they hadn't bothered to try the studio door and found it unlocked, as he had helpfully left it. Whatever the reason, he wasn't going back to Matt Parks's studio to check. Despite his unexpected involvement, this wasn't his problem and he intended to leave it that way.

Donny called mid-afternoon. He was brisk, his voice full of unspoken footnotes to last night's conversation. Lester had heard back from a friend of a friend who knew Tracy who had once partied with someone named Marlon who lived in Hamilton. The extended chain of adolescent relations. An address was forth-coming.

In the meantime, Dan threw together a travel kit and rang up a local hotel. Hamilton wasn't far, but he had no idea whether this would be a quick visit or a longer session trying to coax Tracy into coming home. If he found her. He let Ked know he was going away again, possibly overnight. The comment elicited a grunt of acknowledgement. Dan left it at that and set out.

He thought of Ren all the way down the uneventful stretch of highway known as the Queen Elizabeth Way, wondering what he was up to in Berlin. He also wondered about his sister Ling's tangential connection with Tracy Cunningham. What tied a 39-year-old Asian refugee to a Canadian teenager with white dreadlocks? A love of spliffs and Bob Marley? Somehow, Dan didn't think so.

Rush hour traffic had already started as he wound his way down to the Gardiner Expressway and squeezed into the westbound lane. Though a runt by comparison, and thought of by many as little more than the stopping-off point between Toronto and the U.S. border, Hamilton was also Toronto's nearest rival for size. Competition between the cities was fierce and extended well beyond universities and football teams. Known locally as Steeltown, Hamilton wrapped around the far end of Lake Ontario in an area known as the Golden Horseshoe. If you were from Toronto, you turned your nose up at the industrial sprawl at the other end of the lake. If you were from Hamilton, you had a million reasons why you would never live in that pretentious metropolis lurking seventy kilometres upstream: too close for comfort and just far enough to be considered within striking distance. Smoke-belching chimneys and a flame-throwing up-thrust greeted Toronto commuters approaching Hamilton's skyline, making it appear both formidable and unwel-coming, as though wishing its sister-city's inhabitants a speedy farewell before they'd even arrived. The sen-timent amounted to a two-way street. Sibling rivalry was always good for a laugh.

The address Lester provided took Dan to a room-ing house. It was a sombre-looking place, everything dark and hidden behind rows of glass. There seemed nothing unusual about it. It was the kind of place you'd pass without a second glance, though a girl with white dreadlocks on the premises might give someone pause.

A friendly face answered Dan's knock. He was the sort of boy habitually found on a football field when he wasn't in the local pub. Frat house pranks and a case of beer under the bed.

"Good afternoon," Dan said. "How are you?"

"Cool," came the response. "You're not selling stuff, are you? Because we're all, like, students here. No extra cash for nothing."

"Got it," Dan said. "No, I'm actually looking for a guy named Marlon."

"Ah, Skateboard Marlon!"

Thoughts of the stripper who had won first prize on his unicycle at Slam came to Dan's mind. He pushed them aside. The boy spoke with friendly assurance. There wasn't a hint of suspicion or even curiosity on his face. Queries about Marlon were either not unusual or else this boy felt Marlon had nothing to hide.

"Does he live here?"

"No, man, sorry. Marlon moved out a couple of months ago."

"Do you know where?"

"Shit, he told me where, but I don't remember. It was on the same piece of paper with his phone number, but I lost it. I can tell him you called, though. I usually run into him at the coffee shops."

"Would you, please?"

Dan felt in his pocket for a business card and produced it with little fanfare. The boy took it with scarcely a glance.

"Would you let him know I'm looking for Tracy?"

The face looked blank. "Who's Tracy?"

"I thought she was his girlfriend."

"Nah! Marlon's not into girls." He nodded down at the rainbow-coloured triangle beside the door handle. "At least, he didn't used to be when he lived here."

Dan nodded. Metrosexual casualness never ceased to amaze him.

"Okay, but if you see him please give him my card."

"Sure, will do."

"Thanks."

Dan texted Donny to ask if Lester might have an alternate address for Marlon and his not-girlfriend, Tracy. He got back in his car and drove around the streets, making his way past the Royal Botanical Gardens and up a large hill. He turned and came back just as the sun was setting. Headlights littered the road ahead as an orange glow spread over the city.

The main thing on his mind when he arrived back in the downtown core was supper. Hamilton's gay scene was minimal, Dan knew. He put it down to all the steel workers. But there was at least one gay bar that served food: The Werx. He hoped it had a good menu.

He clocked it from three blocks away. The Werx was the only purple-fronted building in a line of run-down brick warehouses. With a parking lot on one side and a factory on the other, she was the loud girl making a splash among all the Plain Janes in the neighbourhood. In fact, she looked as though she'd worn many guises in her day.

Dan parked and approached on foot. The drag queen at the front door gave him a practised smile. He knew the look: the intent was glamour, but glamour slapped on with a trowel and squeezed into imitation gold lamé with an attempt at Marilynesque curves that bottomed out into something like a mermaid's outfit.

Dan often wondered if transvestites and trans-sexuals were simply a few generations ahead of the rest of the human race, refusing to be bound in time and space by sex roles and fashion considerations.

Whatever the reason, he tended not to cross them. They usually needed little provocation to be friendly or to pick a fight. This one was in a friendly mood. "Karaoke night," she informed him, with a flutter of her oversize eyelashes.

Lucky me, Dan thought. *At least I won't have to sing for my supper. Everyone else will do it for me.* He nodded his gratitude for the information. There was more to come. She pointed inside the lobby to a painting of what appeared to be an Asian drag queen. Half man, half woman.

"That's Alexia Zen," she told him, like an information-booth worker trying to hustle the tourists into a receptive state. "She haunts this place. Don't be frightened if you run into her."

A haunt for the haunted, Dan thought. *Appropriate.*

"I'll do my best."

He opened the door and stepped inside. It felt like home: plenty of dark corners, an Amigos Bar on the first floor, a downstairs pub for the bear-and-leather crowd, and a second-floor disco with a tinselly stage for karaoke evenings.

Dan ordered a burger and beer and sat on a stool, watching the crowd come and go: twinks and DQs playing up on one side, mature men and leather daddies hanging about in a far corner, just out of reach of the harsh lights that shattered dreams and revealed such blights as thinning hair and widening girths.

The burger wasn't memorable, but he hadn't come to Hamilton for the cuisine. He finished his meal and looked around to see what else might be happening. The boy who approached him was far too young to be in a bar, but then business was business. This one looked undernourished and borderline anaemic, but Dan had spent his fair share of time in bars as an underage teenager and he knew the score. He shook his head at the irony of getting hit on by the one kid he felt sorry for, otherwise he would have blown him off with a cutting remark. He bought the boy a beer, politely disengaged himself, and left.

Upstairs, an old Patsy Gallant tune being sung blithely off-key clued him in that the karaoke show was underway. He stood watching from the back, assuming the posture of a permanent non-participant at such events, leaving the foreground to anyone else who wanted it. In this case, anyone else was comprised of two Chers, a couple of Whitney Houstons, and one Maria from *The Sound of Music*. Maria flubbed her lyrics and changed keys with astonishing irregularity, but made up for her minimal musicality with sheer enthusiasm, all the way to *do* and back again.

One after another they took to the stage, giving their all and then some. But the applause was stinting at best, the laughter far too easy. This was a blowsy, hard-to-please crowd with more attitude than chic. They looked like they would be more likely to applaud a fall from the stage rather than anything vaguely resembling talent.

He trailed back down the stairs just as a familiar

face was headed up. The man gave him a startled glance and looked away. Dan couldn't place him. Just another misplaced Torontonian checking out the local flora and fauna, perhaps.

He turned and got a better look at the man as he passed beneath the lights at the top of the landing. Then it hit him: the graceful nose on an otherwise forgettable face. He'd shared an elevator at the hospital with this man when he'd gone for his interview with Doctor Chranos.

Dan reflected on that first sighting where his fellow passenger had seemed undecided about which floor he wanted. And now here he was again in Steeltown, still looking like Mr. Nobody Special in a brown pullover and cream trousers. Maybe he had his own private stalker, a sex fetishist with an eye for something rough. Too bad the guy wasn't his type. But then Hamilton wasn't exactly the place Torontonians came to get laid.

Dan continued downstairs and found a seat. Sure enough, his stalker showed up a minute later. His eyes scanned the room and stopped at Dan.

Dan decided to play easy to get. He nodded. The man looked around as though perplexed. Nobody beside him. Nobody behind. He looked back at Dan and pointed a thumb at his own chest. Sign language made easy.

"Yeah, you," Dan called across the bar.

The man shrugged and approached, beer in hand.

Dan held out his hand. "Dan Sharp."

They shook.

"Paul Gordon." He waited a beat. "Do we know each other?"

"Not really, but I think we've met," Dan said, waiting for the practised look of surprise.

It came quick enough.

"Really? Were you here last night for the big drag show?"

"You don't remember?"

A squint. A passable affectation of someone trying to retrieve a memory. It was a good attempt, Dan thought. And quick. If he hadn't known better, it might have thrown him off.

"When did we meet?"

"About a week ago. We rode an elevator together in the Women's College Hospital."

"Wow, you're right. I was there." He made a show of looking Dan up and down then shrugged. "I'm surprised I don't remember you."

Dan nodded. "I think you had a lot on your mind that day. Who were you visiting again?"

"My Aunt Helen."

Dan smiled. "Right, I remember now. That's what you said." In fact, Dan knew, he hadn't said anything of the sort. He'd simply bumbled about, seemingly not knowing where he was headed. "How is she?"

Paul nodded nervously. "They're, uh, discharging her next week."

"That's great. What did you say was wrong with her?"

"Peritonitis."

"Is it serious?"

"We were worried about renal failure, but it looks like it's going to be all right now."

The unrequested detail for added measure.

"That's good then." Dan looked around the bar. "So what do you think of this place?"

The other glanced about, his elegant nose sniffing out the décor and whatever else he thought it ought to notice.

"Great place. Terrific!"

"You come here often?"

"No, hardly ever."

"I thought you said you were here last night?"

"Uh, yeah, but I just popped in and out."

Dan pretended to be looking around the crowd.

"Some pretty hot guys here, don't you think?"

"Absolutely," Paul agreed, a little too vehemently.

Dan's gaydar was not giving off conclusive results. Usually it zeroed in on anything that offered a clue. Eye contact, hand gestures. This guy was a cipher. Perhaps he was just a gay nerd hopeless at sending social signals, unconscious or otherwise. Or maybe he was really what he said he was, but Dan remained unconvinced. There was one sure way to sort out the *vrai* gays from the nervous straights. He brushed his thigh against Paul's. Paul looked down where Dan's knee was nestled in his crotch.

Dan winked. "Don't mind me. I'm the friendly type."

"Hey, make yourself at home."

Dan took a sip of beer. Paul followed suit. Dan gave him a suggestive smirk. Paul smiled in return. Dan turned up the heat with the knee pressure then reached over and planted a kiss on Paul's lips. He thought he smelled the tang of fear. At first, Paul resisted, then gave in to the bristly smooch. Dan grabbed his crotch and was surprised to feel a fair-sized erection coming on. Yup, he was gay all right. Or at least a willing metrosexual. There was no faking that, as far as he was concerned.

He released his hold. Paul seemed a little woozy.

"Wow," he said, "are you always so forward?"

"Not usually," Dan said, leaning in again to pinch a nipple.

This time Paul flinched. Dan laughed and redoubled his efforts, zeroing in for a good feel, as if he didn't care what he did. Suddenly, he pulled back.

"So where are you staying, Paul?"

Paul suddenly seemed nervous. "At the Premier, but I can't take you there."

"Ah! Got a wife back in the hotel?"

"N-no."

"Then what's the problem?"

"Nothing, I just don't … I don't know you, really."

Dan smiled. "We could change that."

Paul seemed to be thinking this over. "I guess we could, couldn't we?"

Dan set his beer down before Paul could decide.

"Excuse me. I've got to make a pit stop."

He lurched in the direction of the washrooms and locked himself into a cubicle, settling down on the seat.

Inside, he flipped open the wallet. The name on a credit card read PAUL M. GORDON. Same with the next two cards. He kept digging. A driver's licence showed his name to be something quite different. So did an identity card that stated: THE BEARER OF THIS CARD ACTS UNDER THE AUTHORITY OF THE CANADIAN SECURITY INTELLIGENCE SERVICE.

Dan felt sick. CSIS was responsible for overseeing threats to national security. What did they want with him?

Why are you following me? Dan whispered.

He pocketed the identity card and stuffed the rest back inside the wallet, his ears keen for anyone entering after him. He unlocked the stall door. The washroom was still empty. Outside, the hallway was dim. Maria was still busy climbing mountains upstairs. Dan peeked around the corner and saw Paul sitting where he'd left him. He turned and found an alternate stairwell leading out through another part of the bar.

Sixteen

How Gay Are You?

Dan could see the bar entrance from where he crouched between cars in the parking lot. It wasn't long before a flustered-looking Paul Gordon emerged and stood looking up and down the street. Obviously, he'd realized Dan was gone. It was hard to say if he knew he'd taken his wallet as well.

Dan waited till Paul started walking then simply followed. The darkness kept him well hidden. At one point Paul turned and glanced back, but Dan ducked behind a van. When he looked again, Paul was farther down the street. Dan shadowed him to a small boutique hotel. He shook his head when he saw the sign: PREMIER HOTEL. Four stars. Paul had told the truth about where he was staying. *Obviously a rookie*, Dan thought. He was almost resentful that a CSIS agent should be staying at such a good hotel on taxpayers' money.

Dan watched Paul enter, waited half a minute, then followed through the front entrance. The elevator doors were just closing. He stood and watched, hoping that no one boarded on one of the floors above. The counter climbed directly to the fifth floor, paused briefly, then headed back down. No one noticed Dan waiting for its return. The check-in staff had obviously taken him for a hotel guest.

A minute later, he emerged on the fifth floor of an elegant hotel with six rooms per floor. What were the chances he'd get it right before he was discovered? He walked up to the first door and pressed his head against it. Not a sound. He made his way down the hall. Still nothing. An argument issued from behind the next door — a man and a woman, by the sounds of it. Directly across from it, Dan heard a voice.

"I have a small situation. Put me through, please."

Silence ensued.

"It's Ross, sir. I'm afraid he got away from me. I followed him to a bar, but he said he recognized me from the hospital." There was another silence. "Yes, sir, that's what I thought. We talked briefly then he said he was going to the bathroom, but he never came back." A pause. Paul's voice was more serious when he spoke again. "No, you're right, sir. I underestimated him, obviously." More silence, followed by shuffling. "I will, sir. Sorry, sir."

Dan heard keys and pocket change jangling, then, "Oh, shit!" He'd finally realized his wallet was missing.

Determined footsteps headed for the door. Dan

slipped into a stairwell, sprinted down five floors, and across the street before the elevator hit the ground. He was waiting when his quarry emerged from the hotel and headed along the opposite side. The lamps threw shadows all around, people milling here and there. Paul seemed to be heading back to The Werx.

Once inside, Dan gave him time to search for his wallet near where they'd been sitting. Next, Paul turned to the bartender who looked briefly behind the bar then shook his head. He gave up and sat on a stool, looking dejected.

Dan entered, arms extended, and came up to him.

"Paul!" Dan exclaimed. "Where did you go?"

The man's face betrayed fear. "What do you mean?"

You should stand up, buddy, Dan thought. *If I were here to wipe you out, you'd be at a disadvantage sitting down.*

"You left me all alone in this shit heap," Dan said, an audible whine in his voice.

He affected a stagger to show how inebriated he was. A few patrons laughed politely then turned away.

Paul looked bewildered. "I waited for you. You didn't come back," he said petulantly. "I even looked in the men's room."

"Ah!" Dan shook his head and grinned. "I was in the *ladies'*."

Paul shook his head, either in disbelief or annoyance.

"You know these faggot bars," Dan said with a quick laugh. "The only place you're safe is in the *ladies'*."

Still seated, Dan noted. *Not a good idea.*

Paul suddenly seemed to get the joke. "Really? You were in the *ladies'* room? Holy shit. I never thought to look there."

"Well, how gay are you?" Dan asked.

Paul looked mildly offended. "Gay enough."

Dan's voice lowered. "Good to know you know your sexuality. What about your name? Do I call you Paul Gordon or Steve Ross?"

Nothing showed in the man's expression.

"Steve will do nicely, thank you."

"Great, we'll dispense with the cover, then. What the fuck does CSIS want with me, Steve?" Dan held the wallet up to his face. "By the way, you dropped this."

"I did not drop it ..."

He made to take it but Dan pulled back, dangling it over his head. His free hand grabbed Steve's crotch again. Only this time, the grip was not meant to arouse anything but fear and pain.

"Uh-uh. You didn't answer my question. What does CSIS want with me?"

"I don't know," Steve squeaked out, his face stricken.

Dan's grip tightened.

"Careful. I don't want to make you cry in public."

"I'm telling you, I don't know. They just tell us who to follow, nothing more. I swear."

"I'm sorry. I don't believe you." Dan tightened and twisted.

Steve looked as though he might gag from the pain. He grabbed Dan's arm, but Dan held on.

"Better think of something fast before I rip them off."

Steve was nearly choking.

"Tell me something now."

Dan looked over Steve's shoulder. The others in the room were watching the pair openly, clearly undecided whether this was courtship or combat.

"I was told to watch and see who you meet up with," Steve choked out.

"That could be a million people. Who in particular are you supposed to be looking for?"

For a second, he thought Steve was prepared to risk the family jewels for queen and country.

"A woman," he gasped out. "A Chinese national."

Dan let his grip loosen, but did not release him. Alarm bells were ringing loudly.

"I don't suppose it would do any good to ask why?"

Steve shook his head. "I don't know. I'm telling you more than I should. If you want to know then call national headquarters. It's in Ottawa —"

"I know where it is, thanks."

Dan relaxed his grip. He doubted he would get more out of the man.

Steve took a deep breath. His hands went down and massaged his crotch. The pain he'd been holding back suddenly spread wide across his face.

"Fuck, I think you just about crippled me."

He hunched over as though he might throw up.

"Most men pay me for the pleasure," Dan said, to a reproachful glance. "Just curious, are you really gay?"

"Yes," he said. "Not that it's any of your fucking business."

"Good to know where you stand. By the way, you've got a nice cock. Too bad we couldn't have managed a more personal get-together, but then I don't think your superiors would care for that sort of patronage."

Steve glared, but said nothing.

"Don't try to follow me," Dan said. He looked down. "Not that you could right now."

He turned and left the bar.

Seventeen

Skater Boy

CSIS was on his back and there was no further news from Donny. Dan had a moment of indecision as he returned to his hotel, but finally decided to stay where he was for the night. He strode through the lobby and headed upstairs. In his room, everything appeared exactly as it had when he left. The door was locked, the windows bolted. He breathed a sigh of relief to see that his laptop lay untouched. So far as he could tell. Whatever CSIS wanted from him, they would have it one way or another. But they'd have to find him first.

He didn't bother to unpack. There was no need. He wouldn't be staying long enough. In the morning, he would try to find Marlon and settle his business here then leave. He kicked off his shoes and put his feet up on the bed, casting around for something on television. He settled in with good, sensible Miss Marple, who always knew the right thing to do in any situation.

It was probably due to her misanthropic outlook on life, Dan thought. Trust no one and you get to the truth faster. In any case, there was no point in going out and showing his face on the street again tonight. Who knew where Paul M. Gordon — a.k.a. Steve Ross — might be looking for him?

A Chinese national.

That would be Ling Siu all over. But why follow him? He'd barely made a cursory search for her online, apart from one abortive visit to the studio of a self-titled genius photographer who barely recalled if he knew her. Or so he said. Even money hadn't proved an incentive to make him talk. Better make that two visits, he realized with a start. He'd left his card there the first time around. Was that how CSIS connected him to Ling Siu? It struck him that Parks could have been a CSIS informer, though it was unlikely, given the nature of the files he'd found. In any case, it was too late now to find out what Parks really knew about Ren's supposed sister.

Dan's mind was reeling. Given that CSIS was interested in Ling Siu then why had they tailed him to Hamilton, especially when it seemed more likely she lived in Toronto? Moreover, what was the intelligence service's interest in her? Ten minutes of thinking in circles brought him no closer to an answer. Miss Marple would have had it all figured out by now, of course.

He fell asleep with the remote in his hand.

In the morning, he walked around the corner from the hotel and found a diner. Scanning the menu, he saw little that looked appealing. The waitress scowled as she waited for him to choose.

His cell phone rang before he could decide. He saw Donny's name.

"Hello, sweetheart," he said.

"I've got something for you."

"So like you to ruin my breakfast."

"Always glad to help. Lester thinks he may have found where this Marlon kid moved to."

Dan sat up straight. "I'll take whatever you've got. I'm doing this as a favour to her father for passing along a little information a few years ago. I'm not even on a retainer. If I can bring his daughter home, I will more than have fulfilled my obligations."

He shook his head at the waitress, who stood expectantly with pad and pencil poised for his order. She looked even scowlier now that he would not be giving her one.

"Just a coffee," he said, hand over the phone. "One cream, one sugar. To go."

He turned his attention back to Donny. "Sorry, I'm back."

"Have you heard from him since you found the you-know-what at the you-know-where?"

It took Dan a moment to untangle Donny's coded reference to his recent visit to the photography studio. A chill ran down his spine. In fact, he hadn't heard anything from Ian Cunningham since then. He hadn't even stopped to think what that might mean. Now he did.

"I hope we're not looking at the possibility I tipped him off and he paid a late-night visit looking for revenge."

"You said the intruder looked like a woman."

It was a sharp reminder of Ling Siu that only unsettled him even further. Searching for her had got him into this mess. Dan mulled this over. Now it seemed to be pulling him in even deeper. "I don't know that whoever showed up was responsible for what happened. Why would you come back to the scene of a crime?"

"You tell me. That's your territory, Danny boy. All I know is perfume and fashion."

"True."

He took the coffee the waitress offered him, held out a five, and shook his head when she tried to give him change. Suddenly, her smile lit up like a Christmas tree. He made his way out to the street, juggling the phone and coffee while trying to keep his hands from getting burned.

"In any case, I've got an address for you," Donny told him. "Whether you find your girl there is not for me to say. At least it's what you call a 'lead.'"

"Better than anything I've had so far here."

He toyed with telling Donny about his run-in with CSIS, but decided not to risk alarming him any further. Even Donny had his limits.

"I'll end this call with what I usually say to you about these things," Donny said. "I hope you're not getting in over your head."

"You know me."

"Yes, I do, which is why I say the things I do. Just remember you've got a son who needs you alive, so no crazy-man stunts."

"Understood, thanks."

Donny rattled off the address and wished him luck.

Dan retrieved his suitcase and checked out of the hotel. He exited the parking lot, keeping one eye on the road and the other on the cars behind him. With the new address punched into the GPS, he found himself approaching terrain that wouldn't instill confidence in any parent's mind. It looked like the creaky back lot of a *Texas Chainsaw Massacre* franchise. "Wrong side of the tracks" didn't cover it. This was the wrong side of anywhere. The street hovered somewhere between ultra low rent and war-zone chic.

Not surprising, Dan thought. Hamilton was an industrial town, after all, so there needed to be plenty of the down-and-out aspect to make it appear realistic when the tourists and the taxman came calling. At least that's what went through his mind as he rolled past the address Donny had given him.

He parked down the street and backtracked to a ramshackle dwelling that looked as if it would soon be condemned, if it hadn't been already. It could easily have doubled for a building in Beirut during a siege. Debris covered the yard, boards covered the windows.

Dan walked cautiously up the stairs, half expecting one of the planks to give out underfoot and drop him in some dark, dank basement. When he made it

to the top landing in one piece, he stood there looking around. From inside came an excited barking.
Apparently a knock wasn't necessary.

Dan waited. The barking subsided suddenly in
what sounded like a forced manner. His eye caught the
slightest of movements through a crack in the boards
on the window to the left of the door. There was definitely life inside, but what sort he couldn't tell. Perhaps
the canine security guard had bounded up onto the
sofa to check out the intruder.

Dan waited. Still nothing.

He leaned over the railing and peered through the
broken slats till he saw bookshelves, a comfy chair,
an old TV. Home, sweet home. It was dingy, but fur-
nished. Which said someone lived there at least some
of the time.

If there was anyone inside now, they weren't in a
welcoming mood.

Dan made a show of stomping back down the
stairs and walking off along the street. He turned a corner and hid behind a fence where he could watch the
house. Two minutes later, the front door opened and a
slight figure in a hoodie and sweatpants emerged carrying a skateboard and locking the door behind him.

Skateboard Marlon.

The boy threw the board onto the pavement,
pressed down with one foot, and sped along. Marlon
didn't seem to think he was being followed, because he
never looked over his shoulder.

Dan followed the swiftly moving figure down a

lonely road with no one else on it. He had to increase his pace not to lose him. Before long, a destination seemed to be in sight: a phone booth. Didn't all kids have cellphones these days? Apparently not, or else Marlon wanted the call to be untraceable.

The skater dismounted and stepped nimbly on one end of his board, grabbing the other end as it flipped toward him. He carried it into the booth with him. *No sense taking chances in a neighbourhood like this*, Dan thought. He concealed himself behind a van and watched.

The booth stood on a corner in full view. Dan couldn't approach without being seen. He'd have to wait to see what Marlon's next move might be. The kid talked steadily for four or five minutes, glancing around and gesticulating wildly. He seemed to be complaining or arguing. Finally, the call ended. The boy emerged and continued down the street, away from the dilapidated house. Dan didn't want to lose him. It had to be now.

He quickened his steps until he was a few paces behind his quarry then called Marlon's name. Beneath the hoodie, a bruised and beaten face turned to him.

"Can I talk to you?" Dan asked.

"What about?"

The boy looked like a fearful dog trying to avoid a beating.

"I'd like to ask you a few questions about someone I'm trying to find. A girl named Tracy Cunningham."

"Leave me alone. I can't tell you anything," he said, already turning and heading away.

Dan followed.

"I won't hurt you," he said.

"Yeah, that's what the last guy said. So just fuck off or I'll call a cop."

"How about calling Tracy's father? He's a cop."

The boy stopped and stared. "Piss off, why don't you!"

"Not until you tell me where Tracy is."

"How the fuck should I know? She took off when that bastard showed up last night. She didn't bother sticking around when he was beating the shit out of me, either."

"What was he looking for?"

"Her! What the fuck do you think he was looking for?"

"Why?"

"How should I know? He said she owed him. She took off before he could collect, so he decided to take it out on me." He glared angrily at Dan, as though he might be to blame for what he'd endured. "And you can tell her father to fuck off, too. Tracy ain't stayin' at my place no more. Not after this."

"Will fifty bucks make it feel better?"

Dan took out his wallet. The kid stood there, hesitating.

"What for?"

Dan pulled a bill from his wallet and handed it over with his card.

"A simple request, that's all. Give this to Tracy if she shows up again."

"And if not?"

"If not, you keep the fifty and I'm shit out of luck."

There was a glimmer of a smile on the boy's face. He stuffed the bill and the card in his pocket.

"Fair enough," he said. "Now stop following me."

Dan took this as his cue that he would get no further with the boy. If necessary, he could return another day with another fifty.

He wandered back the way he'd come, wondering if the boy could be trusted to pass along his message. If not, it wouldn't be the first fifty he'd thrown away on a lost cause. It crossed his mind to sit and wait to see if Tracy returned, but, judging by the bruises on the boy's face, Dan doubted she would. Someone was playing rough. He thought briefly about the day he'd seen her coming down the steps from Matt Parks's studio. So who did she owe and why?

He went back to the diner, determined to have one good meal before heading home. The waitress, clearly remembering his generous tip, was all smiles upon his return. He found a booth near the back where he could watch the door. He picked up a *Toronto Star* and slouched in his seat.

He'd just been delivered a plateful of grease when a column in the entertainment section caught his eye: Toronto's arts crowd had organized a memorial gathering in honour of a celebrity photographer found dead in his east end studio. There was Matt Parks, smiling in all his glory, looking as if he'd once had an aspiration to be more than just a B-scene pornographer. There were the usual laments about great talent snuffed early, as well as the platitudes from grieving friends and colleagues who thought he had finally "kicked the habit." But clearly they were mistaken, because Matt Parks, Resident Genius, had recently died of a drug overdose.

Eighteen

Not Women's Work

Paranoia struck a home run all the way down the QEW. Dan couldn't get back to the city fast enough. A simple look into a photographer's files had yielded far more than he'd anticipated. Granted, it had been a surreptitious look, not to mention illegal, so he could hardly complain to the police about it. The obituary had unsettled him more than he might have expected.

On the way back, he kept reminding himself that everything would be okay when he got home. Even if it wouldn't. *Starlight, star bright, first star I see tonight* ... He pictured Matt Parks's head thrown back against the wall, eyes staring dead ahead. Definitely not a drug overdose.

Who killed him seemed secondary at this point. The real question was who would want to turn a brutal murder into an accidental overdose, an artist's clichéd leave-taking from a life of suffering and self-proclaimed genius? The dots collided with a flash: CSIS. Who else could engineer such a thing?

Dan suddenly realized he was checking his rear-view mirror with manic frequency. Once, he looked back and felt his heartbeat quicken when a driver resembling Paul M. Gordon, a.k.a. Steve Ross, pulled up behind him. It wasn't him, of course, just his own overactive imagination.

He tried Ked three times on his cell as he approached the city. The call went directly to voicemail. Which probably meant he was at school. Or out walking Ralph. Though he could still be home in bed. Dan had long ago given up trying to figure out the complicated schedule of a high school junior. *Pick it up, buddy!* Why didn't they just make kids go to school and stay there all day long? All of which probably meant there was nothing to worry about, even if CSIS had been tailing him to see who he met up with. *But why? Why? Why?* The voices were clanging in his head. Still, a real live voice on the other end of the line would have gone a long way to relieve his worries.

An accident outside Burlington held up the drive for more than half an hour. This, coupled with the usual sludge of traffic heading into the city made it take twice as long for Dan to return as it had been to arrive. *One more reason never to go to Hamilton*, he mused, watching the lines of cars snaking ahead of him. The urgency of his feelings made the wait intolerable. Now that he knew he had CPTSD, his anxiety shot through the roof. It was like weather reports with wind chill added. Even if the temperature read minus five in real terms, once you knew it was minus fifteen with wind chill factored in, it just made things feel that much worse.

He took in a huge breath and exhaled with relief when he spied the CN Tower spiking the horizon. It was like the first sighting of Oz glimpsed far down the yellow brick road. The closer you got, the more real it seemed and the more it glowed. Before you discovered all that lay beneath its glitter once you reached it, of course.

He felt his shoulders relax as he turned off the expressway onto Leslie Street, closing in on home. And then he was in his driveway, opening the car door. All was quiet. That was not necessarily a bad sign, he told himself. In fact, it should be a good sign. If there were a problem, he would be greeted with silently rotating lights on the tops of emergency vehicles and a concerned face coming to head him off before he entered to find his son lifeless on the kitchen floor, the innocent victim killed by CSIS because his father, their intended target, had conveniently been away when they struck. It wasn't when the sirens were blaring that you had to worry. It was when they weren't.

Ralph greeted him with his usual, hi-how-are-you-today tail-wagging routine, as though to say all was well in his world so it should be the same the world over. Dogs had it easy. *Where's my next meal? When do we go for a walk?* Simple things that seldom varied.

All would be well, Dan thought, once he'd gone

room to room and checked for minor changes, signs of disturbance. If he found none, his anxiety would vanish as long as his CPTSD held itself at bay. He pictured it like a dog lunging at the end of a chain, just waiting to be released.

He walked stealthily through the house to the kitchen. *Why am I sneaking around my own home?* he wondered. A flyer on the table caught his eye: a purple pamphlet about discussions and prayers at a local mosque. The print was in English and some other language that registered as squiggles to Dan's not-so-discerning eye. Arabic, of course. Even if he couldn't read it, he could recognize it. *Why is this here? Why now of all days?* He turned it over, hoping for a note from Ked. Nothing to say where he was or why the flyer had been left for him to find. Since when did Muslims go door-to-door proselytizing like Jehovah's Witnesses? Ked must have picked it up somewhere. His son had never shown the slightest interest in religion. It was odd, but not necessarily anything to worry about in itself. At the moment, he had more compelling issues to consider.

Something caught his attention. He stood still and listened. Voices came from the living room. He opened the door and walked in.

Ali looked up from the sofa. Ked sat on his right.

"Ah, Daniel. I was just telling Kedrick about the Quran," he said, with a disarming smile.

He stood and extended a hand. Dan shook it, wondering how his world had suddenly become so unfamiliar. His face must have said a thousand things, most of them not compelling. Ali seemed to realize he needed to explain his presence.

"A boy needs to know about these things when he has Muslim blood."

Dan wasn't aware of any such need.

"I believe his mother has discussed such matters with him," he said, in a voice not entirely free from strain.

Ali's half-apologetic look said that such things were not women's work. Or maybe Dan imagined it.

"I don't mean to interfere," he said with what sounded like total sincerity, yet here he was sitting in Dan's house discussing an extremely personal and politically charged subject with his son.

"Ked is free to follow whatever belief he sees fit."

Ali spread out his hands, as though saying that was all well and good, *but*. It was the unspoken *but* Dan didn't like. It implied a great deal without saying anything in particular. It might be saying that Dan was a Christian, and therefore not a true believer. True believers were not Christian. Nor were good Christians gay. Infidels were more likely to be gay, of course, and the children of infidels needed to be rescued before they turned into infidels themselves. But that was putting words in Ali's mouth, where few had emerged. Dan didn't know what to think, except that he was startled to find a near stranger sitting in his house discussing the Quran with his son.

Dan looked to Ked. "Why aren't you at school?"

Ked looked relieved by the question. He nodded and turned to Ali.

"I need to go to school now," he said.

Ali stood. "Of course. We will talk again."

"Sure, thanks for dropping by."

Ked left the room. Dan heard him running up the stairs.

Ali looked at Dan. "I hope you don't mind my taking an interest in Kedrick. He is a very intelligent boy."

His voice was soft, deferential. So deferential that it seemed to be mocking Dan's concern.

"Yes, he is a very smart boy. But I would prefer to know before people come to my house," was all Dan could think to say. "I would also like to know what you're discussing with my son, to make sure I'm in agreement with it."

"Of course." Ali smiled.

He held out his hand again. Dan ignored it.

Ali nodded. "I hope that you and I might meet again someday soon."

Dan saw him to the door and closed it behind him just as Ked rushed down with his knapsack.

"How did he end up here?" Dan asked.

Ked seemed startled by the question.

"He just called and asked if he could come by to drop something off."

"A pamphlet? The one on the kitchen table?"

"Yes."

"How did he get your cell number?"

Ked shrugged. "He said Mom gave it to him."

"I see."

"I thought it would be all right to let him come over. I would've asked first, but you're never around to ask."

Dan left the comment hanging there with all it implied: a good father did not abandon his family to go off searching for lost boys and girls in other cities, leaving his son on his own at home for anyone to prey on.

"I thought you didn't like him."

"He's not as bad as I thought." Ked watched his father, challenge hidden in his eyes. "Don't you want me to talk to him? I thought you said he was going to be part of the family."

Dan felt shaken by the unspoken accusation. He had never denied Ked the right to choose his own path. "Of course you can talk to him. As long as everyone's okay with what you're discussing."

What to tell his son? That as smart as he was, there were still some things that were over his head? That religion was a glitter that got inside you in moments of weakness, twisting and shading things in a million different ways they were never supposed to be shaded in by people who were interested in power, despite what they may have said about your salvation? That good people were the humble ones who did not try to sway your thoughts by any means other than through personal example? All of the above, likely.

Dan had never pretended to be holy or pure, but he believed in goodness and had seen through all the ways it could be corrupted and twisted out of a person. He also knew that the paths of so-called righteousness were exclusive and narrow, despite what anyone said or believed.

"I don't know anything about the Quran. You and Mom never talk about religion."

"That's because we're not religious, not because it's forbidden."

Ked stood there, defiance written all over him. Defiance for an absentee father, defiance that there should be a prohibition on what he could talk about and with whom. When had his son turned into an alien? Dan wondered. Perhaps it had been building up all along and he'd just never noticed it before.

"You'd better go to school."

Ked turned and went out without another word.

Dan's initial thought was to call Donny, but he decided to address his concerns with Kendra first. He dialled her work number. She sounded distracted when she answered.

"Got a minute?"

"I … yeah." She sounded unsure.

"I just got home and found Ali sitting in the house with Ked."

There was a pause.

"Oh. Well. Ali mentioned that he wanted to get to know Ked better. Is there a problem?"

"No, just that I found it odd I didn't know about it first."

"I guess Ali thought Ked would tell you. I'm sorry if it seemed odd to you."

"It's just …" He stopped and tried to imagine how he sounded. Paranoid? Jealous? "They were discussing religion."

There was a silence.

"Is that a problem?" she said at last.

"I don't know."

"Ali is somewhat serious about his faith. He was probably just sounding Ked out on it."

Dan waited. He wasn't sure what he was actually concerned about, so it was hard to know what to say.

"Would you prefer he didn't discuss religion with Ked? Is that it?"

"No, that's not it."

"Good. Because I think Ked should be the one to decide that for himself, don't you?"

"I guess, but —"

"Then what is it?"

"I don't know."

"You don't like Ali."

It was a statement and a challenge.

"It's not that."

"Well, do you like him?"

Dan wasn't going to be cornered by the question.

"I don't know him. Maybe when I get to know him better I will like him."

"But you don't have a problem with him?"

"I just … don't know him."

"Good, because I don't want him to become a problem between us."

Dan felt a sinking feeling in his stomach. In fifteen

and a half years, he and Kendra had not had a single argument over Ked's upbringing. Now, suddenly, with a new person added to the mix it all seemed fraught with potential complications that Dan had never really considered.

"I'm sorry, I just … I don't know. It was just odd to come home and find him here."

"I'll make sure you're properly informed the next time Ali and Ked get together, all right? I've got to go."

He heard the edge in her voice. It seemed impossible that he had known her all these years and suddenly felt as though he might not really know her.

"Okay. Sorry. It's not a problem. Please just let me know what's going on beforehand."

"All right. I have to go."

She hung up.

If he'd felt perplexed before, he was worried now. As far as child-rearing was concerned, he never expected to find himself on the other side of an issue from Kendra. She was the most modern Muslim woman he'd ever met. The most modern woman of any sort, in fact, and progressive on all fronts. Till now they'd agreed on everything important: gay rights, women's rights, human rights. But suddenly it was staring him in the face: he'd fathered a child with a woman from a completely different culture than his. It only made sense at some point that those cultures would have to intersect and possibly conflict. The real surprise was that it hadn't happened before. Dan had raised Ked largely on his own all those years by choice, but Kendra was still his mother and had never taken any less of a role in his upbringing when it came to that. She would always be his mother, even if she moved to a distant part of the globe. It only stood to reason that she would want to include him in her life, no matter what direction it took.

He picked up the phone and pressed autodial.

Donny answered right away. "At last," he said, by way of an opening. "How did it go?"

An image of Skateboard Marlon flashed before his eyes. "I didn't find her, but give my thanks to Lester. The second address was the right one."

"Was the duchess out to tea when you arrived?"

"No, she'd fled the premises. Someone was on her tail, by the looks of things, only the calling card he left wasn't the kind you stick in your wallet. The boy I talked to had been beaten up."

"Drugs?"

"My guess is not, though it seems money was an issue."

He hesitated.

"I never like your pauses," Donny said.

"Me, either. I met someone while I was away. Not exactly what you'd call a friend."

"But not quite an enemy?"

"Remains to be seen. I was tailed by a guy from CSIS while I was in Hamilton."

"*The* CSIS? Are they even for real?"

"They're for real. As far as I could tell."

"What did he want?"

"We didn't get into the nitty-gritty. From what I gather, and I won't discuss the circumstances under which the information was obtained, though I'm proud to say it was a bit painful for him —"

"I'm not liking this —"

"You won't, so I will spare you the details. In any case, it seems he was there to see if I met up with an Asian woman."

The penny dropped.

"The one you're looking for?"

"That's my guess. I don't know for sure. If so, then it was the same one who also had a connection with a photographer who is now being eulogized in the arts section of the *Toronto Star* as having died of a drug overdose."

"A drug...?" Donny's voice was all seriousness and dire warnings. "Now I really don't like this."

"Nor I, but I don't know what to do about it." He paused again. "I'm sorry to involve you in any of this."

"You have to talk to someone and I am currently available."

"There's more."

Donny made a noise of incredulity.

"You've only been gone one day. How could there possibly be more?"

"Nevertheless there is, but they're not related. When I got home, I found Ked sitting in the living room discussing the Quran with Kendra's new beau, Ali."

"Jesus."

"No, not exactly."

"So what were they talking about? Was it a discussion on comparative religion?"

"I'm not privy to that. It just upset me to come home and find him sitting here. Ked pretty much called me an absentee father when I tried to discuss it. Apparently, he doesn't get his religious chats at home from either of his parents, so he's getting them elsewhere."

"Is that what he said?"

"More or less. When I tried to discuss it with Kendra, she got upset at the thought that I might be criticizing Ali."

Donny snorted. "I'd be criticizing anyone who showed up in my place unannounced and tried to discuss religion with Lester without my say-so. What are you going to do about it?"

"What can I do? I can't banish the topic from home. I've never censored him before."

"Maybe it's time to start."

"You know I won't do that. He's old enough to make up his own mind about things."

"What's this Ali guy like?"

"Apart from having serious sex appeal, Kendra says he takes his faith seriously. From what I can tell, he's not too traditional. He drinks. He doesn't have facial hair."

"Okay, so not a fanatic. Maybe. Hey, I have no problem with a little comparative religion, but you'd better keep your ears open. Next thing you know, he'll be taking Ked with him to the local mosque."

Dan flashed on the flyer on his kitchen table.

"That's what I worry about. What will I do if it leads to that?"

Donny was stern now. A pep talk was building.

"You know how I feel about that. Religions take no prisoners. They want your soul. And they don't mind killing you to get it, if need be. Don't let him go there."

"Shouldn't that be Ked's choice?"

"Oh, don't be so fucking bend-over-and-screw-me Canadian. I'm tired of being told Islam is a peaceful religion when around the globe they oppress and murder women in the name of honour. They also kill gays and just about anyone else who does not agree with them. Remember Theo van Gogh? How is that peaceful? And you want your son to be a part of that? Give your head a shake. And don't tell me it's just a handful of fanatics. Have you heard of the Muslim Brotherhood? They're hardly a minority. You know I'm all about freedom of choice, but don't point a good kid in the wrong direction. Not until you see some major changes first. And that won't happen in this century."

"Thanks for the confidence booster."

Donny sighed. "Listen, I'm just telling it how I see it. It's not confidence you need right now. You've got a shitload of things to worry about, from the sounds of it. Though I doubt Islam is your biggest problem at the moment, with CSIS on your doorstep."

The conversation ended on that note. Dan hung up feeling even worse.

Nineteen

Don't Bug Me

With Ked at school, Dan began a thorough a search for surveillance equipment. It was just beginning to sink in what he was up against. He tried to recall extended periods of time where he and Ked had both been out of the house together and realized that included just about any weekday when he was at work and Ked at school. Gaining access to the house wouldn't be difficult. He didn't have a burglar alarm; he simply had Ralph. He cast a suspicious glance at the dog. He'd always thought Ralph a patriot, one who would defend his home under any circumstance from any invader. Was he complicit in something? Had a nice man with a juicy piece of hamburger cooked to specification — Ralph preferred well done — been by for a visit, dropping a morsel of food with one hand and stashing a listening device along the underside of a book shelf with another? If so, Ralph wasn't owning up to anything.

Going through Ked's room required extra care. Not only did Dan feel he was betraying a trust of sorts, he also felt like a spy in his own home. Setting aside baseball caps and Star Wars memorabilia, moving things one inch to the left or a few to the right, making sure everything was exactly as it had been when he started. Nevertheless, he would deal with it when the time came if Ked accused him of going through his belongings.

He'd pretty much covered all the rooms in the house before concluding it was futile. A bugging device could be hidden anywhere or nowhere at all. As far as he could tell his computer was untouched, though that was the likeliest place to start. He had a good idea what intelligence agencies were capable of: hijacking hard drives, installing software to track keystrokes. Still, he wasn't that worried about his home computer. "Go ahead. You won't be thrilled when you read the crap on there, if that's what you're after," Dan murmured aloud, as though someone might be listening. On the other hand, if it was private conversations they were monitoring, CSIS wouldn't have to leave any equipment behind. A cellphone could be tapped remotely by activating an internal microphone. It wasn't even necessary for it to be in use. Simply having it on your person was enough to overhear you planning a felony or making a few pertinent inquries about the sister of a client who'd disappeared at Tiananmen twenty years earlier. They could even listen in on private chats in cars being driven through remote Canadian wilderness via the vehicle's built-in emergency tracking systems. These days, nowhere was safe.

While he searched, he again went over all the possible permutations of what could have alerted the security agency to his search for Ling. He'd left his business card when he visited Matt Parks, of course, but he'd also made some fairly straightforward attempts at locating Ling on the Internet, accessing various databases to see if he could find her by name, though in all cases he'd come up empty-handed. In fact, there was no telling when or where his search might have triggered an alarm. All of which begged the question: why was CSIS interested in her? What bothered him more, however, was why they thought he was worth tailing. The obvious answer was that they believed he had found her or at least knew where she was. Clearly, he'd stepped in something smelly and there was no polite or simple way of stepping around it at this point.

The only bright spot on his horizon was Ren's imminent return. Or it would have been but for all the things he now faced with locating his sister. He needed to have a talk with Ren as soon as possible. While he was charmed by his tales of imaginary meals and missing heirlooms, he needed Ren to see things as they were. With CSIS keeping an eye out for the woman he believed to be his sister, chances were that Ling Siu was something more than a simple Chinese refugee. Putting aside whatever radical student politics she may once have been involved in, the woman Ren wished to find could not simply be the same girl he had loved and lost all those years ago.

The complications grew when he thought about what Ren meant to him. Despite their disparate backgrounds, Dan felt they both had things to gain by creating a life together. If you were able to share a meal and have a laugh with someone you cared for, from such humble beginnings a relationship could be born. He tried to remember the last time he'd met a kindred spirit he longed to share his life with. Trevor, of course. In reality it wasn't so long ago, though sometimes it felt like forever, and it had been all too brief.

He'd just left off with his search when he heard an insistent knocking at the front door. Either someone was panicked or feeling important or both. He opened it and found himself staring at a face that took him a second to recognize as Ian Cunningham's. He'd never seen the man out of uniform before. The displacement of the man and the role caught him off guard.

The surprise barely had time to register when a fist flew at him. In that moment, a second fact registered: the Ian Cunningham facing him looked slightly deranged. Dan ducked the blow and head-butted Cunningham in the solar plexus, sending both of them flying into Dan's shrubbery. Dan straddled him, prepared to continue the fight, but it was soon apparent his opponent was in no condition to put up a struggle. He reeked of alcohol. As Dan held his fist over Ian's face, the body beneath him went limp.

Dan got to his feet with difficulty, pulling Ian up with him. The cop went into defensive mode, holding his hands up to ward off potential blows.

"What the fuck, Ian?"

The off-duty policeman was mumbling, his sentences barely coherent. When it became clear he wasn't going to continue his fight, Dan dropped his aggressive posture.

"Are you going to tell me what this is all about?"

Ian stared at him. He looked as though he hadn't slept for some time. "Why didn't you tell me?"

"Tell you what?"

For a moment, Dan thought he was referring to what he'd learned in Hamilton. In fact, he'd hardly had time to let anyone know Tracy Cunningham might be in more danger than it first seemed.

"What that bastard was up to."

"I thought you knew!"

"I was only guessing."

"It was a surprise to me that he'd been involved in escort services. In fact, you were the one who told me."

That much was true, though Dan wasn't about to say how he'd confirmed the truth about Matt Parks's activities. He waited as Ian stood unsteadily before him, straining to catch his words. Something about the flood coming when you least expect it. He hoped he wasn't going to be treated to a sermon on top of everything else. A homily from a police officer who had just assaulted him was the last thing he needed right now.

"Ian, if you promise not to try to hit me again I'll invite you in for a coffee. We can chat inside."

Ian's expression registered the offer. He nodded and mumbled again. Dan held the door open and they entered.

Five minutes later, coffee in hand, Ian's confusion seemed to be clearing up a bit. He had stopped his mumbling and replaced it with a mournful sighing that was no less distressing as far as Dan was concerned.

"She's always been able to twist me around her little finger, eh?"

They were talking about Tracy. Dan nodded and sipped from his coffee while Ian spoke. He wanted Ian to talk his way through this without being led, a technique Dan was familiar with from his own counselling sessions when his anger threatened to get out of hand.

"It's since her mom died," Ian said. "I always let her have her way after that. I can't bear to say no to her."

Dan knew the scenario well enough. You never wanted to say "no" to your own kids, though you wished like hell they wouldn't ask for things that weren't in their best interests. There was a fine line between letting them make their own mistakes and pitch precipitously over a cliff while you agonized over whether you'd just ruined a life by allowing a child to make a simple choice.

He let Ian stumble through his litany of regrets as a parent, the constant vigilance that attended any work in progress, which is what a child's life surely was. He wasn't sure if it was time to reveal what he'd discovered in Hamilton. That seemed to call for a larger plan of action. In the meantime, it might trigger more anger. Dan was still stuck on the question of what Ian had or had not done in regards to the demise of the late photographer and pornographer. He wasn't even sure Ian knew about Parks's death. Unless, of course, he was responsible for it.

The question could wait, but there would come a time when he would have to ask. He went to the kitchen to get a second cup of coffee for both of them. When he returned, Ian was slumped against the back of the couch, his mouth open as he snored away.

On days like this, Dan felt like everybody's big brother. He went up to his office to do some work. When he came down an hour later, Ian was gone. He'd penned a single word on the back of a sales receipt and left it where Dan could find it.

Sorry.

Twenty

CSIS

Dan didn't need to find CSIS. CSIS found him in a food court in the basement of the Toronto Dominion Centre. There were two of them. Dan recognized Paul M. Gordon, a.k.a. Steve Ross, looking his usual dowdy self, munching on a donut. The second agent was regulation nondescript, dressed in perfect business attire. So perfect you would pay more attention to the clothes, the sunglasses, the Gucci watch. All the accessories, rather than the man himself. Except in this case, as it turned out, the mannequin inside the clothes was the real accessory. An afterthought to the couture. You weren't supposed to notice him. Once out of his presence, you took away only the impression of a genteel, well-turned-out man, but got no closer to the truth than that. Steve Ross was obviously an amateur compared to this guy.

They sat quietly next to him, one on either side, Styrofoam cups steaming in their hands. Perhaps they preferred this surreptitious meet and greet over an official get-together at the CSIS head office which, rumour had it, was located far underground beneath the Air Canada Centre. Dan was amused to think of the pattering of basketball players aiming at hoops while the heads of Canada's hard-sleuthing spy industry dreamed their nefarious dreams far below. It seemed appropriate: it was a Canadian game, after all. As for the two men facing him, he tried to guess their game. The choices were few and none seemed good.

"Hello again," Dan said to Steve. "Happy coincidence?"

"Don't kid yourself. You're easy to find. We could have nabbed you at that cheesy diner the other morning."

"Too bad you didn't. I was saving my hash browns for you." Dan gave him a big grin. "How are your testicles, Steve?"

"Fine. No thanks to you."

The other agent watched him with a cool gaze over his coffee cup. His silence was more formidable than Steve's bumbling garrulousness.

"Are you here to warn me about the perils of too much caffeine or do you want something?"

The new agent nodded. "We're here to give you some advice, Mr. Sharp. After that, we'll disappear. Bottom line is, we were never here. We've never met."

Dan nodded to Steve. "A bit late after lover boy and I exchanged business cards in Hamilton."

"That never happened, either, if you want to continue in your career," the man said softly, as though offering a hot tip on the races.

"I was actually thinking of applying for a counter position at McDonalds."

"You're not doing yourself any favours."

Dan sipped at his coffee. It burned his lip, but he wasn't letting it show.

"Shoot."

Steve placed an envelope in front of him. Dan picked it up and slit it open. A shot of the woman from the Kowloon Bakery calendar slid out. These days, people seemed to be passing him pictures every time he turned around. This one was highly pixelated, black and white, possibly taken with a surveillance camera. It showed her from the shoulders up, set against a plain concrete background. She looked furtive, as though trying to avoid unwanted attention. In any case, it was clearly not a publicity shot unless the photographer was going for a top ten list of potential bank robbers.

"Do you recognize this woman?"

"Possibly."

"We understand you've been looking for her. Why?"

Dan considered how much he was willing to divulge. They'd obviously made a few conjectures about his work and were waiting for him to fill in some blanks. They might or might not believe him, no matter what he said. In any case, he knew they had the ability to make his life hell if they chose. He opted for simplicity.

"I've been hired by a client to find her."

The new agent blinked. "For what purpose?"

"I understand he misses her."

He laughed. Dan knew better than to mistake this for a lightening of the mood.

"Okay, here's the score," the agent said, all traces of mirth vanishing behind his expression. "We're having a look at your background. And I mean a good, hard look. If you have secret connections with the Chinese government, we'll find them sooner or later. Is there anything you'd care to tell us now?"

Dan suddenly felt less amusing.

"You think I'm a spy?"

"If we thought that, you wouldn't be sitting here enjoying your freedom. We want to know precisely why you're looking for this woman and what your client wants with her."

Dan leaned forward and looked him in the eye: straight-on body language. It said that whatever he told them was the truth. Of course, with a little practice it was also the best way to drop a lie undetected. They would know that, too.

He nodded at the photograph.

"My client believes this woman is his sister, Ling Hao, who disappeared during the Tiananmen riots in 1989. He thinks she lives here now. It's a simple case of a family member looking for a long-lost loved one. That's what I specialize in."

"Then there's nothing more to it?"

Dan nodded. "That's correct."

"Do you sleep with all your clients?" asked the newbie.

Dan felt his heart drop to the floor. He was tempted to kick it aside before it got stepped on.

"First time for everything."

"Apparently."

Steve leaned forward now. He seemed to exude a bit more confidence in the company of his spiff-looking partner. They were putting the squeeze on him, the old one-two power play.

"What do you know about her?"

"Nothing. I haven't been able to locate her. I don't even know if she is my client's sister for sure. He hasn't seen her in twenty years."

"Our guess is your client has defection in mind. We believe he wants out of China and he thinks his sister is the key. If she is his sister."

Dan waited. He wasn't about to serve up Ren's personal musings on citizenship and the hardships of queer life in China. "I know nothing about that."

"Your client is a high-profile, up-and-coming diplomatic representative for China."

Dan opted for a blank look. "Point being?"

"He's here on a trade mission for the Chinese government. His sister — if she is his sister — is a spy. This could be one of the most politically sensitive situations Canada has seen in decades."

Dan nodded. "I'm listening."

"We can't have your client associating with known spies while he's here talking with our government ministers, regardless of what he does or does not know about her. We also can't risk a messy public defection of a high-profile individual."

"Fair enough, but as I said, I haven't located her, so he can't associate with her. For the same reason, I also can't tell him what she may have become, for good or for bad."

The new agent tapped the photograph.

"She works for the Chinese Ministry of State Security. Her operative name is Ling Siu, though she goes by several names — Ling Hua, Ling Chang, Chunlan Wu, and others. That's why you haven't been able to find her. Her code name is Jade Butterfly."

Ren's story of having given his sister a family heirloom flitted through his mind. He wondered if the name was meant as a joke on her part. *If so, a not very funny joke*, Dan thought.

He nodded at the pudgy agent. "And Steve Ross here is also known as Paul Gordon. He could even be called the Blue Butterfly of Love, for all I know. So what?"

The other agent's face was ugly now. "This isn't a joke. We wouldn't be sitting here with you today drinking bad coffee if it weren't true."

Dan shrugged. He suddenly understood Ked's reflexive action on being questioned. "What am I supposed to say?"

"You might start by asking what we want from you."

"Okay, what do you want?"

"Information."

Dan felt his impatience get the better of him. "I just told you, I don't have any."

"But you could get it."

Dan's eyes flickered from one to the other. He didn't like where things were heading.

"We want you to help us find out what Ling Siu is up to."

"And how do I do that when I don't even know how to find her?"

Steve cleared this throat. "We can arrange for you to find out."

Dan stared in disbelief. "If you know where she is then why haven't you done something about it?"

"Simple," the other agent told him. "We have no reason to do anything about her presence yet."

"This is all sounding a bit ludicrous," Dan said. "This is Canada, not the Far East. What's she supposed to be doing here? Are you going to tell me she's part of some sort of international hit team?"

"No, we would already have nabbed her if we thought that," Steve said. "If she were Russian then I'd say she was more likely in Canada to assassinate someone. Ling Sui is into information espionage. You must have heard the scandals. The Chinese are stealing secrets from corporations and from our government."

Dan took this in. "What sort of secrets?"

"Technology, mostly," Steve replied. "Western corporations invest millions in research, then China comes along and helps itself to the best of it. Surely you know that the Chinese economy is now one of the strongest in the world. From extreme poverty to extreme affluence in a few decades. It's not a coincidence. They're in a death struggle with the Americans, who are currently at their lowest ebb in years."

"Let the giants fight it out," Dan said. "Does it matter to us?"

"Don't be naive," Mr. Spiff said. "It matters a lot, in the long run. When it comes down to it, which country would you rather have running the Internet? The Americans may be brutal when it suits their purpose, but at least they're on the side of freedom."

"Their version of it, anyway," Dan said. "But let's not quibble over the facts."

Steve sighed. "What has your client asked you to do when you find his sister?"

Dan shook his head. "Just to find her. He wants to know where she is."

"What is his name?"

Dan considered lying for a moment then decided to play along.

"His name is Ren Hao."

The two men exchanged looks again.

"Shouldn't you have that in her file if she's a spy?" Dan asked.

"We do," Steve said. "Is he paying you to find her? Or are you doing it for the sex?"

"I'm not a prostitute."

The other agent smiled sourly. "Not lately."

Dan's mind reeled. They even knew his history as a street kid newly arrived in Toronto.

Steve placed a file on the table and began to read: "Chinese Agent, known as Ling Siu and several other aliases, born January 14th, 1970, briefly attended Peking University where she excelled in languages. She was an A-plus scholar, but got involved in student politics during the Tiananmen riots. In the aftermath of the riots, her parents were imprisoned and tortured for anti-government propaganda. They were blamed for the disappearance of their daughter following the massacre. Both parents were given thirty-year sentences, but these were suddenly commuted after less than a year."

Steve closed the file and looked Dan in the eye. "We think she joined the Chinese intelligence services in exchange for their freedom. She showed up in Canada four years ago. Most of her operations are classified, but I can tell you she is now a high-level espionage and sabotage expert. One of the best in the field."

The other agent studied Dan's face intently. "What do you think?"

Dan returned his stare. "Frankly, I'm shocked to think that CSIS would hire a couple of gay guys."

Steve looked distinctly embarrassed.

The other agent rolled his eyes. "For the record, CSIS doesn't discriminate." He paused. "What I meant was, does that report sound like she could be your client's sister?"

Dan rubbed the bridge of his nose then stopped,

trying to remember what it was body language for. Fear? Deceit? Apathy?

He looked over and said, "Could be. He said his sister was a scholar and that she disappeared during the Tiananmen riots."

"We agree with your client. We think it's the same woman."

Dan shrugged again. He was tiring of their game. "That may be. Why should I help you with anything?"

The other agent gave him a sharp look.

"Ever heard of the Patriot Act?"

"Yes, it's an American invention. It effectively allowed the U.S. government to do whatever it wanted in the name of stopping terrorist threats, be they real or imagined, in the aftermath of 9/11."

"So you don't like it?"

"Of course I don't. It abrogates civil liberties."

"Ooh — abrogates. Big word."

"Would you like me to dumb it down for you?"

"Thanks, I know what *abrogates* means."

"So then what?"

"It's all the more reason for you to help us, so we don't end up with a Patriot Act here."

Dan waited, staring them down. He took a sip of coffee. It was cooler now.

Steve watched him. "What we're saying is that we want you to help us catch a Chinese spy on Canadian soil. It would be a coup."

Dan looked around at the other shoppers sitting in the food court, most of them bored with their lives and their purchases and their fast-food lunches. At that moment, he would have given a lot to be in the shoes of almost any one of them.

"Sure it would. And it would help you guys cozy up with the CIA, but who's to say if that's a good thing? So I repeat: given what you say might be even partially true, why should I help you?"

"It's not so black and white," Steve said.

"Politics never are, which is why I distrust them. You never know who you're actually helping win the war."

"Let me put it this way: at the moment, America is losing billions to the Chinese every year. Our economy is directly linked to theirs. If we look like we're hosting Chinese spies, our economy is going to suffer in whatever way the Americans can come up with to hurt us. Need I say more?"

Dan was not entirely convinced, but he didn't think it a wise choice to turn CSIS down outright without at least hearing them out.

"You would have to prove it to me first."

"We can do that. We can put you there. Surreptitiously, of course."

"Oooh — surreptitiously. Big word."

The second agent turned to Steve. "You were right. He is an asshole."

Dan shook his head. "Listen, I'm a busy guy. I can't afford to do double-time for CSIS at the moment. Tell me why I should help you."

The other agent leaned closer and looked Dan in the eye.

"For one thing, we can help you find Ling Siu. After that, we might even arrange to get your client out of China and help him resettle here. If he wants that."

"As a favour to him?"

"No, Mr. Sharp. As a favour to you. We understand you like your new client."

"He seems like a nice enough guy. I can't say I know him that well."

The new agent smirked. "I'd say you're getting there pretty fast, but that's not my point. My point is that bad things happen to nice guys, especially when their reputations get tarnished by news from abroad."

He paused meaningfully, letting Dan fill in a few gaps about the Chinese government and its harsh repression of dissidents. Dan had no doubt they could do considerable harm to Ren on his return to China.

"We suggest you think carefully about it."

"And if I don't agree?"

The second agent's lip curled. "We might have to revisit the night you paid an unscheduled visit to a certain photographer's studio recently."

Dan felt a distinct chill at the words.

"He was in a bit over his head, don't you think? In a bit deeper than just escorts, I mean. Not something you want to get mixed up in. With any luck, you won't." The agent stood. "Think about it. We'll be in touch. When are you seeing your client again?"

"Next Thursday," Dan said. "He's out of the country at the moment. But you already know that, don't you?"

"Yes." He smiled. "Don't cancel, if that's what you're thinking."

Dan nodded. He'd been thinking exactly that.

"Just keep things as they are with no change." The man's expression said he was hoping for good things, but expecting bad. "If all goes well, you won't be seeing me again. Paul here ..." He gave an ironic smile. "Or rather, Steve, will continue to be your contact."

He held out a hand. Dan declined to offer his in return.

Shake hands with the devil? No thanks.

Twenty-One

Closely Guarded Information

Ked was on his laptop in the living room when Dan got home that evening. The boy looked up, grunted a greeting, then turned back to his screen. It seemed like years since they'd had a good father/son talk, Dan thought, apart from the brief discussion of hormones at breakfast the previous week. Since his queries about Tracy Cunningham, Ked seemed to be nurturing a grudge against him. Either that or the conversation following Ali's visit had left him resentful. Whatever the cause, Ked was on edge whenever Dan was around. Suddenly, it was as if there were unspoken rules being broken, invisible lines crossed, "No trespassing" signs he was ignoring everywhere. *Fucking teenage hormonal over-sensitive everything*, Dan thought. Had he gone through the same shit at that age? No doubt, but he'd been too busy being slammed around by an alcoholic father to notice. Not that his father hadn't loved him, apparently, as his aunt pointed out years after his father's demise. But still.

Ralph sniffed the air sympathetically, as though to say he had a handle on what was going on, but really wasn't in much of a position to help, all things considered. Dan decided to make an overture and see what came of it.

"Are you interested in a curry tonight?" he asked. "I'll cook."

"Ate already," Ked mumbled. "Thanks."

"No problem."

Dan went out to the kitchen and started a pot of rice then returned and sat across from Ked and stared at him till he looked up.

"I want to apologize, if you think I'm interfering in your private affairs," Dan told him.

Ked glanced at him warily. Dan felt as though he'd been named as a potential suspect in any number of teenage offences.

"I was concerned about your schoolmate Tracy."

"I know."

"I still am, in fact, but that doesn't excuse my snapping at you the other night."

Ked relaxed ever so slightly. Dan took this as his cue to continue.

"I also don't want you to think I'm neglecting you when I have to go out of town suddenly. The truth is, I don't have the means to hire somebody to do it for me. So when the calls come, I have to go. It's as simple as that."

"Not a problem," Ked said quietly.

"As for Ali, it surprised me to find him sitting here with you discussing a very serious subject. I'm your father. If you want to have these discussions then you might try me. I'm open to it. I understand religion is not a thing to be taken lightly, even if I don't have a … a personal interest in the matter."

Ked nodded without looking at him directly.

"Is your Muslim heritage something you feel you would like to explore further?"

For the first time, Ked looked at him directly. "I don't know," he said.

"Fair enough, but if you do, I'd be happy to explore it with you. Or perhaps your mother should be the one to talk to about it. Would you be comfortable doing that?"

"Maybe."

Short answers seemed to be the most he could hope for, Dan realized, but he wasn't going to lose his temper over it. If Ked felt uncomfortable, or even if he was just unwilling to talk to his father about it, then so be it.

Dan stood.

"I just want you to know you can talk to me about anything at any time. Is that understood?"

"Yes."

"Okay. Good. I'll leave it with you then."

He turned and went out to the kitchen, feeling as though he'd been dismissed.

* * * *

Dan didn't hear from CSIS for another two days. He was beginning to think they'd decided he wasn't worth their time when he received an email suggesting a meet up to discuss "that fishing trip." Dan scrolled down. "Looking forward to it, pal." It was signed, *Paul from Hamilton*.

It was their game, Dan knew, but that didn't mean he couldn't play it his way. Ren would be returning from Berlin in a few days. He would want a report on Dan's findings. Dan was tempted to postpone the get-together, but CSIS had warned him not to change his plans. The more he thought about it, the more he hoped the woman he was chasing would turn out not to be Ren's sister or, at the very least, that he might dissuade Ren from his pursuit of her. The latter was unlikely, given Ren's convictions, but he could hardly tell Ren about his concerns with CSIS.

Still, there were things he could suggest. Twenty years was a long time. Even Ren would have to admit that the woman he wanted to find might have little or nothing to do with the woman he'd lost in the Tiananmen riots. Given his conversation with CSIS, Dan thought it likely that the real Ling had died at Tiananmen and someone taken her identity. If by some miracle she turned out to be his sister, whatever she'd gone through between leaving China and transplanting herself in Canada might have succeeded in completely erasing the person he had known.

Steve met him in the food court of the Eaton Centre. He seemed to have a taste for fast food in public spaces. His plate was piled with pineapple chunks drowned in a garish yellow sauce poured over battered chicken, with fried rice on the side, in what passed for Chinese cuisine. Dan wondered if the irony of his choice had occurred to him or if he was merely taking advantage of his partner's absence to chow down on junk.

Their meeting was brief and to the point: CSIS had arranged for him to attend a charity fundraiser hosted by some very rich philanthropists invested in the information technology industry. Ling Siu would be there, looking to meet some heavy-duty IT contacts.

Steve was less aggressive without his partner. He seemed more like the rookie making mistakes all over the place whom Dan had confronted in Hamilton. He passed Dan another envelope, sliding it toward him across the table.

"Offer her this," he said. "It's a titbit of IT research that will make you seem as though you're the real deal. She won't pay you for it. It's just a way of saying hello. Tell her there's more where this came from. If she likes it, she'll get back to you."

"How do I know she'll even talk to me?"

"We'll have one of our people tip her off that you're trying to sell information. She'll be looking out for you. Besides, you've got what she likes." Steve looked him up and down. "Physically as well as on paper."

Dan ignored the comment.

"Then what? Do I ask her to get in touch with me again?"

"Your contact info is in there." He shook his head at Dan's concerned expression. "Don't worry. The info isn't real. Everything has to come through us, but it will look like it comes from you. Your name is Max White. You're an IT developer. We've even set you up with a fake website and a Facebook page. You've already got a couple hundred friends. We'll keep you posted on whatever we tell her."

Dan watched him poking at his food. He speared a chunk of pineapple and popped it in his mouth.

"You're in no danger," Steve assured him. "As long as you do what you're told."

"You'll forgive me if I say I don't believe you."

Steve smiled. "What choice have you got?"

Plenty, Dan thought, though he wasn't about to voice the opinion.

"What am I supposed to do when I meet her?"

"Just give her the envelope. Once you put this in her hands, we'll see if she bites. In the meantime, it doesn't do to ask too many questions."

"Why? Because you don't want to know the answers?"

Steve shook his head. "No. Because you don't. Don't ask, don't tell. The less you know, the better off you'll be."

"I've heard that one before. What's the catch?"

"The catch, as you probably guessed, is that once we provide diplomatic immunity to your chum, you'll have to give him up."

Dan was dumbfounded. "That wasn't in the bargain."

Steve looked carefully around and leaned forward. He spoke softly. "You need to think this through clearly. We are going to provide your friend with diplomatic immunity, but we can't protect him forever. The Chinese government will come looking for him sooner or later. He has to disappear. I thought you were smart enough to figure that out for yourself."

Dan sat back, his mind reeling. Helping Ren assured that he would lose him forever. He felt as though he'd been kicked in the head.

Steve pushed his plate aside and stood. "I'll be in touch soon. Just keep the channels open."

Twenty-Two

The Bridal Path

The Bridle Path was Canada's most affluent neighbourhood by a long shot. Home to the swank and elite, the uptown borough housed mansions on two- and three-acre lots. Dubbed Millionaire's Row, the Path was lined with expensive cars of all makes. Dan felt like a poor cousin as he pulled up across from one of the larger homes. The only other vehicle that seemed out of place was a white delivery van with tinted windows parked a little ways down the road. He wondered if they were already watching him or if they were too busy drinking coffee and thumbing through magazines to notice his arrival.

This wasn't a part of the city Dan spent much time in. Settled by the horsey set back in the 1930s, lately it had become home to international celebrities, a ruling business class, and not a few members of the Russian mafia. Bad taste, high prices, low class. Cheap hookers in designer dresses. The wrapping didn't change the content much. When Radovan Karadjic, former president of the Republika Srpska a.k.a. the Butcher of Bosnia, was on the run from the war crimes tribunal in the years after the Bosnian War, it was not infrequently heard in injudicious whisperings between servants that he was here, enjoying a life of relative freedom and comfort on one of the Path's many grand estates.

Christened the Bridle Path in honour of its intricate equestrian runs, the neighbourhood's true name had been obscured and misspelled in favour of the notion that it was good place for weddings, where brides-to-be might be found traipsing about in idyllic bliss at all hours. Neither of which was true, but then most public misconceptions were founded on idyllic notions of one sort or another, Dan knew.

Whatever the reason for the misnomer, he arrived on a bright afternoon dressed in a smart jacket, cashmere sweater, and casual slacks, chosen by someone he'd never met and which had simply showed up at his door the previous day. The clothes fit perfectly, framing his physique to every advantage. Someone clearly had his measure, as well as his measurements, down to the size of his powerful biceps. When he donned the outfit, he didn't look like the sort of man who had come to spy on one of the guests. But then, that was the point.

The roster of invitees was impressive: attachés, diplomats, philanthropists, and high-powered businessmen. Big money and big talkers. Dan walked up to the gate and presented his invitation. The guard looked him over with the equanimity of a parking-lot attendant taking a ticket, registering that Dan's dress conformed to the accepted standards of such a swank event, and allowed him in. He closed the gates securely behind him, as though to dissuade anyone without proper attire from entering. *That's equality for you*, Dan mused. *You might be the low-born son of a Sudbury miner, but if you look the part and have the credentials to back it up, you will surely be included in the world of the haves.*

He was escorted into the red brick Georgian manor, noting the Chagall hanging in the entrance and a bronze sculpture that might have been a Rodin. There were other pieces he couldn't identify. Donny would have recognized them, no doubt. His escort handed him over to a second-in-command, the sort used to greeting the rich and making them feel as though the world was theirs. He guided Dan through the house, ushering him down a long hall with more artwork and elegant furniture, past a showroom that might have been a joke featuring a soda fountain and gleaming ice cream bar. *A little something for the kid in all of us*, Dan mused, as they passed through to a whirl of guests on a festive lawn.

The backyard was ablaze with fashionable colours. The crowd mingled restively, drinking and laughing as they circumvented a kidney-shaped pool at the cen-tre of the yard. Waiters with white linen draped over stiffened arms offered appetizers on silver trays, while a jazz band blew intricate rhythms at the far end of the lawn where the visitors had arranged themselves like pieces on a giant chess board. *I see England, I see France, I see Belgium's underpants* ...

Dan had little idea what constituted small talk in the world of diplomats and entrepreneurs, but thought it might amuse him to find out. He stood at the edge of a gathering and overheard one man say to another: "I know for a fact he spent a million restoring it. I would have turned it over three times by now. Even if it was a good investment, he's blown the budget sky high. He never knew when to leave well enough alone."

Dan recalled the joke about the sure-fire formula for becoming a successful businessman: *No brains, no education, buy low, sell high*. He passed on to another group. This clutch seemed to be composed of CEOs and accountants. "Out of all the billions of corporate wives to hit on, I happened to stumble on her!" Followed by incredulous laughter.

Dan left them as they pondered the whims of fate and adultery. A buzzing in his ear alerted him.

"Heads up. Your girl just entered the game."

He turned slowly, but at first saw no sign of his quarry. Suddenly he caught the lone figure striding through the glass doors and onto the back lawn. His heart skipped a beat then subsided into its dull, thudding regularity. She was glamorous, a classical beauty in a black strapless gown. The Jade Butterfly.

He flashed on the photograph of a teenaged Ren with his sister. Sure, it could be her, but then again maybe it wasn't. Dan thought of Angelina Jolie. There must have been a time in her life when she was mousey and awkward, an ugly duckling teenager, despite having blossomed into a total knockout by the time she bowled Brad Pitt over. Perhaps Ling, too, had simply grown into her destiny and embraced it. Because if Angelina was a 10, Ling was an 11. But what had turned a fearful, trembling girl into a confident, glamorous woman? Money, possibly. Leaving China, sure. Espionage training, more likely. Still, you couldn't invent beauty. Sex appeal was something else again. But the latter, Dan knew, was largely a matter of attitude. Women had swooned over the Greek tycoon, Aristotle Onassis, even when he was long past his prime. Famous women, important women, had thrown themselves at him. Maria Callas and Jackie Kennedy. Neither needed to pretend to fall for him in order to get their hands on his wealth and prestige, since both had their own and were already far more famous than him when they met.

Until Dan saw Ling in the flesh, he hadn't actually believed in her, he realized. She had remained a figment of some imaginary abode, a waif or a foundling. But now that he'd laid eyes on her sweeping beauty, he knew she was real. Whatever she had been as a teenager, at that moment she looked every bit as attractive as the man who believed her to be his sister.

He watched her scan the crowd, as though looking for someone she knew. Her gaze touched on him lightly then passed over. Not her type after all, Dan mused. She headed to a tennis court. Dan followed her with his eyes, but didn't approach. No sense in being overeager. He would let her get settled in and then casually wander by.

A waiter swooped in to fill the void of empty fists, serving up a tray of bubbly, claret, and other nectars. Dan watched as Ling grasped a stem, raised it, and took a sip. Others approached, no doubt drawn by her glamour. A stocky figure in a tuxedo was led toward her by a man intent on doing his hostly duties. Dan felt a tinge of jealousy. That's what hosts did, after all. But he found himself wanting to be presented to her as well.

She was impeccably stylish. Every move, every gesture spoke of grace and breeding. Dan was surprised how well she carried it off. She looked as though she'd been born to the role of glamorous beauty, rather than some waif from a poor background. When she smiled she appeared to be in her element, captivating everyone around her.

Dan was distracted by a short, abrasive little gnome who introduced himself as a Russian cultural ambassador. Dan's lack of smile or effort to charm seemed to have the opposite effect of what he'd intended, as if the man were drawn to sulkiness and disdain, and felt he'd met a kindred spirit. He had little to say other than to comment on the poor quality of the vodka and deliver a snivelling aside about Canadian operatic productions being nothing compared to their Russian counterparts. Dan couldn't disagree on either count, but wished the man with the diminutive stature and the towering superiority complex would pass along and leave him to his observances.

A figure stood at the centre of the gathering, comanding attention with his raised hand. Taking the opportunity to slip away from his captor, Dan recognized the man who had introduced Ling to the tuxedo, both now lost to view. Their host thanked his guests for attending and asked them to give generously to his foundation aimed at reducing illiteracy in developing nations. A noble cause, the suits and gowns seemed to concede, their jewellery flashing, pricy hairdos and couture evident in every direction.

A voice spoke over his shoulder.

"Enjoying the spectacle?"

He turned and found Ren's lookalike by his side. Seen close up, she might almost have been his twin. She was one of those rare creatures whose looks improved with proximity. Her cleavage was suggestively framed by the folds of her dress, yet without stealing focus from exquisite cheekbones, pouting lips, and taunting eyes that boasted they could have you any time they wanted. If Dan had been heterosexual, he might have swooned. He looked her over discreetly, but there was no sign of a butterfly ornament, not even a demure anklet. There were few places on her artfully clad figure where such an object might have been concealed. Nearly everything, it seemed, was out in the open.

Dan nodded and tried to conceal his surprise. "I feel like I should be out skeet shooting. What do they say about conspicuous consumption?"

She smiled. "I don't know. What do they say?"

"That it's the pursuit of the leisure classes, I think."

She tilted her head inquisitively, as though recognizing him at last for the peasant hidden among the gentry and about to instigate an open revolt.

"You're not a self-made millionaire then?"

She was toying with him, pulling him in close, like a praying mantis showing a distinct fascination for her chosen mate.

"Not yet, but still hoping. For now, just a lowly worker bee. I develop software. Highly specialized, of course, or I wouldn't be here today to gawk at the wealth. How about you?"

She sipped from her drink and made a show of looking over the crowd. "I'm a woman of both pleasure and leisure."

Was that flirtation, Dan wondered, or just a clever figure of speech? What exactly was he supposed to read into that remark? The envelope was burning a hole in his pocket. Despite his flattering costume, he hadn't felt overly sure of his role here today. He wasn't an IT expert. It would show if he needed to impress her with his expertise. This whole spy business wasn't something he would consider as a career. Chances were he wasn't the right man for the job, no matter what CSIS thought. If it were up to him, Dan wouldn't have left things in the hands of an amateur.

"I think of myself as a consumer for the leisure classes," she continued, as though sensing his discomfort and wanting to reassure him. "I'm a sharer of information. I believe in liberating things from the private sector."

This was ringing bells for him. She had practically declared herself a modern Robin Hood or at least a Maid Marion. If ever there were a cue, that was it. Dan made a show of studying her face.

"Can't have too much of that, if you ask me. I believe in spreading the wealth around, too. I might have something to offer if you're in the market."

She gave him one of the demurest smiles he'd ever received. And that included from a long list of hopeful lovers.

"What might that be?"

"Some interesting research I've been working on that would satisfy your most exacting criteria."

The smile held. There was no change in her features. Clearly, this was a woman who had learned to control her expressions a long time ago.

"I'd have to see a sample first, of course. Gratis."

He produced the envelope and passed it over. She took it and tucked it into her purse.

"My contact info is in there," he said.

"Naturally."

She held out a hand.

"Pleasure to meet you, Mister …?"

Her touch was warm and soft. Something in him tingled as it had when he first saw her brother.

"White. Max White."

Her gaze seemed to swallow him whole. Their mating dance was nearly complete.

"Ling Tu."

Dan tried to recall if that was one of the names CSIS had mentioned.

"I'll be in touch if I think we have common interests," she said.

"Naturally," Dan replied.

They parted on the lawn. Dan stood there watching as she headed for the house. The back of her dress was cut low to the waist. Her hips swayed gently. She didn't once look over her shoulder. The entire encounter had taken less than two minutes.

An hour later, Dan was back in the Eaton Centre. Steve sat across from him, looking smug. He hadn't bothered with the pretext of buying coffee. He preferred face-to-face meetings, he said, when Dan queried why the need for another get-together so soon.

"We can't have this stuff floating around in an email," Steve told him. "You get to tell me what she said in person. That way I can go back to my superiors and report what happened."

"I thought you had it all on audio tape."

"We need the visuals, your impressions of her, that kind of thing."

Dan had plenty of visuals, but suspected they weren't quite what Steve had in mind. He went through the meet-up, describing the location and the conversation he'd had with Ling, her quick leave-taking once he'd passed along the envelope. Steve seemed pleased by the account.

"You'd make a good agent," he said.

"No, thanks."

Steve shrugged. He had an oily, grating manner that was beginning to get on Dan's nerves.

"So here's what's next," he said, eyeing Dan. "When your client comes back from Berlin, we're going to help you arrange a meeting between the two of them. Once he makes a positive ID and tells you whether Ling Siu is really his sister or just some woman the Chinese government has set up in her place, we will provide him with papers to help him stay in Canada permanently. Agreed?"

Dan nodded. He still hadn't accepted the bit about having to part with Ren for good, but he wasn't about to voice his hesitation. If there was a way around it, he would find out. If not, he'd do what seemed best for Ren.

"We're counting on you," Steve said. "I'd like to hear from you as soon as your client returns. Send me an email once you've seen him to let me know all is well. Then we'll arrange for them to meet."

They parted. Outside, the sky had turned grey. Dan made his way through the crowd of workers escaping their daily drudgery and heading for streetcars and subways. It was past seven by the time he reached his office. Inside, the building beat like the heart of a dying man, faint and faraway, a morgue for the lost, lonely and misbegotten.

Sylvia had taped a note to his door. A young woman had been by asking for him earlier that afternoon, but left without leaving a name or message. Dan couldn't think who it might be. A brief P.S. asked whether he would prefer lemon tarts or brownies the next time she got the urge. He grabbed his files, scribbled LEMON! on the note and dropped it on her desk on his way out.

He'd just reached the exit when he saw the light beneath the warehouse door. If he hadn't come down the back way he would have missed it. No one was supposed to be there at that hour. Perhaps a late shipment had necessitated an after-hours pickup. He leaned his ear against the door, but heard nothing.

He tried the handle. It was unlocked. That was unusual, even when the office was open. The firm's shipments were often valuable and the neighbourhood was prone to theft. He pushed the door open. A light came from the far end, but nothing moved in his line of sight. There were no workers busily moving crates or hustling to finish the job and get home. Dan wondered if he should phone security to alert them that the space had been left unsecured. Someone might come in to work in the morning minus his job, but that wasn't his concern.

The warehouse was a Wi-Fi dead spot. There was no reception inside the walls. Not a good place to be caught in a bind, he noted, not for the first time. That meant he'd have to go outside to make the call. A flash of paranoia told him this had something to do with CSIS or Ling Siu or somebody he definitely did not want to come into contact with alone.

He turned to leave when a head popped out from around a pile of crated goods. White dreadlocks.

"Hey!" she said, as though it were just another casual meeting.

"Hi."

She was sitting on the floor in black jeans and a green khaki jacket. Very *guerrillero*. If she'd had a cigar, she would be smoking it.

"Are you Dan?"

"Yes. How did you get in here?"

"Some guys were bringing in boxes. I waited till they weren't watching and then sneaked in."

She looked as pleased as a teenager discovering the party punch has alcohol in it.

"I'm Tracy."

"I know. You got my card, then."

She looked half doubtful and half curious. "What card?"

"My business card. I gave it to your friend Marlon the other day."

"Marlon? Shit no. I never talked to Marlon after some creepy guy showed up looking for me."

"Yes, I heard about him. How'd you find me then?"

"Lester messaged me on Facebook. He's a cool dude."

Lester the Diligent. Dan took out his card and offered it to her. She looked it over then stuck it in her back pocket.

"He beat him up, in case you're wondering."

"Who?"

"Marlon. The guy who came to find you in Hamilton hit him."

For a moment she looked frightened. Then she giggled.

"Shit."

"Whoever is trying to find you could be following you on Facebook. It's probably not a good idea to get Lester involved, if you don't have to. You know what I'm saying?"

"Yeah, okay." Her face took on a shadow of wariness. "You know my father, right?"

"Not well, but I know him. He asked me to find out where you went." He hesitated. "What are you involved in? Can you tell me what you're running from? I saw you leaving Matt Parks's studio last week."

"Oh, that." She rolled her eyes. "I said I would do escorting, yeah? Nothing wrong with going around town on a date with some guy with lots of money if he wants to take me to a restaurant or whatever. But I never said nothing about the other."

"What other?"

She screwed up her face and dug her fingers into her hair and scratched.

"They wanted to put me on a plane to somewhere. I said I didn't have no passport. They told me they could get me one. That scared me."

"Is that why you went to Hamilton?"

"I didn't know they'd come after me and bother Marlon. Shit!"

"When did you last see Matt Parks?"

She thought about it. "Last week, I think. Probably the day you saw me there. Yeah, I didn't go back after that. I don't want to see to him again. He'll just ask for his money back. Why?"

Dan watched her face. The question seemed genuine.

"Because he's dead."

She suddenly looked shaken.

"Whoa! How?"

"It doesn't matter. But you've taken money from someone who wants you to live up to your agreement, whatever that is."

She nodded, much less insouciant now.

"They will look at it as a business agreement and expect you to keep up your side of the bargain. Even if what they're asking you to do is illegal, they could be very difficult people to deal with."

She looked defiant as much as scared. "I can't help that."

"It's probably too late to give back the money. Why don't you go home to your father?"

She shook her shaggy head.

"I can't. He'd kill me if he found out."

"He won't kill you. He wants you to come home. You'll be much safer with him than on your own."

"Safe?" She stood and began pulling on her jacket.

"What are you going to do? Where will you go?"

Dan reached out a hand. She backed off suddenly.

"It's okay. I got a place to stay."

"Where?"

She looked as though he'd just asked her if she liked blood pudding. She shook her head.

"I'm going to have to figure some shit out. I'll be fine."

"Can I do anything to help?"

For a second she looked as though she might cry.

"Tell my dad ... I don't know. Tell him I'm okay."

Dan very much doubted that. She turned and was gone.

Twenty-Three

Family Matters

Ked was out when Dan got home. No note, no phone message. Had he gone somewhere with Ali? Kendra promised to tell him of any future get-togethers between the two, but he hadn't heard from her since the morning he accused Ali of interfering in family matters. The lack of communication in itself wasn't unusual. They didn't speak every day or even every other day, unless there were issues to be considered. They weren't best friends, they had simply parented a child together. Now, however, the silence weighed heavily. It felt fraught with the weight of things unspoken, of things not being discussed. He called and left a message: *Just calling to say hi.* His voice was unconvincing. It would have made even him suspicious. When she called back half an hour later, she sounded cool. She wanted Ked to come over for lunch later in the week. With Ali. It wasn't something she would normally have felt the need to make a request for. Dan wondered if she were trying to make him feel guilty. Behind her inquiry, he sensed resentment that he might be trying to impose rules about her access to their son.

"I'm assuming you have no objection?" she said.

He had no intention of restricting her access to Ked and, knowing she would be there, he didn't even have an objection to Ali's presence at the proposed lunch. In fact, he wasn't sure what he was afraid of, other than the possibility that Ked's current rebelliousness might boil over into unspoken resentments between father and son that could not be easily resolved. This was exactly the sort of thing that kept Dan in work, when family disagreements became so pronounced people felt there was no way out but to cut ties. He didn't want that for his family.

He looked out the window. A wishbone of a moon held in the sky.

"No, I have no objection," he said softly.

His initial meeting with Kendra had been almost as improbable as their eventual co-parenting. In university, Dan's infatuation for Kendra's brother, Arman, had brought them together. The rest had been a combination of curiosity and hubris, the latter mostly a result of trying to cement his friendship with Arman. Keeping the child had been Dan's idea once Kendra disclosed her pregnancy, though he'd been surprised when she went along with it. He realized later that he'd been key to helping her escape the double bind of both her family and culture. Neither of them truly belonged anywhere:

he a single father and gay man, she an at-arms-length mother and indifferent Muslim in a slowly deteriorating Christian culture. They were both outcasts, infidels looking at the world through the slats in a fence.

Apart from the non-Islamic name her mother had bestowed on her, plucked from the pages of some romance novel she'd been reading at the time, in all other ways Kendra's upbringing had been strict and traditional. She'd rebelled, but secretly and silently — Western pop music, modern clothes, and makeup — when out on her own, while remaining outwardly obedient at home. She was adventurous and bright, embracing an opportunity to study in the West even while remaining critical of what she thought of as its self-indulgent excesses. She saw how other girls her age gave up their independence to marry and vowed never to go that route. She was too smart and keen-spirited to be under anyone's thumb. Dan was her first experiment in non-Muslim dating. While she found him refreshing, she hadn't taken him seriously. Then Kedrick came along to change everything.

She sounded defensive over the phone. "Whatever impression you may have formed of him, I just want you to know Ali is one of the kindest men I've ever contemplated having a romantic involvement with …"

She hesitated. Dan wondered whether to say something soothing or let her complete her thoughts. He waited.

She continued impatiently. "I just don't understand what your objection is to him."

"I don't object to him," he said, trying for an understanding tone. "I just don't know him. He pushed a few of my buttons, but that doesn't mean I think he's a bad person."

"I can tell you he's a very good person. The fact that he's a devout Muslim doesn't mean he can't be sensitive to the issues we care about."

"I wasn't suggesting that. I know you're a good judge of character." He tried for a bit of humour. "After all, you picked me to father your child."

She wasn't buying it.

"He's not just kind to me. He tithes a percentage of his earnings to charity. He has a very deep respect for humanity."

"Then he's probably what you say he is. It's just —."

"Just what?"

"I don't want Ked exposed to a religion that discriminates against gays or women or minorities —"

"That's every religion in the world, not just Islam!"

She was exasperated.

"I know that. I'm sorry. I don't even know what we're arguing about. I just have these worries."

"Every parent worries whether their child will turn out all right. That he won't grow up to be a murderer or a thief or a lot of other things. We have given Ked every kind of encouragement to be the best person he can be. I suggest we sit back and enjoy the good he has brought us rather than worry about any bad that can possibly occur."

"You're right."

After graduating from university and finding herself a success, Kendra had announced her intention to stay in Canada. Her family quietly accepted that she was lost as far as tradition went — just another child who had been exposed to the modern world and caught in its web. She was not recast as the Daughter of Shame, unlike many girls who sought non-traditional lives, but it was understood she was now beyond their reach. She was also fortunate in that she had no younger sisters waiting for her to marry and clear the way for them. Arman, on the other hand, had accepted the terms of an arranged marriage and was surprisingly happy with the choice. If Kendra's family had known about Kedrick, however, it would have changed things radically, so she arranged her life that they would never find out. Returning to Syria for her infrequent visits required a total act of deception, but she bore up well and had no regrets, as far as Dan could tell. Now, it seemed, she wanted more from the personal side of life. Ali was the temptation she was currently contemplating.

One look at him told Dan why: he was attractive, masculine, and well-off. In other words, a great catch. Still, he hadn't contemplated that an addition to the family might mean a disruption to its affairs inwardly, if not outwardly. Perhaps Kendra was ready to give up the ruse of being entirely self-sufficient and happily single.

"So you have no qualms if Ali and I have Ked over on Tuesday?"

"None. Sorry I made an issue out of this."

"Thank you."

They ended the conversation amicably. Dan was headed upstairs when the phone rang a second time. He hurried to his office to take the call.

It was Ian Cunningham. Dan's first and somewhat optimistic thought was that the cop was calling to apologize again for the scene he created the other day. His second thought was that Tracy had heeded his request and gone home to talk things over with her father, putting her faith in him to protect her from whoever had beaten up Marlon and felt she owed him a piece of her future. The same person who had offered her a passport and a trip out of the country. After a few seconds on the line, however, it was clear Ian hadn't called with glad tidings.

"She was here," he said, his voice choked with emotion. "It was about an hour after you called me to say she'd been by your office," Ian said. "I thought she decided to come home to stay, but ..."

He was struggling to speak.

"You argued," Dan suggested lightly. "And she left again."

"Yes."

There was a heavy intake of breath.

"Maybe she'll think about it and come back when she cools off."

"She won't."

There was an anguished cry on the other end.

"What is it, Ian? What happened?"

"She took my gun!"

Dan felt the panic hit him even as he urged calm, telling Ian to do the right thing — the *necessary* thing — and report the theft. He listened as Ian tearfully detailed a distressing conversation with his daughter where she told him what she'd been up to and how he'd cringed at every word. Dan knew the father's grief. He thought of Ked and how he would feel if it were his son who'd gone over the edge. Whatever transpired between fathers and their children, Dan thought, it was a wisdom he was rapidly losing his grip on. He stayed on the phone another quarter of an hour without once asking the question that lay uppermost on his mind: what did Ian Cunningham know about the circumstances of Matt Parks's gruesome death?

Twenty-Four

The Colour of Smoke

It had been two days since Dan's encounter with Ling, two days since Tracy stole her father's gun. Not much else had been on his mind in between. He made no further progress in either direction apart from increasing his worry about what Ian might actually be capable of doing to sort things out on his own. Dan just hoped whoever had been harassing Tracy and her friends didn't make the mistake of showing up on Ian Cunningham's doorstep looking for compensation.

Today he had another concern: Ren's return. He'd heard from CSIS. He was to meet with Ren, letting him know he'd had contact with his sister, then report to Steve afterwards. He watched the clock, counting down the minutes. He didn't have long to wait. Ren called at six to say he'd just come from the airport. Dan listened as he described his flight: turbulent, but pleasant; the weather, clear and calm; Berlin's architecture, inspiring and eclectic. It was like a formal dance with intricate footsteps, a fandango in 5/4 time. Finally, Ren got around to saying he was eager to meet.

Dan agreed to come to the hotel. Meanwhile, stalking his mind throughout the conversation was everything he now knew about Ren's sister. His impulse was to break things off immediately, to tell Ren he'd found nothing because the trail had gone cold. Next, he would regretfully say he could no longer have Ren for a client, that it would be a waste of Ren's money and Dan's time to continue. Even that they should not have also "the more personal," as Ren had so charmingly put it, if only to distance him from whatever fallout might occur. But CSIS had warned him not to change anything, not to break any arrangements between them. So he would go to the rendezvous and see what happened.

The night clerk nodded a friendly acknowledgement as Dan entered. He realized he'd become a known quantity, the whooshing elevator now a familiar ride rather than the novelty it had been only recently. Upstairs, the harvest inset in the rosewood slots yielded a galaxy of delicate star fruit.

Ren met him at the door dressed in jeans and red T-shirt, looking very Western indeed. Dan stood there, resisting the urge to enter, fearing where it would lead.

"Please come in," Ren said with a slight bow.

Perhaps he thought Dan's hesitance a slight formality rather than a wariness of making things worse for both of them by being there. Ren closed the door and put his arms around him, holding the embrace.

"Welcome back," Dan said finally.

Ren released him and stepped apart. "Thank you. It is most pleasant to be here. Canadian people are much more welcoming than many other countries I have visited."

Where Dan might have been touched by the admission, he was determined to push such emotions aside.

"That's because we stole it from the Natives," he said facetiously. "Deep down we're all aware of that, so we make up for it by being welcoming to foreigners. Don't mistake that for generosity."

Ren took his hand and pulled him deeper into the room. "That is an intriguing thought."

Dan felt his resistance melting. "Some would call it cynicism, but there's truth in humour."

"This is so." Ren nodded. "I was aware of another intriguing thought while I was away."

"What's that?"

Ren smiled. "At first, I could not tell what it was. It seemed to me when I arrived that something was out of place, something not quite right."

"You didn't like Berlin?"

"No, I like Berlin very much. However, I sensed that something was missing." He looked meaningfully at Dan. "You, tough man. What I missed was you."

Dan found himself unable to answer.

Ren smiled again. "The heart is surprising, is it not?"

Dan nodded dumbly. "So I'm told. I hope you got your work done while you were away and didn't spend all your time thinking of me."

"Much was accomplished, yes. There were many meetings with diplomats and government representatives. It occurred to me that a diplomat's situation is remarkably similar to the plight of the homosexual in China. It is as if we are all trying very hard to remain unnoticed so that we may go about our business without being observed. We are like smoke. You can see right through us, but there is no colour to discern. We must hide our true desires. Only then can we do our work effectively. Especially for people from such countries as China. We must be what we are told to be or else we can be punished."

Dan thought of the second CSIS agent's threat to tarnish Ren's reputation unless Dan did what they asked. "Sounds like a difficult job."

Ren nodded. "Yes. I must do many things I do not like doing. Such are the perils of being a government employee."

"Shall I tell you what I've been up to?" Dan asked quietly.

"Excuse me. I have been dominating the conversation. Please have a seat."

Dan pulled out a chair and sat. Ren perched on the edge of the bed across from him and watched.

"I think I have a lead on your sister," Dan said at last.

Ren nodded eagerly. "I am happy to hear this."

"Do you remember the missing girl I mentioned? The one who is a friend of my son's?"

"Yes, I do recall this."

"I followed another lead on her that took me to Hamilton."

Ren started to interrupt, but Dan put up a hand.

"I know you wanted me to work exclusively on finding your sister, but the two cases are related. I thought it would be wise to follow up on the first and see where it led. So far, I haven't been able to discover why they're connected, but I will."

Ren looked perplexed. "I do not understand."

"Nor do I — yet. I've been thinking about your sister," Dan ventured. "How will you be sure it is your sister?"

Ren gave him a curious look.

"I can know for sure it is Ling only when I see and talk to her."

"I meant, what if she denies she is your sister?"

"She will not do this," Ren insisted. "Why would she say she is not my sister?"

"The woman you believe is your sister seems to have accumulated a variety of aliases ... false names."

"Then you must have already found her," Ren said astutely.

"I don't know. I've been in touch with someone who may be the woman you're after, but you will have to determine if she's the right one."

Ren was very still. His eyes searched Dan's face for understanding. "Please explain."

"I have been in touch ... by phone," Dan lied.

"Then you must take me to her."

"I can't just hand over a total stranger." Dan

paused. *And I can't tell you what kind of danger I'm leading you into, either*, he thought, feeling the sting of his betrayal no matter what he chose to do.

Ren's eyes showed disappointment in Dan's refusal, disappointment that life had given him a family and taken it away again.

"I will try to arrange something," Dan said.

"When?"

"I don't know. Soon. How will you know for sure it's her?"

Ren smiled shyly. "I will ask if she has kept the jade butterfly and watch what expression she makes. That will tell me everything. The butterfly was a symbol of our love for one another. We agreed that if we should separate, it would remind us of one another." For a moment, he seemed too distraught to speak, then he continued. "At the time we were not thinking of revolution, but just of the possibility of living elsewhere. I have always hoped she kept it as a sign she is waiting for me somewhere, but I never heard from her again. If she is alive, she will remember this one thing. She will have it, I am sure. If it is not Ling then she will not know what I am talking about."

His eyes misted over. Dan got up and sat beside him, putting an arm around his shoulder.

Ren reached up and took Dan's hand. "When my sister left, I endured months of pain and recrimination. Was this my fault, I wondered? I had no wish to harm my sister, but she vanished because I allowed her to follow our friends through Tiananmen Gate."

"You will achieve nothing by blaming yourself," Dan told him.

"Yes, I know. Still, I cannot help this feeling of guilt. It haunts me."

"Ling may no longer be the person you remember her to be. She may have become involved in things you don't know about. What if … what if someone has purposely taken her identity?"

"You mean it is possible there is someone who looks and sounds like her, but is not her in the most intrinsic ways? A counterfeit?"

"Yes," Dan said. "Something like that."

"Please, I must see her to know for sure. Will you help me?"

"Even if it is Ling, I still can't guarantee she will want to see you," Dan added.

Ren nodded. "I understand. She may have her own reasons, as you said. Although I am confident my sister will want to see me, I confess I am also a very possessive person. For this reason, I value certain things and I do not like to lose them. If Ling will not see me — then I should like you to ask her for the jade butterfly to be returned."

"I will do that," Dan said. "I promise. If she won't see you then I will find a way to get the butterfly back, if it's at all possible." He hesitated. Was it too soon to complicate things further? His doubts dissolved. He had to do something, and quickly. "While you were away, I was also thinking about immigration. I might be able to get you citizenship here."

Ren shook his head. "Sadly, this is not possible. I have just learned I must return to China at the end of the week."

"For good?" Dan was stunned to hear this. "Why? I mean, why now?"

A shadow fell over Ren's face. "I received a very official call in Berlin. I feel that something has happened, but I am not sure what. Perhaps I have displeased someone in charge."

For a second, Dan wondered if CSIS had double-crossed him. He recalled their fears of a diplomatic faux pas. Had they leaked something to the Chinese officials so they would recall Ren before he could unwittingly cause damage or embarrassment to their government?

"Could it have anything to do with your sister? If they heard that I've been searching for her —?"

"It is possible, though I don't know how they would know this."

Dan looked deep into Ren's eyes. It didn't matter how or why or for how long. What mattered was being with him.

"There won't be time for a diplomatic route to get you citizenship, but I could marry you. I know it sounds crazy, we hardly know one another. It's just that I want more for us. I want us to be together. Please — I need you to think about this."

Ren put a finger to Dan's lips to stop him from talking. "I want us to be together, too. You will stay the night with me?"

Fuck CSIS, Dan thought. "Yes." He nodded. "Yes, I would like that."

"We can wake up tomorrow in each other's arms." Ren smiled. "Just like in the American cinema."

Just like happily ever after, Dan thought. Did it ever happen in real life? He wasn't betting on it, but it wouldn't hurt to try. "Let's do that."

Ren went to the room phone and dialled.

"This is room 1101. I have a breakfast included in my package. I would like it left outside the door at 7 a.m., please." He paused. "For two. Some rolls and cereal and eggs with sausages. Also, some fruit, I think." He glanced at Dan. "Oh — and coffee. Lots of it."

He hung up and turned to Dan.

"Who are you, tough man? Why did you come into my life? Now everything is changed for me so quickly."

"I'm just a guy who is becoming very smitten with you. A guy who is looking for a good man to share his life with."

"I am your good man," Ren said with a laugh.

Dan's gaze travelled around the room, taking in the lighting fixtures, the painting frames. He couldn't see anything that looked like a camera. As for sound, even next-door neighbours sometimes overheard the amorousness of other hotel guests. He could only hope that whoever might be listening in were otherwise engaged or just too tired to be interested. He took Ren's pass key and dimmed the lights.

* * * *

In the morning, Dan felt more relaxed and light-hearted than he had in a long time. He sat up in bed beside Ren. Together, they peeled an orange, feeding one another the segments.

"How do they make it without seeds?" Ren asked.

"That's one mystery I haven't been able to fathom," Dan said.

Ren passed him his coffee. Dan took a few sips and stood.

"I have to go," he said. "But I am going to make this happen, one way or another."

"I trust you," Ren said. "Perhaps, if you are successful, there will be future happiness for us together."

Dan dressed and headed out. The air was already warm when he hit the street. He felt like a stranger in his own city: the business world was on the move, briefcases on every corner, smokers standing under awnings with their prop coffees, eyes blinded by morning sunlight. The mournful tapping of a cane came down a long hallway leading under City Hall. A man lay curled over a heating duct, fetus-like, his sleeping bag a wind-blown leaf. At some point, Toronto had stopped wanting to be New York and started acting like it. That was when it all went wrong, he felt.

He thought about his next move. He'd have to arrange things quickly for Ren to stay in Canada. Once they were married they would go away for a while. Ked could stay with Kendra until they resettled elsewhere. Then Dan could send for him.

The idea was crazy, he knew. Steve Ross had been

right when he said there was no way to guarantee Ren's safety if they stayed together. If the Chinese government made a fuss, he might suddenly be whisked away by diplomatic forces beyond anyone's control. The results could be disastrous in diplomatic terms.

A shimmering haze hovered over the pavement. Dan watched as a bus forced its way along Queen Street and came up to the curb, pneumatic lifts hissing as it stooped with the wounded dignity of a circus elephant waiting for the conscripts to board, then, groaning, made its way back onto its feet again.

He needed to find a way to make things work out for them.

Twenty-Five

Set Up

Steve Ross sat reading a newspaper at the same table in the underground food court where he'd sat with his partner two weeks earlier. Dan slid into the seat across from him. His stomach was cramped from too much coffee and not enough sleep. Or maybe it was just from too much worry.

Steve caught the dark circles under Dan's eyes.

"The boyfriend came back, I take it?"

"As expected."

"We didn't hear from you last night."

Which didn't mean they hadn't been listening in, Dan knew. He wondered just how much Steve had heard of their conversation.

"I was busy. Then I fell asleep."

"That's fine. It's time to move things along with the sister. By now she will have surveyed the material and either found it to her liking or decided to drop you.

From the email we received this morning, it's clear she liked something, only I'm not entirely sure what. She's got a cozy little love nest picked out for your next rendezvous." He appraised Dan over the paper. "You're quite an accomplished flirt, so I'm sure it won't hurt for you to lead her on a little."

"Yeah, too bad it doesn't pay. So tell me again: what's in this for me?"

"We've already discussed that. We will provide safe diplomatic passage for your boyfriend when this is all over. And you get to go home and sleep safe and sound in your bed all alone. Maybe we will have that date after all."

"I still don't know why you want me to do this."

Steve smiled grimly. "I thought we already resolved that issue. In any case, you'll be doing your country a favour. Any other questions?"

"Did Ling Siu kill Matt Parks?"

Steve's mouth gaped open. Obviously, it wasn't the question he was expecting. Maybe he was hoping Dan would confine his queries to spyware etiquette. Still, the murder was a major unresolved issue. CSIS knew he'd been at the studio the night the photographer was killed. They had to know that Ling Siu was there as well. Why make a murder look like an accidental overdose? Someone had gone to a lot of trouble to do that, but Dan still wasn't ready to hang the rap on Ian Cunningham.

"It's not clear who killed Mr. Parks. But it wasn't Ling Siu, in case you're worried about your safety.

She's not a killer, though she likes to act tough. What did you make of her connection with the photographer, by the way?"

It was a good ploy, Dan thought, taking him into their confidence and asking his opinion on the situation. Guaranteed to blow a lesser man's ego into the stratosphere and quell his fears at the same time.

"Nothing except what I told you. My client found a picture of the woman he believes to be his sister on a public website. The photographer in question was Matt Parks, a sometimes *artiste* and pimp for some high-class erotic acts. Still, that doesn't mean there has to be a connection between Siu and his murder."

"You're right, it doesn't."

Dan hesitated then decided to go for it. "It occurred to me that the sex industry is pretty tame these days. People don't often get killed over it. It's not something CSIS would normally get involved in, but it also strikes me that CSIS probably doesn't cover up a great many murders, trying to make them look like drug overdoses."

Steve held his gaze, but said nothing.

Dan continued, "As for Ling Siu, the photos Parks took of her weren't pornographic. They were taken in a casual set-up."

"So you don't think their connection was a coincidence?"

"Since when do international spies take time off to model for third-rate photographers?"

Steve's face was a blank. "I don't have an answer

to that. Perhaps you could ask her when you meet up with her tomorrow."

"What do you have answers for, Steve? I'd really like to know why I'm playing jockey for CSIS."

Steve smiled. "All will be revealed in time."

"Right. And in the meantime, how do I know I'm not digging my own grave by helping you out?"

Steve wasn't smiling now. "You ask too many questions for a man in your position." He pushed another envelope across the table. "All you have to do is meet with her and hand her the envelope. You're starting to gain her confidence. If she accepts this, then we will arrange to have your client meet with her and, hopefully, identify her as his sister. After that, you'll never have to see her again. As agreed, we will arrange to get your boyfriend diplomatic immunity and whisk him somewhere safely away from here." He paused. "Unless you're having second thoughts?"

Dan glanced at the envelope and back at Steve. "What if she suspects something? Surely, if she's a spy she's going to be suspicious."

"We've given you a perfect cover story. You're feeding her all the right material. She's in an active market and the contact who suggested you is someone she trusts."

"Who is that?"

Steve screwed up his face. "I can't tell you that."

"How am I supposed to know what to say if she starts asking for more detailed information?"

Steve looked gravely at him. "Tell her whatever you think she wants to hear. It's your show."

Two security guards were looking them over from the other end of the food court. Did they suspect terrorists at work in their home territory? Since when did security guards worry about anything more serious than checking the occasional lock on a door and tossing out beggars and pick-pockets?

Dan picked up the envelope, weighing it in his hands. It was lighter than he'd expected.

Steve gave him an address and mentioned a time. "Good luck," he said, getting up from the table.

Dan turned away, feeling sick with helplessness.

He returned to his office and set the envelope on his desk. It was an ordinary manila envelope, the kind that could easily be replaced. He went to Sylvia's desk. She'd left a Tupperware container of pastry with his name on it. He lifted the lid and took one out — the promised lemon — then opened her filing cabinet and removed an envelope exactly the same colour and size as the one Steve Ross had given him.

He went back to his office, turning the idea over in his mind. Without thinking it through, he tore open the envelope and stared at the USB drive in his palm. Now he stopped to consider. The problem, he realized, wasn't that CSIS would know he'd opened the envelope. But they would know he'd read the data the instant he used a computer connected to a network. The drive would be encoded with an .exe file to help them trace it or send out a warning signal if he so much as inserted it in a port.

An old laptop lay on top of the filing cabinet. It wasn't connected to the Internet. He inserted the USB drive and turned it on. The machine hummed and whirred before Dan remembered the mouse didn't work. He unhooked his current mouse and connected it.

After several moments, the screensaver whirled into view. Dan found himself staring at his son at last year's birthday party. Ked was relaxed and smiling for the camera. He was jolted back to that moment in time. What had changed so drastically between then and now? How had he gone from being a favoured parent to a source of suspicion and sullenness? If it knew anything, the photograph wasn't talking.

He glanced at the pop-up menu. There was a single file labelled CX2-SUB. It could be anything. He clicked on it, but the file refused to reveal its secrets. Just like his son. Whatever it contained could probably be opened by someone savvy with computer encryption, but that wasn't him. Maybe Lester could do it, but Dan wasn't about to involve a sixteen-year-old boy in CSIS business. For now, he was stuck.

He shut off the machine, slid the USB stick into the new envelope, and sealed it. Unless there was a code built into the file alerting a reader to previous attempts at opening it, no one would be able to tell the difference. Then he sat at his desk and thought about what he was going to do.

Ten minutes later, he had a plan. He would meet Ling Siu at CSIS's request, but he would play the game his way.

Dan closed his office, taking the envelope with him. He headed downstairs to the warehouse, went in and opened his safe. There wasn't much inside it, apart from a copy of his will and a few odds and ends he was saving for a later date. He lay the envelope with the USB drive on top of everything else. If Ling Siu wanted it so badly then he was going to make a trade: IT information for a jade butterfly.

Twenty-Six

Araby

The hand-woven rug adorning the entrance was a gift from King Hassan II of Morocco. Red and gold tones dominated, patterns hinting at undreamed-of splendours from the land of the Berbers, with its perfect blending of European, African, and Asian cultures. The restaurant was neatly divided for privacy, individual dining areas separated by gauzy curtains. If you were versatile enough, you could make love in one of them without being discovered. You could also kill someone. Dan wondered what Ling had in mind for this meeting.

She was already seated when he arrived, a martini perched on the table before her. He had thought she might prefer to arrive second, using the opportunity to pass him by if she didn't like what she saw, but it seemed she was certain about wanting the meeting to occur.

She greeted him affably, like a cherished friend or even a fiancé. Her hand reached out and touched him reverently, as though touching precious silk or an altar cloth. If she was a killer, Dan thought, she was the most disarming one he'd ever met, but something in her eyes warned him not to get too close.

A hypnotic beat rippled the air. Dan was aware of curtains breathing, of street noises drifting in from outside. On arriving he had noted two entrances, front and back. It seemed a perfect place for slipping in and out of. A waitress drifted by in a belly-dancing outfit, her ample flesh moving to the music. Dan was amused by the touch of exoticism, but kept his eyes in their proper place as she set a plate between them. Olives and cheese, hummus, and baba ghanoush.

Ling looked up and smiled. She wasn't hungry, but told him to go ahead. Judging from her figure, Dan doubted whether she ever truly indulged in solid food. She watched him as she sipped her martini. The breakfast of champions. Or so he'd been told.

The music swirled, evoking the sounds of the desert. Camels and caravans disappeared over horizons, water spilled into wadis, rose in the air, evaporating along with the secret language of oases and desert birds. It would serve to cover their conversation. She hadn't chosen the place at random, he realized. No one would overhear what a man and woman might be discussing over a plate of hors d'oeuvres and a splash of gin in crystal.

She asked about his background, casually, as

though not really interested but feeling compelled to ask for politeness' sake. Dan told her what he'd been briefed to say, describing the IT firm he supposedly worked for, putting no great emphasis on any one aspect in particular. She didn't seem to find anything unusual in his work history or the fact that he had access to highly sensitive material.

He watched as she spoke. Always, he came back to that exquisite face. Grace, beauty, and airy lines suggested a marble altar or the curve of the Madonna's hand as she held her child in some medieval painting. It was her brother's face, but redesigned as a woman's. The only difference was her eyes. They mocked him. They said that love could be happy or bitter, sensual or extravagant, but it had to be acknowledged before time ran out because there was so little of that, and anyway wasn't it better to enjoy today than worry about what was to come tomorrow? Because, really, what else was there beyond right now?

Then Dan asked about her background. The change was instantaneous. She pursed her lips and looked away.

"Who I am is not your business," she said. "You should know the rules."

"Forgive me, but how do I know I can trust you?"

"How do I know I can trust you?" She smiled. "Maybe if we slept together it would put us on a different footing, but I doubt it. Anyway, I need to keep my distance."

"I didn't think spies really slept with one another."

It was an ad hoc remark. As soon as it was out, Dan regretted using the term so blatantly. She didn't seem to notice, or at least not to mind if she did.

"It's one of the perks. I don't get many." Her eyes looked him over. "You're a sexy beast. I bet a lot of girls would sleep with you for free."

Her leg stole across the space and rubbed against his. He half expected to hear her say, *I like you, tough man*. She leaned forward just enough to suggest that something was happening between them. Dan felt drawn deep into those eyes that resembled Ren's but for their sardonic tone. Her perfume hung in the air. He could taste her lips even before they softly brushed his, then quickly slid away again as she leaned back. He resisted an urge to check to see if she'd just picked his pocket.

Dan was mesmerized, exactly as he'd been the night he met her brother. She was smiling, toying with him. He'd been told to flirt with her, but it was she who was flirting with him. He was surprised how much he welcomed it. Very surprised.

"For now, let's stick to business," she told him. "What have you got for me?"

"A USB drive with some highly valuable information that might turn you on even more than I do."

"Show me."

He shook his head. "I didn't bring it with me."

Her eyes flashed. "Then what the hell is this meeting all about?"

"It's about information consolidation. I need to know what I'm getting for my product."

"You'll get paid what it's worth. I have to ascertain its value first, which I can't do until I see it."

"You've already seen the initial offer. I have the key that opens the rest of it."

She looked as though she might pout. "I don't like this," she said.

"What choice have you got?"

"All the choice in the world."

Her hand dipped into a shimmery bag and pulled out a tiny pistol. Despite its size, Dan had no doubt that at that range it would do permanent damage.

"Now let's drop the act and talk properly," she said.

She's not a killer, though she likes to act tough, Steve had told him.

"Should I put up my hands?" Dan asked.

"I don't know what game you're playing, but you'd better come up with some answers. I don't think you're selling information at all or you would have brought it with you. Who are you? How did you find me?"

"I heard about you through the usual channels."

"That could mean anything. Name names."

Tell her whatever you think she wants to hear. Then it came to him: "I saw you at Matt Parks's studio the night he was killed."

The look she gave him was wary, but not surprised.

"What were you doing there?"

Challenge her, he thought. He knew it might piss her off, but if she hadn't shot him by now, then she wasn't going to.

"I might ask you the same," he said.

"Not good enough. For all I know, you might have killed Matt."

"So might you, but we both know neither of us did the killing."

She waited.

"Then what were you doing there?"

"Looking for information."

Her look was scornful. "Matt bought information, he didn't sell it. What sort of information were you after?"

He was scrambling now. "I was trying to find you. I knew I had something you wanted. I thought Matt would have your contact info, but when I asked him he wouldn't divulge it. He wanted to be the go-between to get his share. I went back alone to go through his files. That's when I saw you. Only I got there first."

She was studying him. Her eyes were busy decoding his words, his body, all the signals he was giving off, trying to determine where the truth lay. If anywhere.

"Greedy little Matt," she said. "I dropped him when he got into the escort business. Too dirty, too small-time."

"So what were you doing there?"

He waited. The gun remained where it was.

"Erasing the traces. I wanted to get rid of the photos he took of me for that stupid calendar. I can't believe I let him con me into it. At one point, I even thought I loved him. How ridiculous was that?"

Dan tried to picture the voluptuous Ling with the

skanky Matt Parks. It was a rough fit. "And here I thought you were moonlighting as a supermodel."

"So what do you really want?" she asked.

"What we discussed. Money in exchange for some highly valuable information. And something else." He paused. "I have a client looking for something very specific. He thinks you might have it."

"What's that?"

"A piece of jewellery."

Her face showed a minimum of curiosity, but nothing more.

"Really? What might that be?"

"A jade butterfly."

The gun swung determinedly up and stayed a few inches from his face.

"What is this?"

"We can make a deal," he said, trying for an easy tone.

Her eyes narrowed, wary, an animal cornered. "What deal would that be?"

"It's simple," he said. "I'll give you the information in exchange for money and the butterfly. My client says he gave it to you. Now he wants it back."

"He said he wants it back?" Her breath came out in a whisper.

"Yes."

"Did he tell you what it is?"

Dan tried to look noncommittal. "A family heirloom."

"I don't believe this. Who are you really?"

Her hand was shaking. *Not a good sign*, Dan thought.

"You know my background. The rest is unimportant."

"Yes, you're a guy who doesn't seem to exist outside of a very cheesy website. And these days anybody can buy Facebook friends with a convincing history."

Fucking CSIS, Dan thought. *Can't they get anything right?*

Her voice rose. "Leave here now or I will kill you."

Whether or not she would actually go through with it seemed secondary to the fact that he'd overstepped his bounds and they both knew it. Dan exited the restaurant and stumbled out onto the streets, looking around as he went, convinced that every other person hanging about was a CSIS agent following him.

He tried to clear his head, to think. The butterfly had to be far more important than Ren let on to send her into such a panic. What now? He would have to lie to Steve to buy time until he could decide what to do. He could simply say Ling hadn't showed up or that she hadn't accepted the USB stick. Would he buy it? Maybe at first, but sooner or later Ling would tell her contact the deal had fallen through because of him. Because he'd pressured her about the jade butterfly. Before long, CSIS would realize there was no money forthcoming over the proposed sale and therefore nothing they could pin on her. Then they would make him pay. They could make sure Ren was shipped out of the country with all kinds of incriminating evidence to cause trouble for him when he arrived back in China. For his part, the threat of Dan's visit to Matt Parks's studio still loomed over him. If it came to that, he could likely prove he was innocent of the murder, but he'd still be up on charges of break and enter. Not to mention the effect it would have on his personal and professional reputation. Either way, he was screwed.

He still had an ace up his sleeve: the USB drive hidden in his safe back at the warehouse. Whatever was on it, CSIS would not be able to blackmail him so long as he could prove he was being coerced to do their dirty work.

Twenty-Seven

A Good Man

The dream was a killer. Literally. One moment he was floating high in the air, looking down. The next he lay prone on the warehouse floor, looking up with a vague notion that he was waiting for Tracy Cunningham. But it wasn't Tracy who appeared; it was Ling Siu. She stood over him, swaying seductively. Dan felt her hands on his chest, drawing him up with superhuman strength. She set him upright and kissed him. Her lips moved hungrily over his face and mouth as he struggled in her embrace. That was when he glimpsed it: a turquoise butterfly tattooed on her collarbone.

Her expression turned fierce. "Don't look!" she hissed.

The voice was disembodied, as though it came from a distance. Only it was a man's voice, Dan realized, adapting to the dream's logic. He freed himself from her grip and stepped back, but he couldn't make out her face distinctly. One moment he was looking at Ling Siu, the next she seemed to have transformed into her brother.

Ren hovered in and out of sight, demanding to know where his sister had gone. Dan shook his head. "She just disappeared," he explained. Ren gripped his throat and squeezed. "You lost her!" he shouted. Struggling to free himself, Dan lashed out. His arm passed right through Ren's body. Ren's eyes closed as he slid to the floor. Dan glanced down: his fist held a knife.

Ren lay dying on the floor. With a cry, Dan turned the blade on himself and felt the point pierce his belly. He thrust upward, his viscera spilling out, purple intestines uncoiling at his feet. Suddenly, he was in a familiar dreamscape staring at a bucket on a distant shore. He found himself trying to gather his guts in the child's pail, panicked at how they kept slipping from his grasp.

Dan woke, gasping for breath, his stomach tied in knots. He was terrified and half surprised to find himself alive and in bed. It had felt that real. He reached over to the sideboard and gripped the bottle of pills. One hadn't been enough. How many would it take to obliterate the dreams? Four? Six? More than that? He threw the bottle at the waste basket. It missed and skidded across the floor.

He groaned and rolled onto his back. He thought of the dream tattoo, recalling his conversation with Ling the previous afternoon. She'd looked terrified when he mentioned the butterfly. Was it much more valuable than he'd been led to believe? If so, why had Ren lied about its worth? Maybe he didn't want Dan to know its true value, fearing he might be tempted to keep it for himself once he got it from Ling. *If* he got it from Ling. Judging by her reaction, that didn't seem likely.

He got out of bed. The dream had been among the worst ever. Maybe Doctor Chranos was right: he drank to blot out the visions and dull the memories. It hadn't been from a love of alcohol, but a form of unconscious suicide. His defences had come down when he stopped drinking and now the dreams were coming on strong, night after night. He didn't think he could take much more.

He stumbled to the kitchen and made himself coffee. Extra strong. It started to have the desired effect. When he was sufficiently awake, Dan called Donny. No answer. His list of people to lean on in times of need wasn't long, and he didn't feel like confiding in Kendra at the moment.

He found Doctor Chranos's card tucked in the back of his wallet and dialled the number. He was already composing a message in his head when, to his surprise, she picked up.

He identified himself and heard her pause.

"I've been thinking about you," she said. "How are you doing?"

"Not much change. I'm feeling a little worse, if anything, but thanks for asking. I've been thinking of what you said about taking regular sessions with you." He paused. "I still can't afford it, but I can't afford to crack up, either."

"Did something happen?"

He ignored her question.

"Are there other circumstances that might get me put higher up on the help list?"

"Such as?"

"What if I'm a danger to myself?"

She paused.

"That is a very serious consideration. If I felt you were, I would be legally obligated to inform someone of your mental state. Is that what you want me to do?"

"No."

"In what sense do you think you might be a danger to yourself?"

"I committed hara-kiri in a dream. In a nightmare, I mean."

She laughed. "Well, they can't incarcerate you for something you did in a dream. Is that something you think you might contemplate in real life?"

He ignored her again, not wanting to be put off a second time.

"I have this ... this darkness inside me, for want of a better word. I don't know where it comes from, but it comes at me and strangles me every night while I sleep."

He waited, hoping she would give him something — *anything* — to help him find a way to shake off his torment.

Her words were slow and measured. "In my experience, sometimes the darkness is already within us, only we don't always recognize it. In PTSD sufferers, the answer is to accept it as a legitimate part of your makeup rather than some external enemy you're fighting. If you embrace it, at least on a symbolic level, then you might be able to stop struggling with it."

Dan thought it over. In his estimation darkness was a bearing, an inclination, not a pose dressed up in a leather costume. It lay inside you, inhabited you deep down, and took up residence in some subconscious netherworld. A little alcohol or a few drugs, and suddenly the dragon guarding the entrance to the cave lay down and took a nap while the other you came out to play. It explained his moodiness, his snappishness, his anger and impatience. It was a form of possession, the bogeyman your mother warned you about. It was a pail lying empty at the edge of a lake. Only it lay within, waiting for you to let your guard down. Dr. Jekyll, meet Mr. Hyde.

"I can't tell you what to do," she continued, "but I think you need to face your demons and come to terms with what you call 'the darkness.'"

"I've been facing them for a long time —"

"Excuse me, but I think you've been avoiding them. Possibly even denying them. You said you have a drinking habit —"

"*Had* a drinking habit. That's over now."

"Which is why the darkness has come out. You're no longer hiding from it."

"And what happens if I face it?" He paused. "Never mind, I know you can't answer that for me. I won't really know for sure until I do, right?"

"Something like that. If we already knew what was going to happen to us, what would be the point in living?"

He took that for humour.

She went on. "You have a good life and a family who love you —"

"Sometimes I'm afraid I don't really know how to love."

"You said you loved your son more than anything. You also said you have a best friend you would miss desperately if he left you for any reason. I think that's love."

"Maybe, except my son has been acting strange lately, and one day he'll grow up and leave home. His mother and I have been arguing over her new boy-friend. She thinks I don't want Kedrick — my son — to explore his Muslim heritage, but that's not true. My friend Donny has his own life to live, like everyone else. He's not always available, either."

"Those are bumps in the road. It doesn't mean you're alone on it."

He considered this. "I know I'm good at what I do. I just don't know if I'm a good person. A good father, a good lover."

"Look in the faces of those you love and trust. I'm sure you'll see the love and trust reflected back. If that doesn't tell you then nothing will."

He took this in.

She continued. "What I know is this: life does not

deal everyone a good hand. You cannot defeat life, you cannot conquer it, you cannot stop and do it over. You can only accept it and live it for what it is, for good or for bad. But you can't avoid it by hiding on an island or cover it up with alcohol or sleeping pills, as you're beginning to realize."

Dan felt angry at being summed up so neatly. "You're wrong. It's not about avoiding things. It's about what I can bear. Forgive me."

"I'm sorry. I wasn't trying to tell you how you feel." She paused. "You mentioned a man you were interested in when we last spoke. How is that going?"

"It's complicated." He didn't feel like going into it. "He's been out of town. I haven't seen him much lately."

She tried to sound optimistic, a kindly therapist encouraging a lacklustre client.

"Try to stick with it. Although relationships can be fraught with issues — sometimes even dangerous emotions — my belief is that our relationships save us when all else fails."

"That's good advice," Dan said, thinking it was pretty much what Donny had been preaching to him.

"What's his name?" she asked.

"Ren Hao."

There was a silence.

"Say it again?"

He pronounced Ren's name slowly. "My Chinese isn't that good," he told her.

"No," she agreed, as though thinking something through. "Are you sure that's his name?"

"Yes," Dan said. "Why? Am I mispronouncing it?"

"Not at all. You're pronouncing it perfectly." She paused. "Only it's not a name."

"What is it?"

"I think it might be a joke," she told him. "It means, 'The Good Man.'"

Dan felt almost catapulted to his feet. He'd never done a reverse lookup on Ren, whereas normally he would have asked for a full accounting of any client asking for an investigation. He was suddenly faced with the prospect of a client without an identity. *I am your good man*, Ren had told him.

"I … I have to go, but thanks. For taking time to talk to me."

"Call me again if you need to. I'll think about what I can do to get you on a list."

"Thank you."

Twenty-Eight

Cooking for One

No food courts this time. Steve had him on the phone. The message was clear: *Don't screw up again*.

"I don't know what the hell you told her, but you clearly freaked her out. She doesn't trust you. What the hell were you thinking?" he demanded.

"I have my own agenda," Dan told him.

There was a ferociousness to Steve's voice he hadn't anticipated. "Not on my turf you don't!"

Dan paused before he spoke again, his voice clear and cool. "I'm not one of your employees. You coerced me into going along with this. You shouldn't be surprised I'm not too happy about it."

There was a spluttering on the other end.

"She'll meet you in your warehouse at eleven tonight. I've sent you an email with the details. This is your last chance. And bring the fucking USB drive to give her this time. Do it our way or we will make things very difficult. Is that understood?"

Dan hesitated.

"Are you still there?" Steve asked.

"There may be a complication," he said slowly.

"What complication?"

"I'm not sure that my client is who he claims to be."

Steve seemed to be considering the pronouncement carefully. "Are you saying he's not Ling Siu's brother?"

"I don't know."

Dan told him what he'd learned about Ren's name. Steve was quiet for a long while then said, "We have intelligence that suggests your client is not simply a Chinese diplomat, as he claims."

"What the hell does that mean? What is he?"

"It's possible your client has been trying to make contact with this woman for reasons we don't precisely know about just yet."

Dan thought again of the mysterious butterfly.

"What sort of reasons? Are you saying he's a spy, too?"

"I don't know."

Dan groaned. "I have a dinner date with him tonight. What am I supposed to say to him?"

"Listen very carefully. The important thing is that you don't alert him to anything. Don't let him know that you know Ren Hao isn't his real name. Don't let him know you suspect anything. And most of all, don't cancel. Just meet him and try to be as casual as you can."

"How the hell can I act casual with him?"

"Just do what you do best. Have sex."

"Fuck you."

"No, fuck him."

Dan was silent.

"Don't lose your nerve now. Tell him you will put him in touch with his sister. Agree to whatever he wants. Apart from missing his long-lost sister, why do you think he wants to find her?"

"He says she owes him something. A family heirloom. It's a piece of jewellery. He wants it back."

"Then tell him you'll get it for him. Just go along with whatever he wants and make him think you believe whatever he says. We need to catch them in the act."

"What act?"

"Whatever they're up to."

Dan's head was reeling.

"When are you meeting him?" Steve asked.

"Tonight at six. I'm supposed to go to his hotel."

"Fine, that gives you the perfect opportunity to end things early. Tell him you're going to meet his sister. Watch his reaction."

Ren met him at the door dressed only in a bathrobe. He was on the phone, speaking Chinese. He ended the conversation and pocketed his cell.

"A colleague," he said apologetically.

"Everything okay?"

Ren smiled. "Yes, all is good, especially now that you are here, tough man. Please, one moment more."

Dan watched as he peeled off the robe and hung it

on the door then stepped into the shower. The whoosh of water started up. The blinds were drawn, as though he'd suddenly acquired a sense of modesty.

Ren's laptop lay open on the table. Dan touched the mouse pad. The screensaver dissolved, leaving an idyllic Chinese landscape open to view: pink-and-white cherry blossoms, geese flying overhead, towering mountain peaks in the background. Tucked inside the case was a passport. He picked it up and thumbed through it. There was Ren's photo and his name in Chinese and English: *Ren Hao*. It might not be his real name, but it was his official name, as far as the Chinese government was concerned. There was a stamp when he'd entered Canada a month earlier. There were similar stamps for Hong Kong and Singapore. He flipped through the thickened pages. There was nothing on the date he claimed to have left for Berlin. In fact, there was no German stamp anywhere in the document. Nor was there a return entry.

The shower's soft whoosh left off. Dan put the passport back and busied himself with a magazine. After a moment Ren emerged, vigorously drying himself. He wrapped himself in a towel and stood there, muscles glistening.

"Sometimes I forget this is a hotel and not my home," he said. "Everything changes around me, but it still feels like a home when I return here."

Dan was struggling to stay calm, trying not to betray his suspicions. "When was the last time you went back to China?" he asked.

"Last year," Ren replied. "When I go home now, I do not feel comfortable with the old ways. It is like I do not know the people anymore."

"I can understand that," Dan said. "Sometimes it feels like you never really know people at all."

Ren smiled. "Shall I cook for you?"

"Thanks," Dan said, "but I had a late lunch."

"Then if you will excuse me, I have not eaten in many hours."

He went to the kitchen. The sweetish aroma of soy and sesame filled the air. Ren returned with a bowl of small white dumplings. Dan watched as he deftly scissored one with chopsticks and put it in his mouth.

"Pork and mushroom," Ren said, setting the bowl down. "Very tasty."

He reached behind him and opened a cupboard. A long, tapering bottle sat on the shelf. He splashed a dark yellow liqueur into two short-stemmed glasses.

Ren held out both glasses. "Chinese herbal liquor," he said simply. "Good for the digestion."

Dan hesitated, then chose the one in his left hand. He watched as Ren put the other to his lips and drank. Dan raised the glass and sniffed. Something pungent and potent. He drained it and set it aside.

"I found your sister," Dan told him, thinking suddenly of Ling's exquisite beauty and how much she resembled her brother.

Ren's eyebrows raised. "This is very good news. How did you find her? Was it through the photographer you mentioned?"

Dan shook his head. "No, not him."

"Do you know for sure it was her?"

"Yes, I'm sure it was her. She showed me the jade butterfly," he replied, taking a stab in the dark.

Ren gave him a searching look. "She showed it to you?"

"Yes."

"What did you think of it?"

"It's … incredibly beautiful," Dan said. "Like your sister. I understand why you want it back."

Ren smiled. "I am glad you understand. And she has agreed to meet with me?"

"Yes, she will meet with you."

"When will you bring me to her?"

"As soon as I can."

"I am grateful. I knew that you would find her for me."

Ren took Dan's hand and pulled him to his feet. Nimble fingers undid his shirt buttons, the clasp on his belt. Ren's towel fell to the floor. They stood naked together.

Ren seemed to be watching him for a sign. "And now maybe we shall take this to the next level? This fascination for pain we have between us?"

It was formed as a question, but it sounded like a challenge. Ren opened a bedside drawer and tenderly withdrew a knife, fastidious as a stamp collector handling a pre-war rarity. The handle was carved ivory inlaid with silver. The blade lay across his palms. He bowed his head.

"Make me fear you."

Dan took the knife and set it aside.

"I don't want you to be afraid of me."

"Please!"

Dan ran a hand over Ren's chest and down his stomach, stroking the muscles like a delicate vase. Ming dynasty, irreplaceable. When what was wanted was the courage to smash it.

Ren gripped his wrists. "Not easy. Hard!"

He flung Dan's hands aside and snatched the knife. The movement was so quick Dan was afraid he would cut himself. Ren held it between them, blade flat, turning the edge first toward Dan then back on himself. His eyes glowed.

"This is the thrill for us. It is the secret fear of giving up that which we value most: control." Ren smiled his cruel smile. "This is what excites you. How far will you go? How much of yourself will you sacrifice to please me?"

Dan breathed in the scent of fine soap, crisp linen. Clean things begging to be soiled, desecrated. Something roiled up inside him, countering his desire with feelings of revulsion.

"I don't want to hurt you."

"No, tough man, but you want to please me. That is your nature, is it not? I have seen inside your head. If you wish to please me then you must hurt me. In this you shall discover your hidden depths."

"What if I don't like what I discover?"

"Then you must live with the knowledge of who

you really are. You alone know what you are capable of."

"What are you capable of?"

Ren smiled again. "I am capable of many things. As I said, I am a very possessive person. But sometimes I also wish to be possessed. By you."

He pressed the ivory handle into Dan's palm. It fit perfectly as he turned the blade toward Dan and drew it across his chest. A thin red line appeared in its path, almost as an afterthought. Dan looked down at his broken skin, the knife in his hand. He flung it aside and heard it clatter against the wall.

Ren pulled him down onto the bed, forcing them together until Dan gave in to the urge. He closed his eyes, listening for a sound to drown the voices of dissent inside, the slow burn scorching his mind and body. He strained, muscles tautened, until he collapsed with a groan. Disgusted, he rolled over and lay on his back, his chest heaving. There. It was over. He'd tried. It hadn't worked. He hadn't discovered any secret vices or vicarious appetites. There were no repulsive fascinations inside him waiting for release. Despite his rugged looks and threatening countenance, what he really wanted was to soothe, to offer a balm for the wounded. To give pleasure. At least he knew what he was, as boring as it may have been to others. Too much vanilla never hurt a man. He would get up, dress and leave the hotel, never seeing this man again, whoever he was.

Then he felt the click. Something snapped in his brain, tuning into a different wavelength. He threw

Ren against the headboard with the force of a mad-
man. A fury whirled inside him as he faced the task,
remorseless and sobering, of plumbing the depths of
his being. Darkness is a dazzle, a thrill. To the uninitiated it's slyer than sly, cozying up in unassuming
ways until you forget it's there. Slowly, quietly, it
filters into your unconscious, slips inside your mind
and unsettles your thoughts, till it emerges unbidden,
lighting up your darkest nightmares like a full moon
at Hallowe'en.

Something crackled at the back of his brain. The
angels had flown, shedding their feathers for scales.
His train was jumping tracks while an animal anger
pulsed in his blood, veins throbbing, synapses spew-
ing sparks in an orgy of sensation. A welder's torch
catching fire. Anima rising. Danger. A system overload
seared his brain in a netherworld of loathing as he
sought to quell his desires. It was a ride through hell.
He fought it then finally surrendered to it, rising up,
rusted. A shell. A bottomless bucket left sitting on the
shore. His life emptied again and again while he lifted
it and watched in horror as the water rushed out. No
future. No life. No love. Empty.

Grief had made him one of the walking dead.

He saw now that he was right back where he
started, before all the therapy, before all the searching for answers. Lost in his own private hell. You
thought hell was other people? Hell was living inside
your nightmares for so long you come to hate your
own shadow, fearing going to bed each night for who

you might meet there. Nothing to look forward to but some kind of an end.

From a distance, he heard Ren speaking.

"Ah! It was simply your ego I need to bypass to get you to perform," he said.

I'm not a performing animal, Dan thought, though he was unable to voice the words. He was conscious of Ren looking down on him with that beauty you could drown yourself in. Something to make you forget your troubles, to click your heels and never go home again. He lay back and fell into a dreamless sleep.

Twenty-Nine

The Jade Butterfly

He knew he'd find them in the warehouse. The taxi ride over was a torment, each jostle and jolt a minor earthquake. Whatever Ren put in his drink had knocked Dan for a loop. His vision was fuzzy. His fingers fumbled the entry code as the cab spun off. There was no sign of CSIS as he glanced around the empty streets.

Low-energy bulbs cast a sickly sheen on the lobby walls. The office exuded a derelict feel, like the ruins of some ancient civilization recently unearthed by unknown hands and returned to the light after centuries of abandonment. Attempting to sprint down the hallway, he banged into a wall. His head pounded as he approached the warehouse. Whatever Ren wanted from his sister, whatever unfinished business lay between them was about to have its due behind that door.

Dan looked over his shoulder. Still no CSIS. And what was worse, he was entering a dead zone. No way to call for help once he was inside. He reached for the handle and pushed. The vaulted ceiling stretched overhead. It was darker than the day he'd found Tracy waiting for him.

He heard them talking before he saw them. They were at the far end of the room. Ren barely glanced over as Dan approached. Ling was seated at a metal table where the day workers sat and played cards to while away the hours, which in Dan's estimation always whiled themselves away whether you did any-thing about it or not.

At first glance, the pair seemed to be contem-plating one another like lovers sharing an intimate moment in public. It was only when she looked up that Dan saw Ling was terrified. Then he saw the cords. She was bound to the chair, hands and feet. At first, Dan couldn't piece things together. Ren seemed to be supplicating to her, showing her the utmost courtesy and respect, apart from granting her release. His pos-ture was servile, like a waiter attending to the smallest needs of a revered guest.

In a flash, Dan understood: Ren had recreated their childhood game, Going to Kowloon Café. But what did he hope to gain from this? He looked to Ling for a clue. There was a bruise on her cheek. Maybe she'd refused to reveal the location of the jade butterfly.

"I wish to thank you, Daniel," Ren said, address-ing him at last. He was focused intently on the figure before him. "You have brought my sister back from the dead for me."

"Let her go, Ren. Whatever you want, I'm sure she'll give it to you."

"Sadly, I cannot. Not after all this time." He touched his sister's face gently. She flinched. "All this time that I have been waiting for her to return to me."

"I would never return to you!" she spat out quietly.

"No," Ren said. "Nor to your country. You are a traitor. You have betrayed our homeland."

Dan edged closer to the table. Ren raised the knife. It glittered in the light, smaller and more intricately ornamented than the one that had accompanied their bedroom play, but just as deadly looking. Dan froze.

"You see, Daniel? I know how you think. I know how you will react. After all that we have been through, I am inside your head now."

"Listen to me. I want you to leave her alone. I'll help you with whatever you want."

Ren shook his head. "You have done your job. Now I want you to go away."

"Please don't go!" Ling pleaded.

"What do you want from her?" Dan asked. "What can she possibly do for you?"

"She can return what she has taken from me. Something very precious."

"I'm sure she'll give it back to you. Just let her go."

Ren turned to his sister and spoke in Chinese. His voice was gentle, his expression kindly. A look of disgust crept over Ling's face.

"That was not love. What you did destroyed me. I couldn't stand it when you touched me."

Dan felt the revulsion as understanding dawned. "You were sleeping with your sister?"

"We loved one another," Ren said softly.

"So much so that she fled China to escape you and didn't try to make contact once in over twenty years."

Ren turned, his face twisted with anger. "You know nothing."

"Please don't let him hurt me," Ling cried.

Ren turned back to her, his voice a caress. "Let us pretend, sister. Pretend we are at the Kowloon Café. Once again, after all these years. There is so much food. More food than we can possibly want. You can choose anything you wish from a very long and impressive menu. I will make whatever dishes you desire."

Ling whimpered as Ren gestured with the knife.

"Tell me what you wish to have from all these delights."

"I don't want anything from you," she told him.

"Then it is simple. We shall proceed to the end of our dinner together. Now let us imagine the jade butterfly. It is so beautiful, this symbol of our enduring love. I will place it around your neck. It will bind you to me forever."

"No, please!"

"Close your eyes and imagine, sister. Think of the jade butterfly, this symbol of our devotion."

Ling struggled against her bonds as Ren stepped behind her. Bending his head to the knife, he brushed it with his lips then slid it across his sister's throat. Dan saw the startled look on her face, the red ring forming and growing, the convulsions as her body tried to function and failed.

"No!"

The uselessness of that single syllable had never been so apparent to him. Except it hadn't come from him. Nor had it come from the dying Ling or even her brother, who stood watching her.

Dan glanced up, saw the childish face on the upper walkway, saw her eyes wide with terror as she aimed her father's gun. The shot felled Ren instantly. All of this in a heartbeat.

The girl's sobbing sounded in Dan's ears as he ran to Ling and tried to stop the flow of blood with his hands. He saw the light dimming in her eyes, felt her slipping away.

Everything began to move, forms appearing in the darkness as though leaking through from another dimension. Someone went up to relieve Tracy of the gun, shepherding her out the door and away from her ill-advised hiding place. Somehow, Dan didn't know how, Steve Ross was there, pulling him away from Ling's unresponsive body.

"Where the fuck were you?" Dan demanded. "Why weren't you in here sooner?"

Steve looked chagrined as he glanced around. "It doesn't always go as well as you hope."

Dan pulled himself free of his grasp. "You knew this was going to happen?"

Steve fixed Dan with a reproachful stare. "Not like this, no. But we had to let them meet. Even if you hadn't come into the picture, we would have risked it regardless. It's too bad you didn't kill him for us earlier. You could have saved us a lot of trouble."

Others arrived on the scene, moving about in hazmat suits, their feet wrapped in blue plastic.

"Clean this up," Steve directed.

"What?" Dan shook his head. "This is a murder scene. You can't —"

Steve held up a warning hand. "Don't get involved."

Dan watched as one of the men put a finger to Ling's throat. He looked at Steve and shook his head. Next he went over to Ren and did the same.

"Kid's a good shot," he said.

Dan watched as two paramedics began arranging Ren's body, folding his arms over his chest. Ren's face was splattered with blood. The half-moon lips twitched involuntarily. For a moment, it looked as if he were still alive.

Not dead.

Dan sat on the floor and cradled his head. Nothing had been real. Not the food, that was only pretend. Not the Kowloon Café. That was in Hong Kong. Not a Taiwanese businessman. Not Ren Hao. Not even a Chinese diplomat.

And not love. No, certainly not that.

Steve looked around, perplexed. "Just one thing I'm not clear on. Where is this jade butterfly he was after?"

Dan shook his head. "I don't ..." He stopped. He'd been about to say he didn't know, but in fact he did. "It didn't exist. It was a game the two of them played as kids. Everything was imaginary between them."

"Hmm." Steve appeared to contemplate this. "Odd. Though I'm still not sure why he killed Matt Parks."

"Jealousy," Dan ventured. "I think he discovered he had an affair with his sister."

"Hmm," Steve said again. "Anyway, don't feel sorry for him."

"I don't."

Steve nodded to Dan. "You'd better go."

Dan glanced over at Ling. Her head was slumped forward on her chest.

"Will you tell the papers she died of a drug overdose, too? Or will you just say she slit her own throat?"

"We'll tell them whatever we like. We've got an international political situation on our hands and I've got to deal with it. A Chinese agent just killed a CSIS agent."

"What?" Dan wasn't sure he'd heard correctly. "She was CSIS?"

"You heard me: one of theirs just killed one of ours."

"You said she was a Chinese spy!"

Steve sighed, looking down at the bodies. "Yes, that. Well, not exactly true."

"Then she didn't join the Chinese Security Forces to free her parents from jail?"

"No. He turned his parents in when he learned they helped his sister disappear. "They were both tortured and died in jail not long after Tiananmen."

"But you said the sentences were commuted after a year. Ren told me his father survived...!" Dan stopped. It was pointless. Just stories within stories." "You used me."

Steve shrugged. "You're not the first."

"What's to stop me from saying anything about what I know?"

"Don't be stupid. If we thought you were a threat, you wouldn't be standing here now."

One of the men came over and handed Steve a manila envelope. Dan looked over and saw the door of his safe hanging open.

"Close that," Steve said. He turned to Dan. "By the way, there's nothing on this, if you were thinking it could save you."

"So it was all a farce?"

"Yes, it was."

Dan shook his head. "Then how could you not have known about the butterfly?"

"She never mentioned it. We overheard him telling you about it in one of your conversations. I thought it might intrigue you to think it was her code name. And she wasn't dating Matt Parks, either. She was investigating him, no matter what her brother believed. That's how she ended up at his studio the night he was murdered."

"She let him photograph her. She said she fell in love with him."

"Cover story, probably. But if she did fall for him then she overstepped her bounds."

"Did she know it was her brother you were after?"

Steve looked embarrassed. "I shouldn't —"

Dan nodded. "She thought I was the target, didn't she? She didn't know anything about her brother till I mentioned the jade butterfly the other day."

Steve sighed. "You nearly blew things for us. It was all I could do to calm her down and get her to agree to meet you again. We knew he would eventually come after her. It was just a matter of time. He let his obsessions get the better of him. A dangerous quality in someone trained to suppress emotion."

"How did he know Ling was here? In the warehouse? I didn't tell him."

Steve coughed. "He replicated your laptop. We think he was following the email trail we sent you."

"How? When could he have done that?"

"Not long after you had him over to your house, is my best guess. You might want to invest in a proper alarm system."

Dan thought back. He'd introduced Ren to Ralph the night he brought him home. Ren would have had no problem getting back into Dan's house on his own on a subsequent visit. Ralph would only have been too obliging to a family friend.

"You knew all this."

Steve said nothing.

"You're a disgusting bastard," Dan said.

"Keep the sentiment to yourself. Don't think that I

won't grieve for a fallen comrade, but that's the nature of the business. Just remember, if you do anything stupid, you could find yourself answering for the murder of Matt Parks."

Steve turned to watch his men restoring and cleaning the room. He glanced back at Dan after a moment.

"Are you still here? Go away. Now."

Dan shook his head in bewilderment.

"I don't know who you are," Steve said. "We've never met."

Epilogue

Found

The barbecue was sizzling, flames shooting up past burgers and sausages before retreating back through the grill. Dan looked around at the overgrown shrubbery, trellises weighed down by the weight of clematises and roses. With all the distractions of the last month, he'd barely looked at it. Suddenly there was a jungle in his backyard.

Donny glanced over from the barbecue, waving a long-handled spatula. He was wrapped in a long, green apron with a floppy chef's hat on his head. It was the most unfashionable Dan had ever seen him.

"Happy birthday!" Donny called out. "The others will be here any minute."

Dan wandered over. "Thanks for arranging all of this," he said.

"Your son had a big part in it, so be sure to thank him, too."

"Will do. I'm not sure I'm in the mood for a party, but I'll try to fake it."

"Okay, so not a birthday then. Happy cake and candle day." He cocked an eye at Dan. "You're taking this awfully hard. Life isn't over yet."

Dan hadn't divulged the full story to Donny. He'd simply said that things hadn't worked out between him and Ren. For the first time since he could remember, he hadn't felt up to disclosing the truth to his closest friend. There was that, as well as the paper he'd signed agreeing not to disclose anything about his recent experiences with a certain secret security organization in return for an admission that he hadn't been involved in any wrongdoing. He had considered holding out ... briefly. But Ren and Ling were already dead. There was nothing he could do to change that. Not signing the paper would simply have left him in jeopardy and done nothing to hurt CSIS, despite anything he might have revealed. It would hold up in court, if it ever came to that.

Donny flipped a burger and looked it over with an appraising eye. "It's probably for the best. I never liked this S&M thing between the two of you. I know you never actually called it that, but it wasn't healthy. Besides, you have a history of dating losers."

Dan gave him a look.

"Apart from Trevor, that is, who was a real gentleman and a wonderful human being. It's just too bad the good get picked off so easily." Donny shrugged. "You're a wounded soul and you need to recognize that. But there's one thing I know — we will get through this together. We are family and that means thick and thin." He flipped another burger. With barely a pause he shifted tone and theme. "If there's anything you're not telling me, I'll assume you have a good reason. Ren wasn't into kids, I hope?"

"No. And his name wasn't really Ren."

"Not Ren? As in Not Philip?"

"Correct."

"Are you still over your head in love with him?"

"No ... I don't think I really knew him at all."

"Ah! Then it *is* worse than what you told me. Let it go. Remember — there are no mistakes, just a lot of bad boyfriends." He winked. "I'd still like to hear the details one day, if you're up to telling me about it."

Dan shook his head. "I can't, I'm sorry."

"Top secret?"

"Something like that."

"Okay, so long as it's not child porn or drugs."

Dan paused too long.

"Tell me it's not," Donny insisted.

"No, it's not. I swear."

"Okay then. More than that I don't need to know." Donny pulled a cigarette from his pack. "Anyway I'm glad, because I wouldn't want to have to tell you off on your not-birthday."

He lit it, exhaled and relaxed visibly.

Dan watched him. "Isn't it time I told you off for once? You should stop smoking."

"Any fool can quit," Donny scoffed. "It takes a real man to face cancer."

The patio doors slid open and Kendra swept through, a vision in yellow. She came up and gave them both a kiss. "My, what gorgeous men!" she exclaimed.

Donny smiled. "We're the ones who should be paying you compliments, sugar. You are simply ravishing."

"Thank you."

Dan looked over her shoulder. There was no one trailing her.

Kendra shook her head. "He's not coming."

"Why? I told you to invite him."

"He's gone." She smiled sadly. "For good, I mean. I let him go. It was too much for me to go back to those old ways, those old values. Every time he started to pray ..." She shrugged. "He was a good man, just not for me. I'm a modern girl, after all."

Dan smiled.

"And there's the proof," she said, gazing across the yard at Ked, who had arrived through the side gate with an attractive young woman by his side.

Ked waved tentatively, as though shy in this girl's presence.

Dan took her in: slender face, dark hair, and laughing eyes. It was intriguing to see his son's taste in women. Ked brought her over and introduced her to his father, mother, and Uncle Donny. There was no unnecessary explaining or even an acknowledgement that they weren't a real family in any way. Because what else were they, if not a real family? Dan found himself unexpectedly thinking of Ling and Ren. *All our broken lives*, he reflected. *What do they add up to?* Maybe it wasn't about perfection or even about the whole, he mused. Maybe it was about how the pieces added up to some kind of continuity over time. Or more than a continuity, a succession of loves and lives. At least there was something to be salvaged from the loss, the relentless trail of disappointments left behind.

Dan looked over at Kendra. She wasn't his wife, but perhaps she was something more. There was a community here in this coming together of a man and woman to make a child. There was something that said maybe this was the way things progressed, how we got better as a country, as a race, and moved forward slowly, however glacial the pace.

Ralph came over to greet the newcomer, accepting her into his domain, his sphere of guardianship. It was as though he knew the place she was being asked to fill in the arrangement. She bent down and scratched his neck. Ralph bounded off, the two youngsters following him for a look at the garden.

"I regret a lot of things in my life, but not you and Ked," Dan said

"I feel the same," Kendra said.

Donny leaned in to confide in them. "Looks like your son has good taste in women."

"Isn't it great?" Kendra asked.

"Oh, by the way," Donny said. "I invited someone tonight." He checked his cellphone. "He'll be here in about half an hour."

"Someone special?" Dan asked.

"Very special. In fact, you've already met."

Dan gave him an inquisitive look.

"Don't tell me ... the Hindu god? Not Philip?"

"Correct, only he's Prabin again. He's trying to get it right this time. He actually wants to try exclusive dating. With me."

"Congratulations!"

"Thank you. Only ..."

"Only what?"

Donny shrugged and looked off.

"I just wish he had a flaw — wide hips, a squat nose — anything to say he's not too impossibly beautiful to have. Alas, I can find nothing. I shall have to wait thirty years for his beauty to diminish to see that happen."

"And this too shall pass ..." Dan murmured.

"What was that?"

"Nothing. But I think it's only fair to remind you of something you said recently: relationships are dangerous."

Donny laughed. "Oh! Don't I know it!"

Dan looked across the yard at his son and the girl. He wanted to warn them both. He wanted to tell them about the shocks and jolts they were inevitably going to have to endure, and how it could destroy your love and deaden your spirit if you weren't careful. Then he thought of himself and Kendra, two disparate spirits who had produced another human being without ever actually being a couple, except in the most modern and transcendental sense of the

word. What did that betoken? Perhaps Ked and this
girl, or some other girl to come, would make something of themselves together. Maybe they could avoid
the wrangling and the fighting, Dan thought, if he
imparted whatever wisdom he had to his son, and
they chose not to think of each other in terms of ownership but in terms of a respectful partnership. As he
and Kendra had, more or less, managed to do. But
then what did that say about marriage? That it was
impossible, after all? That the moment you stopped
viewing it as an agreement and started thinking of
it as something personal you lost the battle? Maybe.
In any case, he was extremely grateful for his family,
who were here out of love and loyalty and respect
rather than need or obligation.

What, after all, was a family? He hadn't a clue.
His past included an alcoholic, philandering woman
who had died from neglect and her own wilful stupid-
ity by the age of thirty, and an emotionally stunted
father whose longest-lasting legacy to his son was a
scar that ran down the side of his face as a reminder
of the senseless brutality that awaited children
who didn't do what they were told. It wasn't much,
when all was said and done. But somehow Dan had
redeemed himself by finding a true and loyal friend
from a culture that was alien to his own, and a
woman, also from another race and culture, who had
given him the son he looked on as his life's greatest
accomplishment. That, then, was a family. And no
one could take it away.

Ralph barked, startling Dan out of his dreary thinking. *All well and good*, he thought. *But right now, there's a party going on.*

That night he dreamed he was on the shore of a lake where his mother had taken him when he was four years old. He couldn't see her, but he knew she was there. He felt the familiar sense of trepidation, saw the bucket sitting on the sand and the water lapping at its sides. The sun glinted down, throwing slivers of light into the air. They reflected off the galvanized steel, the white undulations painted around the rim.

He wondered why he felt drawn to lift it out of the water and clutch it in his arms. Then he remembered: *Don't lose it*, his mother had warned him. *We can never go home again without it.* But he'd left it behind on the shore of a lake, never to see it again. Not long after that, his mother died and his world fell apart. *It wasn't my fault*, he wanted to argue, but there was no one to listen even if he did.

He watched the bucket diligently all afternoon, fearful it would drift away if the waves got too big. He had lost it once before, but now here it was again. He knelt down and saw the water rushing inside in little swirls and curlicues, like a miniature world that contained all the promise of the future. His future. He wasn't going to lose it a second time.

The boy looked up. A lady was approaching from far down the shore. She was tall and beautiful, with a scarf tied around her neck. She seemed to be waving to him. He waved back, unsure of himself. She was a nice lady, he felt. She wasn't his mother, but he thought he knew her.

He watched as she walked right up to him and stood peering down.

"Are you afraid?" she asked.

He nodded.

"Don't worry," she said. "It's easy. You just have to understand that being brave starts when you realize you are no longer in control of everything."

The boy wasn't sure if he understood, but somehow it made sense.

She lifted her arms and laughed. "Yes, it's very easy."

She took his hands and placed them on the handle. He felt her strength pass through into his as she guided him. At first, the pail wouldn't move. It was wedged in the sand. Then suddenly it pulled free with a sucking sound, the shore caving in all around it. He felt a thrill and stood looking down at the bucket he held in his hands, the water sloshing inside. Careful, ever so careful, not to spill it.

Acknowledgements

Thanks to Brian Liu for sharing with me his personal account of the Tiananmen Protests. Thanks also to Louise Welsh for the first chapter title inspiration, to Farzana Doctor for offering her aesthetic and cultural insights, and to David Tronetti for letting me read the entire manuscript aloud to him. I am grateful for an Ontario Arts Council grant that afforded me the time to explore this story and to mine it for its fullest potential.

From *After the Horses*, Jeffrey Round's next Dan Sharp Mystery

Prologue: Toronto — 2010 Immigrants

Her breath came out in white flags as she huffed and chuffed through the snow. February was a hateful month. Inhuman. Icy and frozen over. It wasn't her fault, but that wouldn't make any difference. She was late and it wasn't for the first time. She knew it and he would know it, too. There was no use beating around the bush about it. Her feet trudged along as she willed them to hurry, watching warily for ice patches. No good falling and breaking her neck on top of everything else. That would be worse than losing her job. His words came back to her, spoken in the crisp, precise tones of someone who had learned English later in life: *I need punctual help, Sarah. I don't appreciate dawdlers, even if you're just cleaning my toilet. I expect you to be on time. Please don't let it happen again.*

Please. He'd said *please* at least.

Still, that wouldn't help her. He wasn't a kind man. From what she'd seen, there were no warm feelings stirring anywhere in his depths. Although he hadn't said what would happen if she showed up late again, she had a sinking feeling she was about to find out.

There was a snowman in one of the front yards. It reminded her of his tiny eyes and bushy beard, his round face, and bleak, humourless gaze. What was he again? Something Eastern European. Maleski. Macedonian? At least with some of the bastards she worked for she could have a laugh, even though they all knew very well they were exploiting her status as an illegal. And most of them were immigrants themselves!

All right, she would beg if she had to. Yes, she would beg. It wouldn't be the first time in her life. Long gone were the days when anyone might have tried to extort sex from her as penance. Not that this one ever did. He wasn't interested in her sex. She needed to remind him she was honest. She had that in her favour at least. Not one thing had gone missing by her hand in the two years she'd worked for him. She'd heard the stories from others she worked for, how the previous help had stolen and pillaged from them, taking what was not rightly theirs. If you asked her, they deserved a little extra for all the hours and all the labour they put in. But she would never stoop to stealing so long as she had food to eat and a roof over her head. She was poor, not desperate. She wouldn't allow such thoughts to stain her mind.

She scrubbed their toilets and mopped their floors and wiped their children's bums. She walked their pets and toted their liquor bottles out quietly by the back door so the neighbours couldn't see. There was no end to the services she offered. They all seemed to need something special. This one especially. With his wild parties and the boys coming and going at all hours, in all states of dress and inebriation and zgod knows what else. The tales she could tell, if she had the chance. She didn't condone their behaviour, God knew. She simply had no choice. She took the work they offered at the rate they paid and lived her life as quietly and piously as she could.

She shrugged.

Judge not.

The women were the worst. They expected perfection: floors you could eat off, countertops you could see your reflection in, toilets you could drink from. If they could, some might have asked her to screw their husbands to save them the bother. Some of them would be surprised to know she'd grown up with finery. As a girl, she'd had ball gowns and jewellery and cut flowers in the house. She had manners and once — *once!* — she'd been beautiful. Age had caught up with her, though. Even her hands were dreadful to look at now.

The men, at least, tried to make her feel human while they cheated her of decent working wages. Not this one, though. He was a cheat through and through.

Just like a woman himself, he was! Fancy clothes and expensive haircuts and all the trappings. He once told her how much he paid to have his hair done. She was shocked when he told her. With the cut and the tip added in, he left the shop an hour later $240 lighter in the pockets. And what did he give her for an afternoon's wages? A quarter of that. Without a tip.

It was no wonder everyone stole from him. He was a cheap bastard, no doubt about it. God knows it was true and forgive her for saying so. Once, when she arrived early and found him hungover, he told her about the boys who visited. How they took his baubles and stole his drugs. Boys he met who knew where, who ate his food and drank his alcohol, and still they had the nerve to steal from him. Because they could. And that dreadful one she'd run into early one morning, neither man nor woman. She could hardly countenance that. Nor how some of the worst ones who stole from him continued to come around afterward and help themselves to more. Because he let them. That beat everything! Desperate. He was. She didn't want to judge, but he was a homosexual. One of the Sodomites God saw fit to smite in the Bible.

Filth. And filth would always come to a bad end. There were drugs and diseases and worse. No, it was true that she could not choose her employers, but she could pray for her own salvation. This was God's test. She would not succumb to the temptation to steal, despite his terrible conduct as a human being. For the wages of sin is death.

She turned the corner onto Beatty Avenue, counting the steps to the large grey monolith. Built from stone in the last century. Three separate chimneys. Necessary, no doubt, back when people heated everything with coal and the rich had servants to stoke the fires for them. She shivered, grateful she lived now rather than then. It was difficult enough being poor today, never mind in the old days.

She let herself in the tall iron gates and pulled them closed behind her. Standing beside the gates she looked tiny, a dwarf approaching a witch's house. She crossed herself as she made her way up the walk, carefully navigating the flagstones. A single set of footsteps came and went. Otherwise, the snow lay undisturbed. At the top, she found the keys and pulled them from her purse. Late or not, she couldn't ring the doorbell and expect him to let her in. If she was lucky, he might still be in bed with one of his boys and not notice that she'd arrived — here she checked her watch — twenty-seven minutes late. Why did she have the misfortune to work for a man who obsessed over punctuality? All the others demanded of her was cleanliness. If she was lucky, he might already have left without waiting for her. In that case, she would find the instructions on a sheet of paper laid out on the kitchen table. It was as though she couldn't be trusted to see what needed cleaning. If he was out, he would never know she'd been late unless she told him. Which she wouldn't.

White lies. That's what her mother had called them. Cross your fingers behind your back. The door was double-locked. That only happened when Yuri went out of town, but he hadn't said anything about being away. He was a stickler for security. She knew he'd been burgled twice, because he made a point of telling her. His house was full of valuables: artwork, rare books, beautiful carpets, antique table settings, silverware. The sort of thing you saw in the best houses in Europe. All the doors and windows were alarmed. He made sure she knew that, too.

She took a step back and looked up at the house. Dark and unwelcoming, that's how she always saw it. The windows were exceptionally large, but even in daytime darkness showed behind them all. There was nothing for it but to go around to the back. She stepped off the front porch and made her way through the silent snow to the side and around the back.

No one had shovelled here, either. The snow was well over the tops of her boots. Last week's storm had blanketed the yard. No footsteps showed here. Not a soul had been around to this side of the house. She brushed aside the top of the drift and pulled open the rickety screen door, hoping she remembered the code. He usually reminded her of it when she was going to have to use it to get in, but he'd said nothing about it.

3-4-5-2.

The latch clicked and she pulled hard. That door had always given her trouble. The beep registered her entry. She knew she had twenty seconds to enter the code a second time to shut down the alarm or she'd have security swarming over the premises within minutes. She punched it in and the red light turned to green. Safe.

Inside, all was silent. That could be a lucky break. She looked briefly into the kitchen. Dirty dishes lay strewn on the countertop. He'd had another party, no surprise. She hoped she didn't find naked bodies lying around sleeping on the sofas and in the spare beds. It wouldn't be the first time.

Someone had emptied the ashtrays, at least. Probably the Cuban boy. He was one of the few who bothered to lift a hand around the place. He was polite to her, too. He once told her she reminded him of his mother. He was so masculine, you'd never think he was one of those. She sometimes wondered if it was only because of the citizenship. Yuri had taunted the poor boy by dangling citizenship in front of him at one point, but then they'd argued and the boy had been out of favour for the past few months. Maybe Yuri had changed his mind.

She set her purse on the counter then took off her gloves and coat, laying them on the big blue chair. She shivered. It was cold! She flicked the thermostat and heard the furnace starting up.

Still nothing from Yuri. If he wanted to fire her, surely he would have been there to meet her when she arrived. Or maybe he would let her finish her day's work then give her the sack. All right then, better to get started. She'd begin downstairs. First she cleaned the kitchen — it was messiest there — wiping down all the surfaces and putting on gloves to scrub the dishes, making sure the water was extra hot. The food was caked on and dried. They'd had something Italian — lasagna, maybe. The dining room was in a similar state. From room to room, it was the same story. Usually he cleaned the larger messes between her weekly visits. She thought back. Had he said anything about going away? Nothing came to mind.

The conservatory made her wonder. She'd always thought it a marvel, how you could be in the depths of darkness inside that mausoleum then step through a doorway where all was light, windows stretching up twenty feet and wrapping themselves overhead. Browned, curled petals lay strewn on the floor. Orchids. He was always particular with his orchids. Ice cubes, he told her, when she asked if he wanted her to water them. They were fussy. They required three ice cubes, once a week, per pot. No more. They didn't have soil, he said, just an absorbent material that retained the water after the ice melted. Now, looking over the fallen petals, she thought he had forgotten to ice his plants, strange as it sounded. She felt a sickness in her stomach, casting her mind back to the previous week to recall if she had neglected to ice them. It was true, nearly all the flowers had dropped, only one or two retaining a few blossoms here and there. But if so, how could he not have noticed?

She went to the pantry to retrieve the vacuum, sitting it upright while she trailed the long black cord to the wall and inserted the plug. The whirring noise was comforting. The fallen blossoms were gone inside of a minute, but she hoped he wouldn't blame her for their destruction.

The floor was dusty, but a quick wipe with a damp mop and it looked as good as new. She always appreciated a good floor. So many people overspent on the furnishings and neglected the basics: proper hardwood, good stone counters, solid walls and ceilings.

She looked up. His bedroom lay directly overhead. So far, she hadn't heard a thing. Such a sordid life. When she'd started, he told her to ignore anything that looked like an illegal drug. If she saw anything in any of the rooms or anything being used by any of his guests, she was simply to ignore it. What if he'd taken an overdose of something and lay up there in a coma or worse?

The empty house began to give her the creeps. The chill was still in the air. A phone rang in another room. She stood still and listened to it echoing through the place until an answering machine picked up. She heard Yuri identify himself with his distinctive pronunciation before it clicked over to record the message. She thought for a moment that he might be somewhere trying to get hold of her, but she never answered the house phone. It wasn't him. It was his accountant saying he was still out of town but wanted to confirm tomorrow's meeting. The call ended.

Then he hadn't gone out of town after all, not if he was meeting the accountant. Which meant he was probably still upstairs in bed. She lugged the vacuum cleaner to the foot of the stairs. Carrying it up was always a chore. Of course, he was too cheap to get a second one for the upstairs. She rested for a moment before continuing. Then she saw the stain. A drop on one stair and then another a few stairs above. She looked at it curiously. Maybe it was food, she told herself. Maybe he'd had a late night meal upstairs and not noticed the trail he was leaving behind. But she didn't think so.

She left the vacuum at the foot of the stairs. He hands shook as she continued up. Dead flowers and a house in the deep freeze. Something, somewhere, was very wrong. She felt it in her bones, and her bones were never wrong.

More Dan Sharp Mysteries by Jeffrey Round

Lake on the Mountain

Winner of the
2013 Lambda Literary Award for Gay Mystery

Missing-persons investigator Dan Sharp accepts an invitation to a wedding on a yacht in Ontario's Prince Edward County. When a member of the wedding party is swept overboard, a case of mistaken identity leads to confusion as the wrong person is reported missing. The hunt for a possible killer leads Dan deeper into the private lives of a family of rich WASPs and their secret world of privilege. No sooner is that case resolved when Dan is hired by an anonymous source to investigate the disappearance, twenty years earlier, of the groom's father. The only clues are a missing bicycle and six horses mysteriously poisoned.

Pumpkin Eater

Following an anonymous tip, Dan Sharp makes a grisly find in a burned-out slaughterhouse in Toronto's west end. Someone is targeting known sex offenders whose names and identities were released online. When an iconic rock star contacts Dan to keep from becoming the next victim, things take a curious turn. Dan's search for a killer takes him underground in Toronto's broken social scene — a secret world of misfits and guerrilla activists living off the grid — where he hopes to find the key to the murders.

Available at your favourite bookseller